Susanne O'Leary

Forgotten Dreams

FORGOTTEN DREAMS
Including Marianne's Christmas
By Susanne O'Leary

Cover and paperback formatting by JD Smith Design

Marianne's Christmas was edited by Michael Hearing

You know that place between sleep and awake, the place where you can still remember dreaming? That's where I'll always love you. That's where I'll be waiting. - J.M. Barrie - Peter Pan.

Chapter 1

The stranger watched the wedding ceremony from the back of the church. Uninvited, unknown, but still somehow connected to the small party gathered around the happy couple at the altar. He didn't know them personally; it was the petite figure of the maid of honour that held his attention.

He hadn't seen her for a long time, but there she was—the same hot mess of red curls, huge blue eyes, freckles and full mouth. She wore an ankle-length pink dress, which should have clashed with her colouring, but curiously did the opposite and enhanced her glowing cheeks, luminous eyes and copper hair. Older by fifteen years than when he last saw her, she had a mature beauty that took his breath away.

The couple said their vows, the priest pronounced them husband and wife, and gave the groom permission to kiss the bride. Although this was taking place in a church in Provence, the ceremony and the readings were all in English. As the couple stood at the altar, ready to walk down the aisle, the bride turned to the maid of honour, who handed her the bouquet she had been holding all through the ceremony. Their eyes met and the women exchanged fond smiles.

The stranger stepped into the shadows as the wedding party walked down the aisle into the late autumn sunshine. He didn't want her to see him. It was too soon.

* * *

The wedding reception took place in the outskirts of Saint-Tropez, at one of the few hotels that hadn't closed for the season. The small party of around twenty family members and friends enjoyed champagne and hors d'oeuvres on the terrace while the sun slowly sank behind the Esterel Mountains in a riot of pink and orange.

Late autumn was Molly's favourite time of year in Saint-Tropez. All the glitz and glamour of the jet set receded, allowing the town to return to its true Provençal atmosphere and daily life. She loved falling into the rhythm of out-of-season life, when she could work in peace, taking her inspiration from the colours of the Mediterranean, the ever-changing skies and the wild flowers that appeared miraculously after a few days of rain.

The wedding and her role as maid of honour marked a new beginning for Molly. She was moving out of the house she had shared with Liam and Tommy for the past few years. She would no longer be company for Liam, no longer be a kind of mother to Tommy. Liam's new wife would be doing all that and more. Molly smiled as she watched Tommy pull at Daisy's skirt to ask her a question. Daisy leant down to listen and replied, took his hand and walked with him to the table to sit beside his father through the dinner. He would even go with them on their honeymoon to Corsica. Daisy had insisted, although Molly had offered to mind her little nephew while they were away.

"We're a family now," Daisy said. "I want Tommy to feel wanted."

Liam rolled his eyes. "A honeymoon for three. Not quite what I had in mind."

"It's only for a couple of weeks," Molly cut in. "I'm sure Tommy won't pine too much if he stays behind with me."

"No," Daisy said. "I've promised him that he can come with us. A promise to a child must never be broken."

"What about Asta?" Liam enquired. "Is Molly looking after her?"

"No, she's coming too," Daisy replied. "Tommy will miss her too much. A dog is as much a part of a family as a child."

"This is becoming more like a travelling circus than a honeymoon," Liam complained.

But Daisy put her foot down and won.

Molly smiled to herself and turned to look far out to sea, where the setting sun had turned the clouds a soft pink. *Lovely colours together…rose quartz…could look good matched with light-blue enamel set in silver.*

A hand on her shoulder. "Daydreaming again, sis? It's time to sit down to dinner."

Molly turned away from the view. "Sorry. I was miles away. Planning my next collection and thinking about my move to the house in Gigaro."

"You can stay with us as long as you like, you know that."

Molly reached up and ruffled his hair. "Oh, come on, that would be a huge pain for you and you know it. Two women and one bathroom? Just think about it."

Liam laughed and smoothed his hair back. "Yeah, you're right. Nightmare scenario. But I'll still miss you."

"Nah, you won't. Stop trying to be nice. And don't pretend you've forgotten all those irritations when I was living with you."

"Okay, you called my bluff. I can't wait to see the back of you."

"That's better. But don't forget I'll still be using the workshop behind the house. So if you do miss me, I can still pop in to annoy you and tell you you're bringing up Tommy to be a delinquent."

"Gee, thanks. I'll hold you to that." Liam's face softened. "This is where I should thank you for all you did for me.

Without you, I'd be a bitter, useless drunkard, not fit to bring up a child. Without you—"

"Stop it, you're making me cry," Molly interrupted. "I was there to catch you when you fell. That's what sisters do."

"Only sisters called Molly." Liam put his hand on her arm. "You care too much, you know. You must stop always *helping* people. Be selfish for a change, like the rest of us."

"I'll do my best."

"You'd better. I'll be keeping an eye on you. I'm so happy you're beginning to make a career for yourself. Keep working on that, and ignore any lame ducks you might spot."

"I'll just turn away and whistle a little tune if I see one. I'm quite looking forward to my new life." Molly poked him in the side with her elbow. "Let's go and have that dinner, lover boy. I'm starving. And Marianne promised to do the wedding cake. It's a Swedish surprise."

"I bet it'll taste awful."

"I'd say it will be beautiful, delicious and slimming," Molly countered.

Much later, Liam's speech brought tears to many eyes as he declared his love for Daisy and how she was a 'chuisle mo croi', Irish for 'pulse of my heart.' They were still dabbing their eyes when two waiters carried in a gorgeous three-tiered cake covered in green marzipan decorated with pink hearts and a bride and groom, also made of marzipan, on the top.

"It's called a princess cake," Marianne said in Molly's ear as they watched the bride and groom cut into the green marzipan. "Liam always calls Daisy his princess."

"Looks delicious." Molly helped herself to a slice when they reached the buffet table.

Marianne nodded. "Wait till you taste it. Marzipan, cream, vanilla and strawberry jam on a sponge base. The traditional Swedish cake for every occasion."

Molly glanced at Marianne's slim figure poured into a

blue silk shift. "I bet you don't indulge in that kind of thing too often."

Marianne laughed. "Not every day, of course. But I love it when there is a celebration. "Go on, try it."

Molly took a forkful of cake. She closed her eyes as her mouth filled with marzipan, vanilla and strawberry.

"Mmm, heavenly," she said when she had swallowed.

"Knew you'd love it. How's business by the way? All those women still wanting your fabulous jewellery?"

"Not bad," Molly replied when she had swallowed. "I have a steady stream of orders through my website."

Marianne nodded. "That's great. I saw that feature about you in The Sunday Times last week. That'll bring you a lot more clients."

"It already has."

"Great publicity. How on earth did you manage that?"

"One of my clients knew someone who knew someone at The Sunday Times. Just a lucky break, really."

"More than lucky," Marianne remarked. "And you're moving in with Sophia, I heard."

"That's right. Just until I find something permanent. I felt Liam and Daisy needed their own space. Sophia was looking for someone to share her house. I think she's lonely after her husband passed away a few years ago."

Marianne scraped the last bits of cake off her plate. "Yes, I think that's true. Nice woman but a little odd."

Molly wiped her mouth with a napkin. "Odd? She's fecking nuts. But we get on really well all the same. Probably because I'm a bit of a nut myself."

"Ha, ha, yes, so you are. I prefer to call you eccentric. But that's okay because you're an artist. Sophia is not."

"She was an actress, wasn't she?"

Marianne smirked. "Only in a couple of B movies before she had to throw in the towel when she married Sebastian Ffrench. Funny name."

"It's an old Norman name," Molly explained. "His family came to Ireland in the sixteenth century. They built a castle in County Wexford, and I think the family still owns it. Except as Sophia had no children it was taken over by one of Sebastian's cousins when he died."

"But she got to keep the house here. Who wants to freeze their butt off in an old pile in Ireland?"

"Not me," Molly laughed, licking the last bits of cake off her spoon. "I prefer this part of the world."

"Me too," Marianne agreed. "I'm so happy Klaus decided to spend the winter here. And I love my new job."

"I'm delighted you offered," Molly said. "You're the best business manager. I had no idea you'd be so good at it."

"I was at screaming point with boredom." Marianne laughed and pushed her fingers through her short blonde hair. "Klaus thinks I'm crazy. He has billions, but I still want to earn my own money." She frowned and looked sternly at Molly. "Talking about money, you should consider investing some of yours now that you're doing so well."

"I am," Molly assured her. "I'm already looking for an apartment to buy. Staying with Sophia is just a temporary arrangement. I want to invest my money. Some kind of property seems the best bet."

"Very wise," Marianne agreed. "Real estate around here is a very good investment."

"I know. It'll be fun to look around. I might ask that woman who runs the agency in Antibes to help me." Molly put her plate away. "Oh, look, the happy couple are ready to leave. Let's go outside and throw confetti at them."

They joined the rest of the wedding party gathered at the bottom of the steps, as Daisy and Liam appeared to applause and cheering. Daisy held her bouquet aloft.

"Ready?" she shouted. "All you spinsters down there, catch!" She threw the bouquet high in the air, and Molly watched the bouquet of pink and white roses tumble down and land in her outstretched hands. She blushed and hid her face in the fragrant blooms as everyone cheered and shouted, "The next bride!"

This would have been a perfect, touching moment.

If she wasn't already married.

Chapter 2

Molly was still thinking about rose quartz and blue enamel as she moved into Sophia's house the next day. It helped her with the wrench of leaving a house she loved, where she had been happy and needed, into this big villa, so beautiful on the outside with bougainvillea growing up the white walls in a riot of purple, and old stone steps leading up to the dark-pink door matching the shutters. It sat in a well-tended garden on a hill overlooking Gigaro beach and the azure waters of the bay of Cavalaire.

"There you are," Sophia exclaimed as she flung the door open. Molly could see straight into a large hall furnished with wicker chairs and a worn oriental rug on the parquet floor. "I was just about to call you. I have to go out and I was afraid I'd miss you."

Molly put down her bags and held out her hand. "Hi. Sorry I'm late, but packing up took a little longer than I had planned."

Sophia waved her hand in the air. "No need for handshakes. We're very casual in this house."

"We? You have other tenants?"

Sophia let out a husky laugh. "Just one at the moment and occasionally the odd stray who needs a place to stay for a short while. I need the rent to keep this house you see. But please, don't call me a landlady. I'm more of a hostess, really." She sighed and flicked her heavy chestnut hair from her shoulder in a Miss Piggy gesture that almost made Molly laugh. Tall and statuesque, looking eerily like her namesake Sophia Loren in bad light, Sophia Ffrench was the kind of woman you either loved or hated.

Molly loved her instantly. "I know what you mean. I'd do anything to hang on to this house if I were you."

Sophia nodded. "Quite right. And Sebastian would haunt me forever if I let it go. You were lucky to get the suite, though. But only because the previous tenant had moved out just before we met at your launch." Sophia smoothed her short green tunic that barely reached the top of her thighs. "Do come in. I'll show you to your quarters. I'm just back from the beach, so you'll have to excuse my lack of clothing. Then I have to change and rush out again. Afternoon tea with a friend in Sainte-Maxime."

"The beach? At this time of year?"

"It's quite warm today," Sophia declared. "I love this mellow winter sunshine, and a swim in cold water is very good for the immune system."

"If you don't catch pneumonia."

Sophia shrugged. "No, that won't happen. I'm frightfully hardy. Just like my mother and her mother before her." She grabbed one of Molly's suitcases. "But now I'll show you to your room, and then you'll have to settle in all by yourself. Feel free to wander around the house and gardens and make yourself a cup of tea in the kitchen."

"Thank you." Lugging her other bag, Molly followed Sophia up the wide staircase and across the landing on the upper floor.

"Here we are." Sophia opened a door at the end of the corridor. "Welcome to your new abode."

Molly stepped inside. Her new living quarters were more like a studio than a room. A large space flooded with light with a balcony overlooking the bay, an old-fashioned bathroom tiled in turquoise and a kitchenette with a hotplate, fridge and microwave, all showing signs of wear and tear. The wide oak floorboards creaked as they entered, and a gust of wind made the threadbare green linen curtains flutter before Sophia closed the window.

"There," she said, turning the brass handle. "You have to push at it to make it close."

Molly put her suitcase in front of the tall white wardrobe and looked around. "Lovely room. It's so bright."

"It's a bit out of date. Especially the bathroom. But I didn't want to change the nineteen twenties feel of the house. It's so very Noel Coward, don't you think?"

"Absolutely," Molly agreed, peeping in through the bathroom door. "Love the shell-shaped basin and the big bath. And the bed and wardrobe go so well with the style of the house. Apart from a lick of paint, it doesn't need much of a change."

"I have no intention of changing anything. I don't have the means anyway. But I pretend I'm conserving the house and protecting the cultural heritage and some such rot," Sophia said with a cheeky wink. "Anyway, must dash. Make yourself at home. Go down to the kitchen when you're hungry. Don't know what's on the menu, but Jesus is cooking so it'll be something good, I'm sure."

"Jesus?"

Sophia laughed. "He's Spanish. A friend who needed a room when he ran into some financial trouble and I was looking for someone to share the house with when I found myself alone. I know, the name makes you jump at first, but it's quite common in Spain."

"And he can cook?" Molly said.

"Oh yes. Mostly Spanish food. He's a professional chef, as a matter of fact. You'll see. But if Spanish food is not your cup of tea, that's fine too. Up to you and no hard feelings." She waved at Molly. "Got to go. See you later." With that, she disappeared through the door, leaving a cloud of Shalimar behind.

Molly slowly unpacked and hung her clothes in the wardrobe that smelled faintly of mothballs. She had to take three trips to the car before she had finally unloaded her belongings and put them in place in her new home. Once she was finished, she stood back and looked around the room. With her books and knick-knacks on the shelves, her embroidered cushions placed in the two wicker chairs by the window and the red velvet throw from home on the white bedspread, the room looked immediately more inviting and very much a Molly kind of place. It would be her home while she looked around for something more permanent.

The final item was Liam and Daisy's wedding photograph in a silver frame, which Molly placed on the chest of drawers. She looked at their smiling faces and made a wish for their continued happiness. Not that she believed in wedded bliss. The idea of spending the rest of her life with one person was alien to her and always had been. She hadn't thought much of that trouble she got into years ago, but as she stood there and looked at the wedding photo, a brief flash of those days suddenly shot through her mind, only to disappear just as quickly. A silly thing to do. But not something to wreck her life.

A faint whiff of garlic and herbs made Molly's stomach rumble. She sniffed hungrily. Time to meet the man with the controversial name. Judging by the smell, he *was* a good cook.

After walking through the living room with its shabby-chic interior and a dining room with a huge oval table and tall windows overlooking the garden, she found the kitchen at the end of a long corridor.

She pushed at the half-opened door and peered in. "Hello?" she called.

"Hello," a male voice replied. "Who's there?"

"Me," Molly said and walked into the large, warm kitchen

with an island in the middle behind which a dark, stocky man was stirring something in a big pot simmering on the hob.

"Me, who?" His brown eyes were warm and friendly, and his smile softened a ravaged face with a broken nose. He wore a gold ring in his left ear and a red tee shirt with the words JESUS LOVES YOU.

"Hi. I'm Molly," she said and held out her hand, trying not to laugh at the tee shirt. "I'm the new tenant."

He wiped his hands on the back of his baggy jeans and, after inspecting them, gave Molly a firm handshake. "Hello, Molly. I am—" he gestured at his shirt. "Him."

"Hello, uh, Jesus," Molly managed. "Is that really your name?"

"Yes, and no. I was baptised Jesus," he said, pronouncing it 'hesus' in the Spanish way. "But everyone calls me Jay. Only Sophia uses that name just because she finds it funny. She gave me this tee shirt for a laugh. It could have been worse. She could have called me Maria. That's my second name. I'm officially Jesus Maria. I'll never forgive my parents." His fluent English was only slightly marred by a strong Spanish accent.

"I see," Molly said. "Well, that's a relief. I'd find it weird to call anyone Jesus. Or a man Maria," she added.

"Me too." He shrugged. "I didn't know the name would make people laugh until I went to live in London. Then I became Jay because of all the jokes and silly comments." He gestured at a barstool at the end of the island. "But sit down and chat to me while I cook." He pushed a plate with deep-fried baby squid across the counter. "Here, you can nibble on those while you wait. I have a feeling you're hungry, no?"

"Yes." Molly squeezed lemon over the squid and popped one into her mouth. "Delicious. I love Spanish tapas. So what brought you to France, Jay?"

He waggled his thick black eyebrows. "A woman, of

course. A French girl I fell in love with about twenty-five years ago. We were happy for a while but then it started to go downhill very fast and it ended in 'le divorce.'" He rolled his eyes. "French women, eh? Oh so sexy with the slit skirts, that melancholy air and the stinky French cigarettes. Then the slutty side, and that 'who gives a shit' attitude…makes a man so hot." He sighed. "Well, you know…Isabelle Adjani, Juliette Binoche, not to mention Brigitte before them. Bitches, but irresistible."

"Oh, yeah," Molly said dreamily. "I had a girl crush on them myself when I was doing my art course. I watched a lot of French movies then. I even tried to be like those women, but the cigarettes made me cough, and I can't walk more than three feet in them stilettos. Not to mention the tight skirts. Must be something in their genes that makes them so good at it."

He winked. "Some kind of slut gene, I think. I should have left and gone back to Spain when we broke up. But because of our daughter, I couldn't leave or I'd have lost custody, so I stayed here in this area, only a short drive from where my ex-wife and daughter live. But I don't mind. I love France. Better for work than Spain." His phone rang. He peered at it where it lay on the counter. "Excuse me. It's Sophia." He picked up the phone, and after a brief exchange, put it down again. "She won't be home for dinner. She was invited to supper by some English lord or something. So it's you, me and Andalusian stew for twenty. I hope you're hungry."

"Starving. So…where do you work??"

"I'm a chef at a Spanish restaurant in La Croix Valmer."

Molly nodded. "I know where it is. Lovely village. But how did you end up here, in Sophia's house? Please tell me to shut up if it's none of my business."

"I don't mind telling you. I was friends with both Sophia and Sebastian right from the moment they moved here and came to my restaurant for a meal. More a friend of Sebastian, actually. We used to go for long hikes in the hills together. Wonderful man. Kind and funny. His death was a terrible tragedy. I moved in here just after the funeral. The lease on my apartment was up for renewal, but with my divorce, I had a lot of expenses. Sophia suggested I move in here until I got back on my feet. She needed company, and the rent I pay her helps her, too. Not that she'd admit it," he added with a smirk. "Or that she is the least bit fond of me. We argue most of the time."

"But I'm sure you're good company for Sophia, all the same. It can't be nice to find yourself all alone if you're coping with grief."

His eyes twinkled. "She loves to have someone to fight with. The truth is I adore her."

"How about her?"

"Sophia?" Jay laughed. "She adores me back but hates herself for it. But enough about me. What's an Irish colleen doing in this part of the world? Don't tell me you're here because of a man."

Molly laughed. "Not really. I first came here with my brother and his little boy, but when he got married recently, I felt I had to leave them alone and get my own place. Sophia was looking for someone to rent the studio, so I took her up on her offer. It's a nice spot while I look for my own home."

"So what do you do, Molly? For a living, I mean. Just guessing, but are you some kind of artist?"

"How did you know?"

He gestured at her with the ladle. "The wild hair and the colours you wear. Green and blue with the red boots. It all comes together as an artist look. I like it. That top is beautiful."

Molly glanced down at the soft green cashmere crew neck. "Thank you. I found it in this cute little boutique and couldn't resist it."

"Are you a painter?" he asked. "Or a textile designer?"

Molly squeezed more lemon on her squid. "Neither. I design jewellery. I have a workshop at the back of my brother's house, and I'm looking into opening my own shop or sharing with someone else."

He looked impressed. "And buying your own property? You must be doing well."

"Yes. To my surprise. It took a while but now it seems to have taken off."

He peered at her. "Did you make that beautiful necklace?"

She touched the jade heart set in gold at her throat. "Yes. It's one of my very first efforts. My lucky charm. I always wear it."

"It has brought you luck?"

"I'd like to think so."

"Would you make one for me? I could do with some good luck."

"For you? But I don't make jewellery for men." The look in his velvet eyes instantly made Molly regret her words. "But I do like a challenge," she breezed on. "So why not? I could make you a…" She thought for a moment. "A little Spanish bull?"

He smiled. "That would be perfect. I'd treasure it."

"I'll get started on that as soon as I can."

He pushed a glass of chilled rosé towards her. "Let's drink to the little Spanish bull."

Molly lifted the glass and clinked it against Jay's. "Cheers to the bull."

"And new friends," he said.

"New friends." Molly clinked his glass again and smiled into his eyes. What an unusual man. Sophia was a lucky woman.

* * *

After dinner, they moved to the round table in the sunroom with what was left of the wine and some cheese to round off the meal. Nibbling on Camembert and bread, they gazed out across the silent garden, where the evening mist floated around trees and shrubs, and two blackbirds hopped around on the grass looking for worms.

"Such a quiet, peaceful place." Molly leaned back in her easy chair, nursing the last of her wine.

Jay drained his glass. "I like Provence in the winter."

"Even the mistral?"

"I don't mind it. The strong winds sweep the skies clean, and I love to look at the sea all churned up and foamy."

"Me too. I like the silence in the winter months, the golden sunshine. And the absence of people."

He studied her for a moment. "Are you a bit of a loner?"

Molly shrugged. "Not really. But I hate crowds. I like people but a few at a time will do for me."

"That's a little melancholy for a young woman like you."

She laughed. "Young? I'm thirty-eight."

He smiled and winked. "That's young to an old man like me."

"You don't look old."

"I'm glad to hear it." He leaned his elbows on the table and gazed at her. "Thirty-eight and never been married?"

The question startled her. Nobody had asked her that before. "I thought you were going to say 'thirty-eight and never been kissed,'" she said in an attempt to steer the conversation in another direction.

His eyes rested on her mouth. "No, I can see you've been kissed. A lot. That mouth was made for kissing. Over and over again."

She felt her face flush. "What am I supposed to say to that? Thank you?"

He shook his head and winked. "You don't have to say anything. It was just an observation. But go on. What did you say about being married? Or not?"

She squirmed. "I didn't."

"But you were. Married. Yes?"

"Are you psychic?"

"No." He grabbed the bottle. "More wine?"

"Yes," she said.

He tried to fill her glass but she pulled it away. "Not to wine. About being married."

He raised one of his black eyebrows. "You were?"

She nodded, still looking into his eyes. "Yes. I still am. Married."

"I see. And your husband," he made a gesture with the wine bottle, "is around somewhere?"

Molly dropped her gaze. "No. I haven't seen him for over fifteen years. Don't even know where he is. He might even be dead. In fact, I think he is."

Jay sat back. "I think you have to explain. I'm not nosey but this is beginning to drive me crazy."

Regretting her words, Molly sighed and ran her finger around the rim of her glass. "I'm sorry. I can't talk about it. I shouldn't have said anything."

Jay nodded. "I understand. I feel you've been pushing this away for quite some time. It must be hard to get it out in the open. But I'm willing to listen if you need someone to talk to."

"Thank you. I might take you up on that."

They both jumped at the sound of the front door slamming and Sophia calling, "Yoo-hoo, where is everybody?"

"In here," Jay shouted as he got up to switch on lamps and clear plates.

Sophia's heels clattered on the tiles as she walked through the corridor, across the kitchen and into the sunroom. She beamed at them as she entered and sank down in a chair. "Good evening. I hope Jesus fed you a good supper."

"It was delicious," Molly said. "I'm sure there's enough left over for you. He seems to have catered for a small army."

"No food for me," Sophia protested. "I had rather a lot to eat at that marvellous restaurant in Sainte-Maxime. Their helpings are very generous." She took off her high heels and massaged her feet. "A long night with lots of standing about and chatting before we could sit down. But it was a very productive evening all the same."

"Productive?" Jay asked.

Sophia nodded. "Yes. I haven't told you, but I'm planning to do tours of the garden here during the winter."

"Your garden is lovely," Molly said. "What I've seen of it anyway."

Sophia nodded. "Yes it is. Hard work of course, but it keeps me fit. And," she continued in the same breath, "next summer, there will be an outdoor yoga centre here and a platform for exercising and meditation on the little hill overlooking the beach. So it's all happening," she ended with a satisfied air. "I just have to set it all up."

Jay rolled his eyes. "How perfect. Just like the time you decided to start a kennel for cats and dogs and forgot you were allergic to furry animals. I had to take you to hospital because you got so ill and then explain to the owners why we had to kick out their pets at once."

Sophia glared at Jay. "Yes, I know. It just slipped my mind. But this will be different. It will work, I know it."

"As long as you don't ask me to do the guiding and look after old ladies," Jay muttered.

"You're so negative, Jesus." Sophia sighed. "You never approve of any of my ideas."

"I will when you get one that works," he said.

"Oh, please. Give me the benefit of the doubt. I'm really looking forward to getting stuck into this." Sophia stopped and looked from Jay to Molly. "But I was interrupting something, wasn't I? There are strong vibes here of sharing old memories or perhaps even very personal details that caused pain to one of you."

Jay and Molly looked at each other. “I don’t know what you mean, Sophia,” Jay said, his voice cool. “We were just getting to know each other.”

Sophia’s eyes narrowed. “You were doing more than that. It’s floating around in the air here, like wisps of smoke.” Her eyes focused on Molly. “Your aura is very strong.”

“Aura?” Molly said. “I don’t believe in things like that.”

Sophia nodded. “That’s right. You have a sceptical aura.”

Laughing, Molly got up from the table. “I’m sure I do. My dad used to call me Miss Contrary. Must be the red hair or something. I’m going to bed. Thanks for supper, Jay. It was delicious. Goodnight, Sophia.”

“Good night,” Jay said. “I hope you’ll tell me the story later on. But only when you’re ready.”

“I will,” Molly promised.

“Story? What story?” Sophia asked.

“Oh,” Molly said airily. “Just an Irish fairy tale.”

“With a happy ending?”

Molly shrugged. “Nah, not really. It just ends. Like in real life.”

Chapter 3

The estate agent unlocked the door to the apartment.

"It hasn't been occupied for a while, so it might be a little stuffy," she said and swung the door open.

Molly stepped inside and looked around. Situated on the top floor, the apartment had two bedrooms, a large living room, a study, a modern kitchen and a balcony with views of the hills and the mountains beyond. With a price tag of four hundred thousand euros, it was a bargain in this prime location, just outside Sainte-Maxime.

"Near the main road and the motorway," the agent said. "Very central."

"I can hear that," Molly remarked as she opened the sliding doors to the balcony. She quickly closed them again. "I'm sorry. I can't buy this apartment. It's too noisy."

"But it would be perfect for you," the agent protested, a frown furrowing her smooth forehead. "It's in the area you requested and the size you wanted, and—"

"Yes, it ticks nearly all the boxes. Except the most important one. I need peace and quiet," Molly said, thinking longingly of Sophia's house and the tranquillity of the garden, where all she could hear were birdsong and waves lapping onto the beach.

"You didn't include that in your list," the agent grumbled. "Peace and quiet doesn't come cheap in these parts, you know."

"I'm aware of that." Molly looked at the woman. "Okay, I'll be straight with you. This apartment is a little over my budget. I can go a bit higher if I see something I truly love, but then I have to apply for a loan. I won't compromise on anything, certainly not on the peace-and-quiet aspect. I would be willing to buy something smaller that isn't perfect décor-wise, but I can't take on a wreck or anything that requires building work. This apartment is cute and spacious, but it's too near the road, so it's not suitable at all." Her phone pinged. A message from Marianne to call ASAP. "Excuse me," she said to the agent. "I have to call this person back."

The agent nodded. "Of course. Go ahead."

"Hi Molly," Marianne shouted against the background of voices and clinking of glasses and cutlery. "I'm in Nice in a very noisy restaurant, as you can hear. I had to call you straightaway. You'd better get your ass over here as soon as you can. I'm looking at a guy who has a fantastic business proposal."

"What proposal?" Molly asked, intrigued.

"It's killer deal." Marianne lowered her voice. "He's cute too," she whispered. "And single. Come on sweetie, get in the car. We'll wait for you in the bar at the Negresco. I'll order champagne."

"But I'm looking at apartments this afternoon."

"Forget the apartment. When this boat comes in you'll be able to afford a mansion."

* * *

Two hours later, Molly walked into the bar at the Hotel Negresco in Nice. She spotted the back of Marianne's blonde head at a table near the bar, talking into her phone while a tall man waited patiently. Molly took a quick look at him as she approached. With his thick sandy hair and tall frame, he was certainly cute in a preppy way. He looked up, and when their eyes met, her stomach flipped. Mesmerised by his green eyes, she was rooted to the spot for what seemed like an eternity, until he shot to his feet and gave her a dazzling smile.

"Molly Creedon." He took her hand. "How nice to meet you at last." He wore a dark green corduroy blazer with leather patches at the elbows, a light-blue shirt and beige chinos, all deceptively simple but with that indefinable touch of class. "I'm Theodore Anderson. But please, call me Ted."

"Uh, hello," was all Molly managed before Marianne ended her call and got up to give Molly a kiss on the cheek.

"Hi, sweetheart, here you are at last."

"Sorry if I'm late, but it took ages to get a parking place," Molly said.

Ted pulled out a chair. "Please, sit down. What do you want to drink? Champagne?"

"I'd love a cup of tea," Molly confessed. "If that's at all possible here."

"Anything is possible at the Negresco." Ted clicked his fingers. A waiter appeared as if out of thin air and Ted ordered a pot of Darjeeling and scones for Molly. "Not exactly what I'd call a celebratory drink, but being Irish, tea is the elixir of life for you, I guess."

Molly laughed, warming to this young man. His perfect manners made her feel special, feminine, and the way he looked at her made her blush. "Very true. In Ireland, I'd have asked for a pot of Barry's and everyone would have known what I meant. The best tea in the world."

Marianne made an impatient gesture. "Yeah, yeah, whatever. Ted, you have to tell Molly what this is all about and the great deal you're offering her."

Molly nodded and looked at Ted. "Yes. Please tell me. I don't even know who you are."

Ted nodded. "Of course you don't. I'm sorry. How stupid

of me. It all slipped my mind when you walked in here. You were such a breath of fresh air in this stuffy place with your flaming red hair and freckly Irish face. I recognised you instantly from your website." He cleared his throat. "Anyway, let me introduce myself properly. I represent Harlow & Anderson, the Swedish-American—"

Molly gasped. "You mean H&A? The IKEA of fashion? The global enterprise that has cornered the mass market in clothing?"

He laughed. "Yes, that's right. I'm one of the family members who run it."

"Gee." Molly stared at him. "You're one of *those* Andersons? That's…well...that's incredible."

He smiled. "I know. I mean, I'm glad you know about us."

"Who doesn't?" Molly kept staring at him, trying to take it all in. "So," she said after a while. "What was this…deal you were telling my…Marianne about?"

"Well…" he leaned forward, looking at her intently, "what we would like to propose is for you to design our new jewellery range. A collection of costume jewellery that would go out to all our stores worldwide. All you have to do is design it and then it will be manufactured in China and sold all over the world. It's about you getting into the mass market." He sat back. "What do you say?"

Molly looked from Ted to Marianne. "What do I say? I don't know what to say. Mass market? But I handcraft every piece myself. I've never considered doing this. How is it done?"

"The designs would be different from your handcrafted pieces," Ted explained. "You'd do a range that would be affordable for every woman. The kind of thing that has a lot of class and simplicity but is made with base metals, plastic and acrylic. We looked at your work displayed on your website after reading that article about you and liked it a lot. We think you can do a more popular line that would suit the mass market and our customers."

"Oh." Molly looked at Marianne. "I see. Wow. I'll have to think about this. I have to discuss it with my business manager too."

He nodded. "Of course. She has all the details."

The tea and scones arrived, and Molly busied herself with pouring tea into a delicate china cup, spreading cream and strawberry jam on a scone while her mind whirled. Could she do this? Could she design a line that would be attractive to women all over the world? She glanced at Marianne, who nodded and smiled.

"So what's the actual deal?" she asked when she had finished half a scone.

"I explained it to Marianne and she'll tell you all about it," Ted said. "But just to give you a general idea, we'll pay you quite a generous advance, half of which you'll get on signing the contract and the other half when you deliver the designs. Then you'll also get royalty for each piece sold."

"Sounds attractive enough but I'm not sure it's the kind of thing that would be right for me," Molly said, ignoring Marianne's kick under the table. "But I'll discuss it with Marianne and have good think about it."

Ted nodded. "Absolutely. Let us know what you decide. And if you do want to accept our offer, we'll get the contract over to you. Then our head buyer will give you a call and you can discuss the details." He rose. "I have a few phone calls to make. Maybe you could contact me when you've made up your mind?"

"We will," Marianne said. "You'll have our answer later this afternoon."

Ted nodded and touched Molly's shoulder. "It was nice to meet you, Molly. I hope we will be working together."

"Yes, me too," Molly stammered. She looked at his tall frame as he walked away. "You were right. He's more than cute."

Marianne nodded. "Yes, he is. But you can look into his

lovely eyes later. Let's discuss this deal. You seemed a little hesitant?"

Molly sipped her tea. "Hesitant? Yes, I am. I don't want to jump in at once. I haven't seen their offer yet. I didn't want to look as if I was dying to sign with them. I mean, this is something that could change the way I work. I'm happy with how it's going, so why would I want to get into this kind of thing?"

"Because you could make a lot of money. The advance is a hundred thousand," Marianne said. "And as much again when you deliver the designs. Then a ten-percent cut on each piece sold. They have four thousand stores in sixty countries worldwide." She sat back and picked up her glass of white wine. "Your collection for them will be in every one of those stores. You do the maths."

Molly choked on her tea. "Holy shit! Really? And a hundred thousand? Euros?"

"No, coconuts."

"Shut up while I try to digest all of this. So," Molly said after a while, "I get a hundred thousand euros on signing and another hundred thousand when I deliver the designs? Plus ten percent on each piece sold?"

Marianne gave her a thumbs-up. "Bingo."

"Oh. Okay." Molly thought for a moment. "I know this will seem weird and even grasping, but if that's their first offer, maybe we could stall a little? Not because I'm greedy but it just feels a bit amateurish to take the very first offer without a little negotiating first."

Marianne looked at Molly with new respect. "You know, that's a very good idea. Why not let them sweat for a bit? After all, they came to you, not the other way around."

Molly nodded. "Exactly. Of course, I'll take their original offer if they stick to that, but why not play a little hard to get?"

Marianne winked at her. "Especially as he's so hot."

Molly grinned. "Yeah, that too."

Marianne picked up her phone. "I'll tell him."

"What are you going to say?"

Marianne held up a hand as she listened to a voice on her phone. "Ted? Hi, it's Marianne. Listen, Molly is still considering your offer. It's a big step for her to take, and there's a lot to take into consideration. She'll have to take time off her usual work for this, which means a loss of earnings and possibly a risk of losing some valuable clients. We've also had a query from one of the bigger couture houses for their spring collection, so..."

"We have?" Molly asked.

"Shh," Marianne hissed. She listened for a while. "Of course. I understand. But we need to know soon so Molly can get herself organised." She nodded and smiled at Molly. "Great. Thanks, Ted. I'll ask her and tell her to call you back about that." She hung up.

"What did he say?"

"He said he understood and that he'll talk to the board about a possible increase of the advance. Good thinking there, my friend. He also asked if you'd have dinner with him tonight."

"Oh, that's great. I don't care about the money. It's just that I didn't want to take whatever they were offering." Molly stopped. "What was that you said about...dinner?"

"You heard. He wants to take you to dinner tonight. Probably to butter you up."

Molly sighed. "Sadly, I'd say that's the reason. I don't think it's because he wants to get me into bed or anything."

Marianne smirked. "I'm sure that's also on the agenda. What will you say? He wanted you to call him and let him know."

"I'm going to say no." Molly picked up her phone. "Give me his number." When Marianne rattled it off, Molly punched in the number, her stomach in a knot. Ted was very attractive, and she knew instinctively he felt drawn to her. She had seen it in his eyes and felt it in that light touch on her shoulder. But this was business. The idea that he'd ask her out to get her to sign the deal didn't appeal to her.

"Hello?" Ted's warm voice said in her ear.

"Hi, Ted. This is Molly."

"Hi, Molly! Thanks for calling back so promptly. I was just about to check if I could get a table at l'Arôme in the harbour. It's a fantastic fish restaurant with a Michelin star. I believe their lobster thermidor is excellent. That's if you like lobster."

"Love it," Molly said, suddenly hungry. "But…"

"Great. I'll book a table for two at eight o'clock. See you then." There was a click as he hung up.

Molly looked at her phone. "What?"

"What?" Marianne echoed. "I didn't hear you say no to him."

"He didn't give me a chance. Shit," Molly moaned. "Now I have to go to a five-star restaurant looking like this." She gestured at her casual outfit of navy pants and green wool sweater.

"Call him back and say it's not on," Marianne urged.

"And miss lobster thermidor at l'Arôme?"

Marianne looked shocked. "He got a table?"

"He said he'd book one. Seemed like a breeze to him."

"Probably is, too. That man is seriously wealthy."

"Like Klaus?"

Marianne snorted. "Klaus is a pauper compared to him. Or the family, anyway." She peered at Molly. "Be careful. Dating a billionaire can be very tricky."

"I'm not dating him." Molly stuffed her phone into her bag. "He just asked me to have dinner with him so he could talk me into accepting their offer. He'll probably try to get me drunk and then get me to sign the contract."

"Don't be silly." Marianne smiled at Molly. Then she frowned as her eyes drifted to a spot behind them.

Molly turned her head to look in the same direction, but all she could see was an empty chair with a half-drunk glass of beer on the table. "What are you looking at?"

"The man sitting behind us. He seemed to be listening to what we were saying. But he left when I stared at him. I noticed him when you and Ted were chatting. He walked in just after you arrived and sat down in that chair. I didn't pay much attention until he kind of cocked his head towards us as we talked."

"What did he look like?"

Marianne shrugged. "Can't really remember. He was tall with dark hair. I just caught a glimpse of his profile. In his forties, I'd say. That's all." She shook herself. "I'm probably imagining things. It was just that he seemed so interested in you."

"He probably just thought I look strange." Molly got up. "Anyway, I'll have to go shopping to see if I can find something to wear for this weird date. I won't have time to drive back to Gigaro to change."

Marianne made an impatient gesture. "You're fine as you are. That sweater is very pretty and the jade heart is sweet. You might try to see if you can find a pashmina to throw over it and slap on a bit more make-up. But other than that, it's okay. It will send Ted the right signal. You're not trying to seduce him and it's strictly business."

Molly sighed wistfully. "My first date with a hot billionaire and it has to be strictly business."

"Stay strong," Marianne warned.

Molly straightened her back. "I'll try. 'Strictly business' will be my mantra."

Chapter 4

The pashmina Molly found in a boutique near the Negresco was perfect. Woven in a paisley pattern of pastel colours of green, pink and blue, it couldn't have been a better match for Molly's outfit. It cost an arm and a leg, but with the deal she was about to sign fresh in her mind, Molly handed over her credit card without hesitation. The butter-soft cashmere settled on her shoulders like a whisper of warmth, and she walked out of the boutique feeling as if she was being hugged by and angel. Then she went into the Guerlain shop next door and, with the help of the sales girl, applied make-up that enhanced her eyes and gave her cheeks and extra glow. The rosy lip gloss the girl suggested picked up the pink hues of the Pashmina and gave Molly's lips a new pout, which made her giggle.

"Discreet, yet sexy," she said to herself as she looked in the mirror.

"Pardon?" The sales girl asked.

"I was just talking to myself," Molly said in French. "C'est très chic."

The girl nodded. "Oui, madame. It makes you very pretty."

Molly paid the girl and walked out of the shop, repeating her mantra during the ten-minute walk to the restaurant. The streets were emptying and the traffic noises died down to a low murmur. The sun had set and the sky darkened to a deep blue. The lights in the windows of the apartment blocks came on and Molly could see into elegant living rooms with high ceilings and panelled walls. Some of the rooms had beautiful paintings or floor to ceiling bookcases crammed with books. The balconies overlooked the Promenade des Anglais and the Bay of Angels. What a beautiful place to live. Maybe she would be able to afford an apartment there one day. Outside the restaurant, Molly stopped for an instant and pulled the pashmina around her more tightly as if it was magic cape that could protect her from harm. Strictly business, she said to herself sternly yet again.

Her stomach in a knot, Molly opened the heavy glass door and stepped into the elegant interior, where tables covered in white linen were set with gleaming glassware and silver cutlery. She sniffed hungrily as wafts of delicious food met her nose. Most of the tables were occupied, and as she stood there scanning the room for Ted, a maître d' in black and white glided up to her.

"Madame has reserved?"

"No. I am joining someone. A Mr Theodore—"

"Anderson?" he said, looking immediately more welcoming. "Of course. He is already here. Let me take you to the table. Please follow me." He strode across the restaurant, Molly in tow, until he came to a stop at a table by the window, where Ted was already standing, waiting for her. He had put on a tie and exchanged the corduroy jacket for a navy blazer.

"Molly, welcome. So glad you decided to join me."

"Hello, Ted." Molly sat down on the chair the maître d' pulled out. She jumped as he snapped the linen napkin open and placed it on her lap.

Ted straightened his tie and pulled down the cuffs of his shirt. He cleared his throat. "Just to explain why you're here…I didn't ask you out to talk you into signing that contract. It's your decision, and I wouldn't want you to feel you were pushed into it."

Molly took the menu a waiter handed her. "Why did you invite me then?"

He opened his menu. "I just wanted to get to know you better."

"I'm flattered." Trying to look cool, she scanned the long list of dishes. "And hungry," she added.

He laughed. "Me too. How about that lobster thermidor?"

"Hmm, no. A bit rich. I think it's a shame to cover up delicious lobster with cream and cheese." She looked up at the waiter who had just appeared, notebook at the ready. "I'll have the lobster salad in raspberry vinaigrette and garlic mayonnaise on the side," she said. "Then I'd love a big steak with some chips."

"Chips?" the waiter said.

"Yes," Ted cut in. "We call them French fries in the US. Don't tell me you don't do those here."

"Ah, oui." The waiter sighed. "Les frites. It's not on the menu, but we have pommes alumettes that we do for children."

"That sounds good," Molly said. "And the steak should be medium rare, which is a little pink in the middle."

"We say *à point* here," the waiter said, scribbling on his pad. "And monsieur?"

Ted grinned at Molly. "The way you said that sounded so delicious, I'll have the same." He looked at the waiter. "Make that twice."

"And the steak?" he asked "*A point*, like Madame?"

"Absolutely." Ted turned to Molly. "Do you have any preference for wine?"

"I'm driving, so one glass will have to do. I'll have mineral water with the lobster and a glass of red with the steak." She looked at the waiter. "You have that?"

"Yes," he said with a pained expression. "I will bring you a glass of Château Margot."

"Driving?" Ted asked when the waiter had left with

their order. "You mean you're going back to Saint-Tropez tonight?"

"Yes, of course."

"Long drive in the dark," he remarked.

"I know," she said crisply. "But I'm used to it." She looked him squarely in the eye. "You weren't going to suggest I spend the night at your hotel? You have this big suite and there is plenty of room or something?"

He looked confused. "No, not at all. I'm staying in the apartment my company owns, and it's a bit crowded at the moment with some family members over here for an event in Nice."

She dropped her gaze. "Okay. Sorry," she mumbled, kicking herself. Of course he wasn't planning anything of the kind. Why was she always so suspicious?

He snorted a laugh. "I'm not that kind of guy, you know. I had no ulterior motives in asking you out, other than for what I just said—that I wanted to get to know you. I found myself having dinner alone, so I thought—" He paused. "Not that I don't find you very attractive, of course."

"Shit," Molly said just as the waiter placed her lobster salad before her. "I don't mean you," she said to him as he looked startled. "I mean me. I mean…" She felt her face redden. "This isn't going very well, is it?"

"Not really, no," Ted agreed, digging into his salad. He speared a piece pf lobster with his fork "I think you just painted yourself into a corner there. You got me completely wrong. I wanted to spend an evening with a woman who isn't from my normal walk of life."

"You mean you're slumming it?" Molly demanded. "I'm the salt of the earth and you want to spend time with a 'real' woman?"

"Are you always this suspicious of men?"

"No. Yes. Not really. It's just that…" She paused. "Well, you're rich and cute and kind of suave. Not the kind of man I'd normally date."

"Oh, I see. You mean you usually go for the poor ugly type?" His mouth quivered as he looked at her.

Molly gave up trying to explain. "Oh, shut up. You know what I mean."

He raised an eyebrow. "Do I? But I'm slumming it, so I'm just having fun, right?"

Molly stuck her tongue out at him. A childish gesture but he brought out the silly side in her. He was difficult to gauge: cool and suave one minute, cheeky and boyish the next. He was probably telling the truth about why he had asked her to dinner. He was on his own and wanted company. They had just met but they clicked instantly, not by so many words but by the way they looked at each other and a curious, unspoken meeting of minds she couldn't explain, even to herself. Maybe Sophia was right and their auras matched or something. The thought made her giggle.

"What's so funny?" he asked.

Molly shook her head. "Nothing. Just a weird thought about auras. My landlady has this theory that everyone has an aura. She says she can see them."

"What did she say about yours?"

"It has a sceptical vibe, or something."

He nodded, a serious look in his green eyes. "It does. You don't take people at face value."

"That's true. I don't. They have to prove their worth first."

"How do I prove mine?"

She looked at him. There was something endearing and vulnerable about him despite his confidence that came from generations of wealth and privilege.

"Oh," she said softly, "you already have."

* * *

Molly had plenty of opportunity to reflect on both Ted and the deal his firm had offered her during the long drive home.

They had ended the evening on a good note and agreed to meet up again at the weekend, when they would drive to Mougins for lunch and a walk in the hills above the town. He hadn't mentioned the business deal, apart from telling her the board had been contacted and there would be a meeting the next day. They would be in touch with Marianne about the final offer. Then he suggested they forget about it.

"If you decide to sign with us, you won't be dealing with me, anyway," he explained. "I was only told to make the initial contact and present the offer. After that, it's out of my hands. I'll be going back to New York in about a week. The board will decide the next move."

"Who's on the board?" Molly asked.

He looked thoughtful. "Have you heard of Charlotte Anderson?"

Molly nodded. "Of course! Who hasn't? She is the head of your company, right? A legend in business. Tough as an old boot, too. Even meaner than that Wintour woman. I've heard she eats her personal assistants for breakfast. Is she a relative?"

"She's my mother."

Molly's hand flew to her mouth. "Shit, I'm sorry. I had no idea. How stupid of me. I do apologise."

He grinned. "No need. I've heard worse things said about her. She and my three older sisters and I are on the board. I'm just an errand boy to them. It's a matriarchal company. I'm the youngest son and the only male in the family since my dad passed away."

"Can't be easy."

He sighed. "Tell me about it. I'm up against the male equivalent of the glass ceiling there. They're pretty scary."

She laughed and he joined in, but she felt he wasn't too happy about his situation. It had to be hard: the only male and the youngest boy too. He didn't said any more, but Molly had a feeling there wasn't much love lost between him and his sisters.

Molly turned on the radio as she reached the exit to Sainte-Maxime. The classical channel was playing Mozart's opera, Così fan tutte, in an old recording with Kiri te Kanawa. Comforting music while she drove down the twisting road through woods of gnarled cork oaks, pine trees and olive groves in the pitch dark. The dark clouds obscured the stars and rain smattered against the windscreen. A filthy night, not very pleasant for a long-distance drive. It would be a relief to see the lights of St Maxime.

Molly gripped the steering wheel and stared into the darkness, thinking hard. *Money*, she thought, *lots of money*. She had never felt she needed much. Enough to live on and a couple of thousand in the bank was what she thought would be enough to feel happy. But the surge in orders during the last six months had earned her much more than that. She was suddenly doing very well financially. And now this offer, which could make her actually wealthy.

But signing that contract would mean having to compromise her own work, her creativity and the handcrafting of individual pieces, which was her greatest joy. Someone would give her guidelines and tell her what to design. It would also mean signing an exclusive deal, locking her into a contract she might find hard to break. None of that seemed particularly attractive to a free spirit like Molly. At that moment, as she drove down the dark, lonely road, the only positive thing about the deal was…Ted.

* * *

"Two hundred thousand," Marianne said and pushed a piece of paper in front of Molly. "I wrote it down so you'd see it in black and white." They were in the cosy living room in Sophia's house, where they were lounging on the comfortable chintz sofa, enjoying a glass of wine and a plate of tapas in front of a roaring fire. It was a blustery day with chilly winds that fed down from the snow-covered Alps. Clouds skittered across the sky like flocks of sheep rushing for shelter. The cold wind sent smatters of rain across the tall windows and they could see shrubs and plants swaying to and fro in the garden.

Marianne pulled her cashmere cardigan tighter and looked out the window. "Gee, it's getting wild out there. The famous Mistral is on the way. But it's usually over fairly quickly." She jumped at a sound from the kitchen. "What was that? Sounded like broken glass. Has one of the windows blown in?" She stopped as someone shouted and then another crash of something breaking.

Molly didn't blink. "No, it's just Sophia and Jay having one of their fights," she said, helping herself to another piece of Serrano ham. "You'd think Sophia is a real cool English lady, but she has a fierce temper and so does he. They fight all the time. Maybe they fancy each other?"

Marianne shook her head. "Not very likely. Sophia would never look twice at someone like Jay."

"Why not? He's very cute and really nice."

Marianne snorted. "Are you kidding? A Spanish chef in a little restaurant up the hill in that tiny village? Of course not. Sophia is the daughter of a real English lord. She grew up on a country estate. They had no money but none of them do these days. They work hard to hang on to their heritage. But despite all that, they don't marry below their status. Sebastian was of the Anglo-Irish aristocracy. I think he had some kind of title like Sir Sebastian, which would make Sophia Lady Ffrench, believe it or not."

"But I do have a feeling they're really close," Molly protested. "And why not? Jay is a very attractive man. He adores Sophia, he said."

Marianne winked. "I think he kind of likes you too. The way he hugged you when we came in was a little more than friendly."

"He's Spanish. They're very cuddly there."

"True. But back to business." Marianne tapped the piece of paper. "This is important. We need to tell them very soon, or the deal is off."

Molly's eyes focused on the figures. "That's a hell of a lot of money. Well done, Marianne. You really squeezed them."

Marianne sighed with mock modesty. "Ah, shucks, it was nothing. So what do you say? Will you sign?"

"Where's the contract? I need to see exactly what I'm locking myself into."

"The contract? They haven't sent the full one yet. I talked to the main buyer, and she told me what the board had agreed. They'll send on the contract. I just thought we could tell them you've said yes. I'm supposed to tell her boss what we've decided before seven tonight. Shall I give the go-ahead?"

Molly sat up on the sofa and looked sternly at Marianne. "No, you can't. I cannot make any decision until I've seen the terms."

Marianne's sapphire-blue eyes widened with confusion. "Why? Isn't it better to say yes now and iron out the details later?"

Molly shook her head. "No. I have doubts about the whole thing and how it will affect my career."

"Doubts? What kind of doubts?" Marianne exclaimed.

"Several," Molly replied, counting on her fingers. "One, how much time will it take away from my clients and my handcrafting? Two, if I take time off from that, will I have to start from scratch again? Three, will I be signing on for one collection, or several? What if my designs don't sell? If it all bombs, it could damage the brand it has taken me so long to build. I think I need to talk to this woman myself first, if you don't mind."

The air went out of Marianne and she slumped, letting out a long sigh. She threw up her hands. "Okay. I see what you mean. I thought we'd be celebrating with champagne, but here you are being all sensible and careful."

"Sorry. We can celebrate later. But right now, I need to speak to that person—that woman, I mean."

Marianne nodded. "She's actually in Nice right now. But I warn you, she's a tough old bird. Not someone you fool around with."

Molly took her phone, ready to note down the details in the notes. "I have no intention of fooling around. Give me her name and number."

"Her name is Charlotte Anderson."

Molly looked up from her phone. "Char—? You mean…?

Marianne grinned. "That's right. Charlotte Anderson. Ted's mother. A legendary old bitch."

Molly felt the blood drain from her face. Did Marianne know how scared she was of taking this big step? How worried she was about losing everything if she made the wrong choice? The devil you know and all that. But now she wasn't scared anymore. She was terrified.

Chapter 5

I don't care if she's the biggest bitch alive and Anna Wintour's evil twin, Molly thought as she dialled the number. *I have to think of my own life and my career. I'm not going to bow and scrape.*

Marianne had left, saying she had to go home to meet Klaus, who was flying in from Munich in his private jet. "I'll be expecting to hear from you when you've spoken to the witch," she said as she left. "Good luck. Don't let her intimidate you."

Molly's stomach churned as she waited for a reply. After several rings, a voice came on the line: "Charlotte Anderson's private office. Amanda Smith speaking."

"Hello," Molly croaked. "This is Molly Creedon. I'd like to speak to Mrs Anderson, please."

"Just a moment. I'll ask if Mrs Anderson will take the call." Molly heard a murmur, then a click and a cold, crisp voice came on the line. "Charlotte Anderson speaking."

Molly cleared her throat. "Good evening, Mrs Anderson. This is Molly Creedon. I'm a jewellery designer and—"

"I know who you are," the voice interrupted. "I also know you're making us wait for a decision about the offer we made you. I hope you're calling to tell me we can go ahead."

Molly gritted her teeth. The woman seemed to think it was in the bag. Did everyone snap to attention when she spoke to them? Probably, but not this time. "Not exactly," she started. "I was calling to discuss the terms. I haven't seen the contract yet. I don't feel I can say yes or no until I know exactly what I'll be agreeing to."

There was a brief pause. Then the cold voice spoke: "The contract has been sent to your business manager. It should be with her tomorrow. Give us a call when you have seen it, with your final decision. The terms on the contract are non-negotiable. We have already increased the advance. We need to hear from you before close of business tomorrow or the deal is off. Goodbye, Miss Creedon."

"Tomorrow? Oh, but—"

"Please don't waste any more of my time," the chilly voice interrupted. "You have exactly twenty-four hours to make up your mind." The line went dead.

"Bitch," Molly growled as Sophia stepped into the room.

She stopped looking startled. "I beg your pardon?"

"Not you," Molly said, glaring at her phone. "This…this bloody piranha in disguise."

"Who do you mean?" Sophia stepped closer and started putting glasses and the plate with half-eaten tapas on a tray.

"Charlotte Anderson, the female business tycoon. Do you know who I mean?"

"Yes, of course," Sophia replied. "Famous for her success in covering the world in shops full of cheap, cheerful clothes for office girls."

"That's the woman."

Sophia picked up the tray. "Why were you talking to her?"

"Long story. I'll tell you later." Molly got up. "Let me help you with that."

Sophia handed her the tray. "Thank you. Could you take it to the kitchen? I'm just finishing up in the vegetable garden before the storm hits. I have to make sure the doors and windows of the greenhouse are secured. And tell Jesus the tomatoes I picked are in the larder. He wanted them for a spaghetti sauce he's making tonight. He's to use the ones in the blue bowl. The others are for chutney. And the last of the season's carrots and string beans are in a box ready for the market tomorrow. Will you be dining with us?"

"I'd love to."

Sophia nodded. "Good. Then you can tell me about this strange phone call. Must dash. The wind is getting up."

Molly carried the tray into the kitchen, warm and welcoming and full of the smell of newly baked bread. There was nobody about. Molly snuck a roll from the baking tray on the kitchen counter. Jay must have done some baking earlier. She spread butter on it and had just taken a bite when he walked in.

"Caught you," he said. "Stealing bread now, are we?"

Molly laughed through her mouthful. "Oops. Thought I was alone. You must have made fifty rolls or something. Didn't think you'd miss one."

"I made those for the restaurant. The oven there is broken. We're trying to fix it. But it's okay. One less won't make a difference."

"They're delicious." Molly wiped the crumbs off her mouth. "Sophia said the tomatoes are in the larder. You're supposed to use the ones in the blue bowl. And the vegetables for the market are in a box in there to."

Jay nodded and started to put the rolls into a paper bag. "Thanks. I'll make up the sauce for the pasta and then you'll have to do the rest yourselves. I'm working tonight."

"No problem. Sophia is securing the greenhouse. It's going to be a wild night."

"I know. But we have a special end of season Spanish night at the restaurant with flamenco guitars and paella. We expect quite a crowd. I hope the weather won't stop people coming. It's the final hurrah for this year. We open again in April."

"Sounds like fun."

He sighed. "For them maybe. But it will be hectic and hot. Great for publicity though. We'll get a feature in Nice Matin, which is worth gold. And local TV too. Someone even mentioned it would go out on national TV. So we have to put on quite a show."

"I can imagine. Gosh, you and Sophia both work so hard."

"Most people do, don't they? Sophia is trying to hang onto this house by letting parts of it and then all the extra bits like growing vegetables and organising garden tours. She also makes jam and chutney and sells it in the market. It's hard work but I think she loves it. She could sell up and move to something a lot smaller, but this house is all she has left of Sebastian. They restored this old house together, and he spent his last year here. Hard work is second nature to her. It's to do with that Protestant work ethic. A life of leisure would seem sinful to her."

"It's a beautiful house," Molly said. "I can understand why she wants to keep it. I know what you mean about working hard too. It makes you feel useful."

Jay put the last of the rolls into the bag. "True, but it's also about achievement and knowing you can support yourself." He looked at her thoughtfully. "It's about pride, and integrity really isn't it? And that can't be bought."

"No," Molly agreed. "It can't." She sat down at the kitchen table watching Jay chopping tomatoes, onion and garlic, frying mince and adding all the ingredients until the smell of baking was replaced by a delicious aroma of the spaghetti sauce. Her mind drifted to the decision she had to make. Would it lock her into something she would regret? It would mean a lot of money. But what Jay had just said about pride and integrity resonated with Molly.

Jay put the lid on the pan. "There. Let that simmer for about half an hour and then it's ready."

"Mmm," Molly said.

"You look like you're struggling with something."

Her eyes focused on him. "Yes, I think I am. Mostly with myself."

* * *

"Prostitution," Sophia said.

Molly blinked. "What?"

"You'd be prostituting yourself if you sign that contract."

"I haven't even seen it yet."

They were in the living room, where Sophia had banked the fire and closed the shutters against the storm that raged outside, enveloping them in the cosiness of soft lamplight and the glow from the fireplace. Molly had just told her about the deal with H&A, and Sophia had looked at her thoughtfully while she listened. "No, but I bet that contract will be so full of clauses and conditions, it will prevent you making your own handcrafted jewellery, for which you are now famous."

"I'll never sign such a contract. I'll have to negotiate, so it's to my advantage, not theirs."

"Hmm." Sophia put a cushion behind her back. "You're very naïve for someone your age. Do you think that lot would ever do anything to someone else's advantage? Especially that Anderson woman."

"Probably not," Molly said glumly. She leaned back against the cushions and stared into the dying embers of the fire. "But I'll have a go all the same when I get the contract. I'll only sign if it's about just one collection. I can do that and have it ready for their deadline on the fifteenth of December, if I work hard."

"Make sure you get a lawyer to go through the contract before you sign anything," Sophia warned.

"Of course. Marianne's lawyer in Nice has already been alerted." Molly looked at her watch. "It's time for the late evening news. Maybe TV three did feature the flamenco night at Jay's place after all?"

"I forgot all about that." Sophia picked up a remote from the table beside the sofa and pointed it at the TV in the corner. "I hardly ever watch TV, but Sebastian put this set in here so he could watch the BBC."

The news came on. Molly and Sophia watched idly while the anchor woman read out the headlines. There was a whole string of news items, mainly about politics and the European Union. Molly was nearly falling asleep, when Sophia sat up and pointed at the screen.

"Look, they're going to show the restaurant!"

Molly woke up and looked. And there it was—the familiar façade of Jay's restaurant. A big crowd had gathered inside, looking as if they were having a good time. The flamenco guitarist was superb, and the music complemented the Spanish atmosphere perfectly.

"Looks like it's a huge hit," Molly said.

"Yes, it does. Jesus will be pleased. Look, there he is," Sophia said as a beaming Jay came into view. "I wish he wouldn't wear that horrid bandana and the earring. It makes him look like some kind of gypsy."

"I think it suits him," Molly said. "The customers seem to love it. Look at that woman kissing him on the cheek."

"Tart," Sophia said with a snort. "But the man beside her is very good-looking."

"Which man?" Molly stared at the screen.

"The tall man behind the tarty woman. I wonder if they're there together."

Molly focused on the tall figure behind the woman who had just kissed Jay. She caught a fleeting glimpse of his profile before the camera moved away and felt the blood drain from her face.

"What's the matter?" Sophia asked. "You look like you've just seen a ghost."

"I have," Molly whispered. "A ghost from my past."

Chapter 6

It couldn't be. Not him, here in Gigaro, this remote part of the Riviera, largely unknown by tourists. What would he be doing here? Is he looking for me? But why after all this time? These thoughts whirled around in Molly's mind as she tried to go to sleep. The flash of recognition as she saw that man on the TV screen had given her a jolt like a punch in the gut. She had been in denial all these years, shutting him out of her mind while life rolled on. As she lay there, twisting and turning, the locked-up memories came rushing back. Once or twice she had thought he might be dead. She could have issued a missing person's report and become a widow after the stipulated time. But even that had seemed unimportant. She lived in the present and the past was the past. Life continued its usual roller coaster way. Sad times and happy times. Settling into a new country. Comforting a very homesick little boy. And now a happy time with Liam married and Molly's career taking off. A new beginning. Molly closed her eyes and willed herself to put all thoughts of that brief marriage back in the box she had kept shut for so long. It's not him, she told herself. It couldn't be. He must be dead. She imagined the lid of the box closing and finally slept.

* * *

"I just got the contract," Marianne said on the phone the next morning.

Molly sat up in bed. "Yes? And?"

"Calm down. I haven't read it all yet. Just the first page. But I can tell you there's an exclusivity clause. You can still do bespoke pieces for private clients, but that's all. No other work for any other designer, even if it's one of the haute-couture collections. So if you get an offer for one of those, you'll have to say no."

"But I don't have offers like that."

"You might."

"And pigs will fly," Molly chipped in. "I have this offer. That's all I know for now. A bird in the hand and all that."

"I know. But do you really want to lock yourself in with them for two years? I don't trust that Anderson woman. Let me read the rest and ask my lawyer to look through it. Then I'll call you back this afternoon, and we can either proceed or discuss anything we're not happy with."

"Perfect. But Charlotte Anderson told me the deadline is five p.m. today. And that the contract is non-negotiable." Molly flung her duvet back and got out of bed. "She made me feel I should be honoured by their interest in me."

"She did? The bitch. Right. Okay, then. I'll call you back at three o'clock or so. Bye for now." Marianne hung up.

Molly opened the curtains and stepped onto the balcony. It was a breezy, sunny morning with just a few clouds on the horizon. Still in her pyjamas, she did some yoga stretches, breathing in the cool, fresh air laden with the invigorating smell of pine and eucalyptus. The stretches calmed her frazzled nerves somewhat, except for a tight knot in her stomach. This was a crossroad in her career. Whatever she decided would affect her life big time. To sign or not to sign? It all depended on what was in that contract. Molly breathed in deeply, did her final down-dog pose, ending with a sun salutation, stretching her arms as high as she could against the bright, blue sky.

The phone rang just as she was coming out of the shower. Still dripping, Molly wrapped a towel around her and picked it up. "Molly Creedon."

"I know who you are," said a cheery voice.

Molly smiled. "Ted? Is that you?"

"Yup. Hey, I know I shouldn't call you before you make the big decision, but I'm leaving for New York in a couple of days, so I thought we could meet up?"

Molly rubbed her hair with a towel. "I don't see why not if we keep business out of the conversation."

"Great. How about that lunch in Mougins? I know a great restaurant there. Four stars and everything."

Molly sat down on the bed. "I'm not that much into gourmet food. How about a hike in the mountains with a picnic? If you're up to that sort of thing, of course."

"Sure," Ted said. "I'm quite fit. That sounds like fun. Will I ask our chef to make up a picnic?"

"God, no," Molly exclaimed. "I'll bring the picnic. You need to see how the other half lives for a change, preppie boy."

He laughed. "Yeah, I guess I do. So you'll be bringing a home-made picnic? And bake the bread for the sandwiches over an open fire?"

"Of course. And I'll milk a couple of goats and make cheese too."

"Sounds really earthy."

"You'll love it."

"Do I have a choice?" He paused and cleared his throat. "I heard you spoke to my mother."

"Yes."

There was a brief pause. "Okay. I get it. Let's keep her out of this."

"Absolutely," Molly said with feeling, wondering if Ted might have been switched at birth. How could this sweet guy be that horrible woman's son? "When do you want to do this hike, then? The forecast for Thursday is quite good—windy, but no rain. We could meet in the main square in Saint-Cézaire. That's an old village on the Siagne. It's near Grasse. Less than an hour's drive from Nice. You'll find it on the map or your GPS. At ten o'clock?"

"Great."

"Bring a warm jacket. It can be cold up there in the mountains. It snowed in the Maritime Alps yesterday."

"Yes, ma'am. See you then."

Molly shook her head and smiled when she had hung up. There was something innocent and beguiling about Ted, despite his suave manners and sophistication. She had a feeling he hadn't had much fun growing up in that hothouse atmosphere dominated by those women.

She kept thinking about him as she got dressed. Funny how she felt so drawn to him and how they seemed to connect, despite being from such different backgrounds. How would working for the firm affect this new friendship? Well, whatever. It was best to leave it up to the stars. She would go with the flow and trust her own instincts. Anyway, the day ahead was full of pending decisions. No time to linger.

On her way to her car and the short drive to her workshop, the phone rang again. Without checking the caller ID, Molly replied, "Don't tell me I scared you off with the goats and all that!"

"Molly?" a hesitant voice said. "Am I calling at a bad time? This is Chantal from Agence du Soleil. Daisy said you were looking for a—"

Molly let out a laugh. "Oh, shit, I thought it was someone else. Sorry, Chantal. It's fine. Go ahead."

"I'm sorry I didn't call you earlier," Chantal said. "But Gabriel and I went to Italy for a few weeks. He wanted to paint the Tuscan landscape in autumn."

"Must have been amazing."

"It was very beautiful, yes. Anyway," Chantal breezed on, "I'm calling you because a new property has come up. I'm not sure it would be what you're looking for, but..."

Molly opened the door of the car and sat down behind the wheel. "What kind of property is it?"

"An apartment in the centre of Saint-Tropez," Chantal said. "Two bedrooms, a living room and large kitchen. It's in an old building just off Place des Lices. Needs a bit of work, I'd say. Very charming if you can believe the photos. I haven't seen it yet but we can look at it together."

"Sounds interesting. When can I see it?"

"How about around lunch time? Twelve thirty or so? I have another property in the area to look at this morning, so that would suit me."

Molly nodded. "That's fine. Give me the address and I'll meet you there at twelve thirty."

"Perfect." Chantal paused. "What was that about goats?"

Molly laughed. "Oh that. I'm trying to teach a very spoiled man about the real world, that's all."

"You're teaching a man something? But that's impossible."

"I like a challenge," Molly said. "How much is the apartment?"

"I think they said around five hundred thousand euros. But I'll look up the price and tell you exactly."

"Ugh, okay. That's a little pricey. Maybe we can offer a bit below that?"

"No," Chantal said. "They said the price was non-negotiable."

"Okay. Can't wait to see it. Bye, Chantal."

"A tout de suite," Chantal said and hung up.

"Non-negotiable," Molly muttered to herself as she drove away from the house. "Why is everything in my life suddenly non-negotiable?"

Chapter 7

The stairwell was cold and dank, the walls grey. The stairs wound themselves up a narrow shaft, passing old doors that looked like they hid gruesome secrets. Molly had serious misgivings as she climbed the stairs behind Chantal. This was not going to be something she would want to buy. She liked Chantal's crisp but friendly approach instantly. With her tall slim frame, short dark hair and classic style, she exuded confidence, honesty and strong ethics. Not someone who would be carried away by the romance of old buildings. This had to be something worth looking at.

Chantal came to a halt on a narrow landing on the top floor. "Here it is," she said and took a bunch of keys from her bag. "Doesn't look very promising, I have to say."

Molly peered through a small window and saw the church tower behind the dusty panes. "Nice view though. What I can see of it."

"There's supposed to be a terrace with views of the harbour." Chantal inserted a huge key into the lock of the old door. "But let's take a look." She turned the key and the door opened with a loud creak. Chantal stepped inside while Molly hesitated on the landing. Maybe there were rats? Or bats? She took a small step into the hall, ready to flee at any rustle or beating of wings.

Once inside, she was instantly surprised. Stepping through the front door was like going through a magic mirror to a different world. The tiny hall with a gold-framed oval mirror over an old white table and a wrought-iron umbrella stand was oddly inviting. There was a slight smell of wood smoke and—eerily—rose petals, as if someone had lit a scented candle not so long ago.

"Come in here," Chantal called from another room. "This is lovely."

Molly went into the next room which had to be the living room. It was an enchanting space, with pale rose-coloured walls, a period fireplace, and terracotta floor tiles, polished by many feet through the centuries. The arched windows led to a terrace with views of the rooftops and the harbour beyond. She looked up at the high ceiling and noticed a faint outline of clouds and something else.

"Oh my God, what's that?" she whispered. "Angels?"

Chantal followed her gaze. "An old fresco. How lovely. This house is from the sixteenth century, so it must be some decoration from that era. Pity there isn't much left of it."

"It's gorgeous," Molly said, still in awe. "It's nice that the image is so faint but still there. As if someone is looking down on me from heaven through a mist."

"That's a lovely thought." Chantal opened one of the French windows. "Let's have a look at the terrace."

They stepped outside into the cold breeze and admired the view of the harbour, framed by the rooftops, and a tall acacia tree in the little square below. There were terracotta pots on the terrace with wilting roses and a large tub with yellowing herbs. Two rusty wrought-iron chairs leaned against an equally rusty table, and many of the tiles were cracked. The wall surrounding the terrace had once been painted a pale pink, judging by a few patches here and there.

"In need of a serious update," Chantal remarked. "Are you any good at DIY?"

"No, but I can learn," Molly said, her eyes on a sailing boat far out at sea. "Can you smell the fresh bread baking in the boulangerie on the ground floor? Imagine waking up to that smell and going down the stairs for my breakfast rolls and croissants."

"Let's see the rest before you fall too much in love," Chantal said. "You have stars in your eyes. That's very dangerous."

Molly laughed. "I know. I fall for romantic buildings very easily. I'm glad you're here to point out the flaws."

"I'll take out my super-strength glasses to find them all." Chantal opened a door off the living room. "This is the main bedroom."

Molly stepped inside an empty room with whitewashed walls and a large window with a window seat. She walked across the wide oak floorboards and sat down on a musty cushion, looking through the grimy window. From this side of the building, she could see the harbour from another angle, and the blue of the sea seemed to come into the room as she sat there. She turned and looked at Chantal. "I want to live here. I'll offer the asking price."

Chantal sighed. "I would normally hold you to that and make you start the buying process. But you're a friend of Daisy and that makes you kind of family. So I will proceed with caution. Let's go and see the rest and then have a chat."

The rest of the apartment was just as enchanting. The bathroom had a roll-top bath and a porcelain basin that looked at least Victorian, if not older, the kitchen cupboards were of solid oak, and, "would look fantastic with distressed paint," Molly chortled.

"You'll need new kitchen appliances," Chantal warned. "That cooker looks dangerous."

"No problem," Molly murmured, caressing the oak panelling on the opposite wall.

When they had finally seen it all, they retreated to a café on the Place des Lices with two huge cups of café au lait and croissants.

"This will be my local," Molly said, looking at the old men playing boules under the acacia trees.

"If you buy the apartment."

Molly stuck out her chin. "*When* I buy the apartment."

"It will cost a lot of money to do it up," Chantal argued.

"But when I have finished, it will add a lot to the value."

Chantal nodded and took a slurp of milky coffee. "That's true. But won't you have to apply for a loan to afford all that?"

Molly beamed. "Nope. I am about to sign a very lucrative contract. With that, and what's in my savings account, I can manage it without a loan."

"I thought you wanted to see the terms first? Didn't you say something about having to deal with someone very nasty? I know you said it could make you a lot of money, but is it worth it if you have to swallow your pride?"

Molly put down her cup. "Chantal, I would sign a pact with the devil to get that place. Go on, get it for me."

Chantal lifted one of her slim, black eyebrows. "Are you sure?

"I've never been surer of anything in my whole life."

Chantal sighed. "All right. I'll get the ball rolling. But don't come crying to me if it goes all wrong."

Molly threw her arms around Chantal and hugged her tightly. "It will go wonderfully right, I'm very sure of that."

Chantal pulled away and looked at Molly. "This feels strange. I felt it when we were up there and I saw you sitting in the window seat. I feel it even stronger now."

"What?" Molly asked, bewildered.

"That it's somehow meant to be."

* * *

"It's meant to happen," Molly said later that day when she called Marianne. "I'm ready to sign that contract. I don't care about the fecking terms. Just let me sign and I'll do whatever they want."

"But," Marianne stammered, "there are a few clauses my lawyer doesn't like. It will lock you in with them for two years with no option to get out. And they have split the advance into four parts payable over the two years."

Molly shot up from her chair in the sun room, knocking over her mug of tea. "That's not what Ted said when he presented the package."

"No, but that's what that Anderson bitch is saying now."

Molly mopped up the spilt tea with a paper towel. "Shit. I need the money now. I want that apartment like I've never wanted anything in my entire life."

"You could take a loan," Marianne suggested. "In any case, is it really a good idea to blow the whole lot on this property?"

"Yes, because it will make me happy."

"Hmm. Okay."

Molly sat down again. "I'll call her."

"Who?"

"The Anderson woman."

"What are you going to say?"

"I have no idea. I'll think of something. I'll call you back." Molly hung up. With what felt like a million butterflies in her stomach, she looked up Charlotte Anderson's private number and tapped it in.

It rang twice, then: "Charlotte Anderson's office. Amanda Smith speaking."

Molly took a deep breath. "Hello. Molly Creedon here. May I speak to—"

"She's been expecting your call. Please hold while I get her."

It only took Charlotte Anderson two seconds to get on the line. "Yes, Ms Creedon?" she barked. "What is your decision?"

"Good afternoon, Mrs Anderson. I'm very well, thank you," Molly said cheekily. "How are you?"

"Let's get on with it," Charlotte Anderson snapped. "Is it yes or no?"

"It's yes."

"Excellent," Charlotte Anderson said in a more mellow tone.

"On one condition," Molly continued, feeling her heart race.

"I said no negotiations or conditions."

"I know, but I only have one."

"And what would that be?"

"That I get the whole advance on signing. If not, no deal. That's it. Take it or leave it," Molly said and hung up. She buried her face in her hands and burst into tears. What a stupid thing to do. She had blown it. They would never agree to those terms. They called the shots and would never back down. Buying that perfect apartment would not be possible, except if she risked it all and took a huge loan.

"What's the matter?" Sophia asked as she came in from the garden with a basket full of apples. "Has something awful happened?"

"Yes," Molly sobbed. "I've just burned all my bridges and the possibility to buy what felt like home for the first time in my life."

Sophia dropped the basked and sat down on the chair beside Molly, putting her arm around her. "But you can stay here as long as you like, you know that."

Molly leaned her head against Sophia's shoulder. "I know. Thanks. But this place was so perfect. A gorgeous little apartment at the top of an old building in the heart of old Saint-Tropez." She lifted her tearstained face and looked at Sophia. "I sat on the window seat and looked out at a little sailing boat in the bay. I heard the church bells and could smell fresh bread from the boulangerie on the ground floor.

And it felt as if this place put its arms around me and whispered 'welcome home'. I know that sounds completely off the wall but…"

Sophia hugged Molly against her ample bosom. "Ah, I know what you mean. Just like when we found this house. It felt as if it had been here, waiting for us."

"That's it," Molly sniffed into Sophia's soft wool sweater that smelled of wood smoke and apples. "But now it's gone because I lost my temper."

"Maybe it's for the best."

"Oh, I don't know." Molly pulled away and mopped her face with a paper towel. "I think—" She was interrupted by her phone. "It's Marianne," Molly said when she picked it up. "Probably to give out to me for blowing the deal." She put the phone to her ear. "Hi Marianne, sorry about—"

"What did you say to Charlotte Anderson?" Marianne cut in.

"Why? Was she angry?"

"No…well, yes, maybe. Who cares? But the gist of it all is that they have now agreed to pay you half the advance on signing, plus another fifty thousand on top of that, and the other half when you deliver the goods. I mean the design of the spring collection, at the end of December. Howzat for good news?"

Molly sat there, stunned. It would come true. She would be able to buy the apartment. She hadn't blown it after all.

"Molly?" Marianne shouted. "Are you okay?"

Molly stared blankly at Sophia, who was listening intently. "Good news," she whispered. She put the phone to her ear. "I'm fine. I'm more than fine, I'm over the moon! Yippee!" she shouted, throwing the phone on the chair, and jumped up and down her arms above her head. "Yes, yes, yes!" She picked up the phone again. "Sorry, but I just had to let off some steam."

"I'm glad you're happy," Marianne laughed. "Anyway, it

means we have to accept everything else in that contract. We're at the shit-or-get-off-the-pot stage. Or we could call it between a rock and Charlotte Anderson. But I bet you scared her. The rich always want what they can't have. You made her think she couldn't have you. That's what clinched the deal."

"I don't care. I just want to sign and get my hands on the money so I can make an offer on this perfect place I saw today."

"Right," Marianne said in a more business like tone. "I'll call them and say we're accepting their offer and confirm in an e-mail. Then you have to go to the lawyer's office in Nice tomorrow morning to do the signing. He'll organise some of his staff to witness your signature. I'll send it over to New York by special delivery. And then it should only be a couple of days before you get the money into your account."

"Brilliant," Molly said, putting a hand on her chest. Her heart was beating as if she had just run a marathon. A dream come true. Her very own home at last. She looked at Sophia. "I can't believe it. I'll be able to buy that apartment and have enough money to do it up and buy furniture too."

Sophia's eyes were sad. "But that means you'll be leaving, just when I was getting to know you."

Molly laughed. "I won't be leaving for a while yet. That place needs a serious makeover. I'll stay here until it's ready to move into. I'm going to do most of the work myself except for plumbing and electricity. So, it'll take months. You'll be throwing me out by the time I'm finished."

"Never." Sophia got up and lifted the basket of apples. "I'm making an apple pie for dessert, so I'd better get started."

"Sounds delicious," Molly said and picked up her phone. "I have to call Chantal and tell her I can buy the place."

Sophia nodded. "Congratulations. I hope you'll be happy in your new apartment."

Molly smiled. "Thank you. I know I will. This feels like a new chapter in my life."

"I like new chapters," Sophia said. "As long as there's a happy ending."

* * *

A happy ending? The words kept flitting into Molly's head all through the following day. She drove to Nice with Marianne to sign the contract, and they had a giggly celebratory lunch at a little bistro nearby afterwards. Chantal had confirmed in an e-mail that the sellers had accepted the slightly lower price she had offered and the purchase was going ahead. Everything was falling into place.

"So, you'll have to work with one of the 'girls,'" Marianne said, making quote marks with her fingers. "The eldest Anderson daughter. A real dragon from what I've heard. She'll be telling you what kind of jewellery they'll want. The 'theme', they said."

"If she's anything like her mother, that's going to be interesting. But I love a challenge," Molly said, with alcohol-induced bravado.

Marianne looked impressed. "You're very brave."

Molly shrugged. "Maybe I'm just foolish? But whatever. I'll deal with those Andersons. I'm a West Cork girl and we don't let anyone sit on us."

"Hmm, okay." Marianne slipped on a pair of glasses that made her delicate features look oddly vulnerable. She picked up a copy of the contract and flicked through it. "I think I know all this by heart now." She handed it to Molly. "Here, this is your copy. Put it somewhere safe."

Molly tucked the contract into her tote bag and got up from the table. "I have to go. I want to finish something for one of my personal clients, and then I'll get stuck into the first draft of the Anderson collection. I'm taking a day off tomorrow. The weather is clearing, so I'm going on a hike in the mountains with Ted."

Marianne lifted an eyebrow. "Ted? Anderson?"

"That's right."

"Uh-huh."

Molly bristled. "What?" she demanded.

"Aren't you playing with fire dating their golden boy?"

"I'm not dating him, for God's sake! We're just friends. I wanted to show him something other than the inside of luxury restaurants and spa hotels. In any case, it's nobody business who I see in my free time."

"Yeah, sure," Marianne muttered. "But maybe it would be a good idea not to broadcast this little friendship for now."

"I wasn't planning to. I'm sure Ted is allowed to take time off now and then without asking his mummy for permission. He is, after all, a grown man."

Marianne flicked her hand. "Fine, fine, I was just being paranoid. Go on, have fun. But don't come crying to me if the Andersons go apeshit."

"They won't."

"Why not?"

"Because they'll never find out."

Chapter 8

Molly couldn't help laughing when she spotted Ted in the village square of Saint-Cézaire. Leaning against the fountain, he looked like an ad for some top-of-the-range outdoor clothing company. Everything, from the red jacket, blue windproof pants and hiking boots was brand new.

"What are you laughing at?" Ted asked as she approached. He glanced down at his clothes. "Anything wrong with what I'm wearing? Thought you said we'd be hiking."

"Yes, we will." Molly pulled the price tag from his jacket. She glanced at it. "Wow, that's one hell of an expensive bit of clothing."

Ted squirmed. "Well, yeah. I had to get geared up in a hurry. I haven't done much hiking lately. Skiing is more my thing." He inspected Molly's weathered jacket and scuffed walking boots. "Your clothes tell a different story."

Molly hitched her rucksack higher on her shoulders and clicked the clasp shut on her waist. "I've been hillwalking since I was seven. My brother and I used to walk in the mountains in West Cork with our dad and then later on in Kerry. Walking is very much part of my life. I love the open air. I can't stand being cooped up indoors for long. I think it must be in my genes."

Ted grinned. "That's why you look so wholesome."

"Yeah, I'm a real little girl guide at heart."

"Girl guide?"

"Girl scout to you yanks."

He nodded. "Yeah, that's you all right. Hey, I heard you decided to sign the contract."

"Already signed and winging its way to New York."

"Great stuff. I'm glad you're going to work with us. What's in that rucksack?"

"Lunch. I said I'd bring a picnic, didn't I?"

"So you did." He looked around. "Nice little village."

"Yes. It's very old. It was built in the middle ages as a fortification." Molly pointed at the church. "That was built in the early eighteenth century so not as old as the rest. But there is a twelfth-century chapel further on. We'll see it on the way to the trail." Molly extracted a map from one of the pockets of her jacket. "We'll take the Grande Randonnée today, as you're not a seasoned walker. It's not too hard and a lovely trail with gorgeous views." Molly squinted at the sun in the pristine blue sky. "Great walking weather. Chilly and a little breezy. They said on the radio it would rain later, but it might miss us."

"Let's hope it does," Ted said. "Even if my jacket is supposed to protect me from any kind of natural disaster."

"It should for that price. Right, let's get going then. Have you got your bottle of water?"

"Yes. I put it in the water bottle pocket of the jacket. There seems to be a special pocket for everything." Ted extracted his mobile phone. "Even a cell-phone pocket. And you know what? I'll put it in the do-not-disturb mode. Don't want to be pulled back into reality on this fabulous day."

"That's a great idea," Molly said and clicked her phone into the same mode. "Let's run away from home for the day."

"I wish it were for good," Ted said glumly.

Molly laughed. "I know what you mean." She put away her phone and started to walk down the main street, Ted following her. They passed the old chapel, the churchyard and a few old houses at the end of the village and were soon in open countryside on a path overlooked by the foothills of the Maritime Alps, the snow-covered tops of which they could see in the distance. The wind blew, the air was crisp, and the foliage of the trees blazed in autumn colours. A perfect day for a walk.

They set off at a brisk pace. They didn't speak, but Molly knew Ted was enjoying himself. He looked around like a child in a wonderland he had never seen before. He soon overtook her and raced ahead, his long legs tackling the steep slopes with an easy stride. Molly ran behind, slightly out of breath both from the pace and suppressed laughter.

He stopped and turned. "What are you laughing at?"

"You," she panted. "You're like a big Labrador puppy out for his first run in the country."

Ted made a face. "Oh great. A gorgeous woman thinks I'm a puppy."

"Sorry. That was meant as a compliment."

"Gee thanks." Ted wiped the sweat off his forehead with the back of his hand. "I'm hot. I have to take off my jacket."

"Me too." Molly peeled off her jacket and tied it around her waist. "The sun is still quite hot, even up here."

"Sure is." Ted followed Molly's example and bundled his jacket around his waist.

"Water break," Molly announced and took out her bottle.

"Good idea." Ted took big gulps from his bottle, coughed and put the cap back on. "Forgot to tell you. I got an e-mail yesterday asking about you. Can't remember the name, but I'll look it up. Mike something. Said he was a journalist for The Herald Tribune."

Molly stopped drinking. "The International Herald Tribune, you mean?"

"I think that's it. Their European headquarters are in Paris. Anyway, he wanted to know if the rumours of you doing a collection for us were true. I said I wasn't in a position to comment but would get back to him if it happened.

I think it was about a feature of your work or something. It could be good publicity."

Molly wiped her mouth. "How could he have found out about it? I haven't told anyone. I got the impression your mother wants to keep it under wraps until just before the collection hits the shops."

"Yes, she does. We're all sworn to secrecy. Could it be your business manager?"

"Marianne?" Molly shook her head. "No, don't think she'd talk to the press or anyone. How strange. Must have been a leak from your firm."

"If it is, I hope they never own up. They'd be out on their ass in no time."

"I can imagine." Molly put her rucksack back on. "Let's get going. Or do you want to sit down and rest for a bit?"

"What do you think I am? A wimp?" Ted stuffed the bottle back into his rucksack and looked out across the valley below. "What a stunning view. I never knew hiking could be this enjoyable. It makes you feel so free and far away from all your problems."

"I love it." Molly looked up at the top of the mountain above them. "The view will be even better from up there. It'll take about an hour to reach the top. We can have lunch there."

"Hold that pose," Ted said suddenly.

Molly heard a series of clicks and turned around to face a camera with a big lens. "So that's what was in the shoulder bag. Didn't know you had a camera. And such a fancy one too."

"Photography is one of my hobbies." Ted put the camera back in its case. "It's more than a hobby, really. If I didn't have to work in the family firm, I'd take it up professionally."

"Why do you have to work in the firm? Aren't there enough women for that?"

Ted's happy expression changed. "I'm the only son. I have

to carry on the name and take charge of the whole thing one day."

"That's a bit old-fashioned, isn't it?"

"I guess it is. But that's just the way it goes with my mother. If I don't toe the line, she'll cut me off without a penny."

Molly laughed. "Are you serious? Your mother runs your whole life? She would disown you if you wanted to do your own thing? And you're too much of a mammy's boy to argue?"

Ted's face darkened. "I don't see that's any of your business." He slung the camera around his neck. "But let's get going." He started to walk very fast with Molly running behind.

She caught up with him around the next bend and pulled at his sleeve. "Hey, come on. I'm sorry I laughed. I didn't mean to call you a mammy's boy. I have this big mouth that runs away with me sometimes."

"Okay," he muttered and pulled away.

Molly trotted behind. "Come on, Ted," she pleaded. "Let's not ruin this fine day with arguments. I'm sorry. I won't bring it up again, promise."

Ted stopped so suddenly Molly bumped into him. "All right," he said in a determined tone. "I shouldn't have snapped at you either. I do have a problem with my mother, but that's not your fault. It's something that has been going on all my life and can't be fixed in a hurry. So, yes, let's leave it aside and enjoy this amazing walk. And thank you for suggesting it." He didn't wait for a reply and resumed his walk at a slightly slower pace.

Molly followed him, looking at his back and broad shoulders that suggested strength but only of a physical nature. His suave good looks hid a tortured soul. Ted was obviously bullied by his mother, and it looked as if it had been going on for years. It didn't surprise her. Her brief conversations with

Charlotte Anderson had given her the shivers. She knew working for the Andersons would be fraught with conflict. But she wouldn't let that woman ruin her relationship with Ted. She might even have been able to help him if she was subtle and didn't tease him. Molly knew that parental abuse could continue into adulthood. It was difficult to stop and even more difficult to cope with for the victim.

They resumed their walk up the hill, continued along a ledge that took them around the edge of the mountain and onto an even steeper gulley which demanded all their concentration to climb, until they reached the top, where they could sit on a flat rock and eat their lunch. Molly took out rolls, Parma ham, tomatoes and two apples from her rucksack.

"Food," Ted stuffed a bit of ham into his roll and took a huge bite. "Beats a four-star lunch in some fancy restaurant," he said when he had finished his mouthful. "Fresh bread, delicious ham and that view. What could be better?"

"Nothing," Molly said and took off her jacket. "And the sun is hot and the sky is blue and we don't have to talk to anyone."

"Even each other?" Ted asked with a catch in his voice.

"If we don't want to." Molly closed her eyes to the sun. "I just want to sit here and breathe this clean air and enjoy the bread and ham. No need to talk at all."

"Good." Ted finished his bread roll, drank some water and then sat back, looking out across the hills covered in umbrella pines and small oaks. The whisper of the wind and a random croak from a raven were the only sounds. Far below, they could see a road snaking around in hairpin bends and the odd car disappearing toward the coast and the throng of houses in Grasse and Antibes, further away in the distance. The blue ribbon of the river glinted as it wound its way through the valley.

Ted muttered something.

"What?" Molly asked.

"I was just saying that I like you. And something else. Something you'll probably think is really cowardly. And fucking childish."

"How do I know if you don't tell me?" Molly said, more startled by the pain in his voice than the sudden expletive. "Go on. I won't bite your nose off."

"I don't want my mother to know we've been seeing each other. It's not that I'm scared of her reaction, but I don't want her to ruin this."

Molly made a thumbs-up sign. "Gotcha. I agree. I don't want anyone to know about…us. I mean there is no 'us' really but…"

Without taking his eyes off the view, he took her hand and squeezed it. "Yes, there is. And it's special and if anyone else knows, it'll ruin it." He turned to face her. "I've never had a real friend before. Someone I can trust and who trusts me. I grew up in a bubble. Do you understand what I mean?"

Molly touched his cheek. "I do. It must be so hard."

He sighed. "It is. Thank you, Molly. Thank you so much."

"It's okay. No need to thank me. I hope I can help in some little way."

"You already have."

"I'm glad." Molly got up and tidied away the remnants of their picnic. It was time to go back and face the real world. She realised that her world was easier and a lot more enjoyable than Ted's, despite all his money. But maybe one day, she would help him burst that bubble.

* * *

As real life with real problems and pressures caught up with her, Molly would remember the outing with Ted as the last calm and trouble-free day. There were so many things to attend to: the deadline for the jewellery collection; the purchase of the apartment, which turned into a legal wrangle with missing deeds and contracts to sign; then, dealing with electricians and plumbers to get her new home habitable, even though Molly had decided to do all the decorating herself; and finally, meeting Karen Anderson, the deputy CEO of Harlow & Anderson and Ted's older sister, to work on designs and style for the mass market collection.

Molly went to the meeting at the H&A luxurious office at a penthouse suite on the seafront in Nice with trepidation. She was sure Charlotte Anderson's eldest daughter would be a clone of her mother. Not someone to be trifled with.

But Karen Anderson wasn't as bad as Molly had feared. Pleasant and business-like, Karen greeted Molly with a warm handshake and a beguiling smile. A rather large woman in a grey, plus-size, wool dress, the only resemblance to Ted was her sandy hair and square jaw. The bulk of her body was the opposite of Ted's tall thin frame. Although charming with a lovely deep voice, Karen exuded confidence, personal success and a strong will. As Molly showed her some sketches she had drawn up, they discussed the general look the collection should have. Karen showed Molly photos of the clothes in the spring collection, and they very quickly drew up a plan for the line and decided on a deadline.

"I'll be sending out a press release later today," Karen said. "So you might get some calls from the press. We already had an enquiry from The Herald Tribune about your work for us, so I'll be chasing that up."

Molly put her sketches back in the folder. "I heard about that."

Karen looked surprised. "Oh? How? Who told you?"

"Ted," Molly said without thinking and immediately kicked herself. Shit, she shouldn't have said anything about knowing Ted personally.

"My brother? When was this?"

"The other day. We... had coffee together in Nice before

he left for New York." Molly looked back at Karen with an innocent air. "We...bumped into each other by accident and then—"

Karen held up a hand. "Whatever. I don't want to know. Ted's private life is none of my business. He's a grown man of thirty-six even if my mother seems to think he's forever twelve."

Molly laughed. "I can't believe that."

Karen shrugged. "It's true nevertheless. She treats us all like children. But he'll be married soon, so maybe his new wife can stand up to my mother."

Rigid with shock, Molly stared at Karen. "Married?"

She nodded. "That's right. He's going to marry Cindy Moore, daughter of Donald Moore, the New York State senator. Big wedding in Long Island at their country home there. It should be a fun event. Mother is very happy. We all are."

Molly swallowed. "When?"

"Two weeks from now. So I'd like to have everything done before that." She got up and held out her hand. "Nice to meet you, Molly. I'll be in touch."

Her knees like jelly, Molly got up from her chair and shook Karen's hand. "Lovely to meet you too. And...tell Ted I wish him the best of luck."

Karen looked suddenly grim. "Thank you. He'll need it."

Chapter 9

"So, this is it?" Sophia said. "You're moving out?" They were in the little greenhouse at the bottom of the garden, picking tomatoes. Molly had just told Sophia she had signed the contract on the apartment in Saint-Tropez.

Molly pulled a large tomato off the vine. "Yes, but not just yet. There's so much work to be done, and I can't move in until the plumbing's been fixed. I want to stay here while I do the decorating and move in when it's all finished if that's okay."

"Of course. Stay as long as you like."

"Thank you." Molly sniffed the tomato. "What a wonderful smell it has when it's just been picked."

"There's nothing like home-grown fruit and vegetables. But how am I going to find a new tenant in the middle of winter?"

"I'm sure you'll find someone. It's such a nice studio."

Sophia looked thoughtful. "Yes. It won't be that hard if I advertise. But I think Jesus said something about a man who was looking for accommodation only last week. I thought he meant just for one night, so I said we're not running a bed and breakfast. I'd hate to get into that kind of business. Hard work and not much return."

"Maybe you could ask him again?" Molly suggested. "It could have been someone who wants to spend the winter here."

Sophia put her basket of tomatoes on the floor. "I recall vaguely it was something to do with looking for someone." She shook her head. "No, that wasn't it. I can't quite remember the circumstances. He had an Irish name, anyway. And he spoke good Spanish, Jesus said."

Molly dropped the tomato. "What? He spoke good Spanish and had an Irish name? Can you remember what it was?"

Sophia looked into the distance. "Hmm, no. Sean, I think. But the last name...something typically Irish but it won't come back to me." She shrugged and put a few tomatoes on the top of her pile in the basket. "Let's take these goodies in and put them in the larder. Then I want to watch the evening news on Sky. Much better than the silly French channels. We'll have a glass of wine and I'll light the fire. What do you say?"

"Sounds perfect." Molly picked up the tomato from the floor. "A glass of wine is just what I need right now."

Sophia looked at Molly over her shoulder as she walked out of the greenhouse. "You do look a little stressed. You've been very quiet since that meeting two weeks ago. Are those people working you too hard?"

Molly picked up her box of tomatoes and added a few cucumbers. "Not really. I'm enjoying doing the designs. I don't have to do more than drawing, and then I'll do some mock-ups before the whole thing is sent to the factory in China. I have quite a tight deadline, but it's not going to be a problem."

Sophia studied Molly for a moment. "Is there something else upsetting you then? You're very pale."

"Just some personal stuff," Molly said vaguely, not wanting to reveal her struggle with the news two weeks earlier of Ted's marriage. Why hadn't he told her? And why did she feel so upset? They had only just met. He didn't owe her anything. But during their hike in the mountains he had revealed something deeply personal, so why hadn't he said anything about getting married? And he had talked about a special friendship that was growing between them. Two weeks, his sister had said. He was probably getting married that very moment. Deep in thought, Molly followed Sophia into the house and helped her sort out the vegetables before settling on the sofa in the living room to enjoy the warmth of the fire.

Sipping wine and idly watching the news about all kinds of disasters, Molly finally relaxed. It was no use turning all this into some kind of drama. Much better not to be too close to Ted, anyway, now that she was working for his family firm. But an item at the end of the newscast made her nearly choke on the wine, as a familiar face came up on the screen. Molly sat up. "What?" she exclaimed. "That's Ted!"

"Yes," Sophia pointed at the TV set. "Look, he's left that gorgeous girl at the altar."

"Shut up, I can't hear." Molly stared at the screen as the whole story was read out. Ted hadn't exactly left his bride at the altar but had announced at a big dinner the night before that he couldn't go through with it, saying he had to leave the family firm as well to be on his own.

"I'm sick of living in a bubble," he said. Then he had apologised to everyone, kissed his now wife-not-to-be and walked out of the five-star hotel.

"His whereabouts are not known," the news anchor said. "It's thought he went to hide at the family chalet in Colorado. His family are very worried about his state of mind. A spokesman for Senator Moore said neither he nor his daughter would speak to the press." Then the photo of a blonde with film-star looks came on the screen, before they moved on to the next item.

"Jesus bloody Christ," Sophia said, looking wildly at Molly. "Did you see that? Did you?"

"Yes," Molly whispered. "Oh, yes I did. Poor Ted."

Sophia turned off the TV. "Poor Ted? What an absolute cad! Why didn't he spit it out before? Why wait until just before the wedding? That poor woman. Publicly humiliated. And just before the election, too. Her father will be shamed and his political career is going straight down the toilet."

"Maybe they were hoping the Anderson millions would help fund his campaign?" Molly mused. "I had no idea Ted was getting married until two weeks ago. But I got strong vibes from his sister it wasn't exactly a love match."

"But the woman is fabulous. What man wouldn't want to get into bed with her?"

"Bed, yes. But marriage is a whole different matter." Molly held out her glass. "Any more of that wine?"

Sophia picked up the bottle from the coffee table. "It's a very strong Rioja. It could knock you out if you're not careful."

"Perfect," Molly said grimly. "Just what I need."

They finished the bottle and were getting ready to move into the kitchen to cook dinner, when they heard the front door slam and Jay shouting, "Anyone home?"

"In here!" Sophia replied.

Jay walked into the living room, unbuttoning his navy wool jacket. "Boozing in front of the fire?"

Sophia picked up the bottle. "What happened? We must have finished it. Now we need dinner to sober us up. What did you have in mind?"

"I thought you were cooking tonight," Jay replied. He peered at Sophia. "But you look a little dizzy, querida. I'll go and rustle up some pasta with that Bolognese sauce I put in the freezer. Would that be okay?"

"Wonderful," Sophia purred. "But I have to go to bed early. I have the first garden tour tomorrow, remember. It's the winter garden in Provence theme. You promised to help out."

"Shit, I forgot," Jay moaned. "I must have been drunk. Are

you saying I have to guide a bunch of old women through your garden tomorrow?"

"They're not just old women. There will be all sorts of people, the tourist office said. They were delighted to have an event to advertise during the winter. There are still tourists around this time of year. They're usually here just to soak up a bit of sunshine and get a break from the rain further north."

Jay nodded. "I know. I think there's a new trend in tourism around these parts. A lot of older people stay here all winter now. We're even thinking of opening the restaurant a few evenings a week, instead of shutting down completely. Saturday evening for paella and then Sunday lunch. We can run it with just me and two waiters. My boss is going to give me his decision tomorrow."

"I hope he goes ahead," Sophia said, struggling to get out of the sofa. "But off you go. We need food. And I need cheering up. Molly is moving out."

Jay paused in the door. "I know. She told me. But as you know, I might have another tenant lined up."

Molly sat up. "Oh, yes. That Irishman Sophia told me about. Can you remember his name?"

"Michael," Jay started. "And the last name…I can't remember. But I have his number in my phone. I'll give him a call. When did you say you were moving out, Molly?"

"In a couple of weeks. It all depends on when the work is finished."

"Okay." Jay fished his phone from his pocket and flicked through the contact list.

Sophia picked up the bottle and the glasses. "I'll put this in the kitchen and then go and have my bath. Call me when dinner's ready."

"Okay." Jay nodded, still looking at his phone. "I can't find it…"

"Never mind. You can tell me later," Molly said. "I might follow Sophia's example and have a bath before dinner."

"Found it," Jay interrupted. "The name is Michael D. Hegarty."

"Hegarty?" Molly's heart stopped. She put her hand over her mouth. "No..." she mumbled. "It can't be. It just can't."

Jay stared at Molly. "You look awful. What's the problem? Who is he?"

Molly stared back at Jay. "He could be…my husband," she whispered.

Chapter 10

Much later, when Sophia had gone to bed and Molly and Jay were tidying up after dinner, Jay picked up a bottle of brandy. "How about a nightcap?"

Molly nodded. "Okay. I think I owe you an explanation. Thank you for not saying anything to Sophia."

"I felt you didn't want to talk about it. And now, if you still don't, I understand. But if you need a shoulder to cry on and a sympathetic ear…"

Molly sighed. "Yes. I think I do. I've locked it all up for so long, but I have felt a great need to talk to someone lately. Probably because I have come to a watershed moment in my life."

Jay nodded. "Yes, I think you have. But let's sit down. Don't worry about the saucepans. I'll take care of them later."

Molly sank down on a chair at the table. "Okay. But I think I'll have some camomile tea instead of the brandy."

"Fine." Jay turned on the kettle beside the sink.

When the tea was made and Jay had poured himself a brandy, he settled on the chair opposite Molly. "So?"

Molly wrapped her hands around the mug of tea. "I'll tell you. It all happened when I was in my early twenties and an art student living in Dublin—a little lost and lonely like all country girls just arrived in the big city. I rented a studio in a block of flats out near the School of Design on the south side of Dublin. I didn't have many friends, but I tried to get to know people and went to the pub with the other students in my year. It was great fun. We became quite a close-knit group. I loved the Friday nights with them. Then one night, we were joined by a guy called Miguel Hegarty."

Jay looked intrigued. "Miguel? He was Spanish? Or half Spanish?"

Molly shook her head. "No. He was from Argentina, of Irish ancestry. There are quite a lot of them there. They're called the Irish Argentines."

"Fascinating. I never heard that. Shows how uneducated I must be."

"Not at all," Molly protested. "Not many people know about them and the wave of Irish immigration into Argentina in the nineteenth century. Even I didn't have much of a clue until I met Miguel and he told me about it. Che Guevara was of that ancestry. His full name was Che Guevara Lynch."

"Amazing. I didn't know that. I never heard about the Irish Argentines either. So that explains his name, then." Jay leaned closer. "But I think we're getting away from the main point and the story of your marriage. If you want to share it with me, that is. No hard feelings if you don't."

"No. I do want to tell you," Molly said. "We've only just met, but it's sometimes easier to tell your deepest secrets to a stranger." She hesitated for a moment. But then, as the silence became too heavy, she started to tell him about her strange marriage and how it had come about.

* * *

Molly tried to remember who had suggested they get married. Miguel was not her boyfriend, just part of the group who went to the pub on Friday nights. He was popular with the girls, who swooned over his dark Latin looks, hazel eyes and long girly lashes. The only Irish thing about him was his last name, a smatter of freckles across his nose and the capacity to put away a large number of pints in an evening. He spoke English with an accent that was a mixture of Buenos Aires and Dublin, which only added to his charm. One night, he stood up and sang Danny Boy, and everyone stopped talking and drinking. His beautiful voice rang out in the crowded pub, and when he had finished, there was a long silence, broken seconds later by applause and whistles.

He sank down beside Molly and grabbed his pint. "Phew, that made me thirsty."

"You have an amazing voice," she said. "Have you ever considered singing professionally?"

He drank deeply, put down the glass and wiped the foam off his mouth with the back of his hand. "Hell, no. Show business? Are you kidding? But thanks for the compliment."

"What exactly are you studying?" Molly asked. "You never said. We're all art students but as far as I know you're not in any of our courses."

"I'm studying engineering at Bolton Street Technical College. Last term and then…" He shrugged. "Who knows? I have to leave when I graduate."

"You do? Why?"

"Visa problems. I tried to get an Irish passport on the strength of my Irish ancestry, but no go."

"But I thought you could get an Irish passport if any of your grandparents were born in Ireland."

He sighed. "Yes you can. Problem is, none of them were. My father's family went to Argentina during that early wave of immigration in the eighteen-twenties. So the first Hegarty in Argentina would be my great-great-great…" he waved his hand in the air, "whatever—granddad. Too far removed to be of any use."

"Shit, how annoying."

"You can say that again."

"Shit," she said and they both laughed. "With knobs on,"

she added, her breath stuck in her throat as he looked at her with those beautiful eyes. “So what are you going to do? Go back to Argentina?”

He looked into his now empty pint glass. “Don’t know. There are very few jobs there. Engineering is quite big in Ireland, especially with some of the American companies that have started up here. I’ve already had offers. But as I don’t have a work permit, I can’t accept any of them.”

“You could apply for Irish citizenship.”

He looked glum. “That takes five years to come through. What do I do in the meantime?”

She looked at him for a while. “Well, there is another option, of course.”

“Yeah, I know. I could marry an Irish citizen.” He looked sideways at her. “Awful thing to ask anyone. And then we’d have to live together for a year as husband and wife before I can even apply for citizenship.”

“Officially, yes. But you’ll be able to work during that time and you can get a social security card.”

“I know all that. Sounds easy. All I have to do is find a woman willing to go through the charade for a couple of years.”

“I’m sure that wouldn’t be too hard.”

“It would be impossible and you know it. Every girl I know is in a relationship or has her own agenda. I’m sure you wouldn’t want to be stuck to me for a few years and not be able to date anyone else. Or risk being found out by the authorities.”

She thought about it. Would she? He was handsome and fun, and she had to admit secretly she found herself drawn to him. But she wasn’t in love with him, didn’t know him well enough to trust him. Going through some kind of scam just to help him get citizenship was unthinkable.

“No,” she said. “I don’t think I would. Sorry.”

He laughed and poked her with his elbow. “Oh forget it.

I'll just have to bite the bullet and go back home like a good boy. Our glasses are empty. How about a refill?"

And they had more beer and a lot more fun until it was time for Molly to go home to her lonely little flat.

* * *

"So you didn't offer to marry him?" Jay asked, his voice pulling Molly back to the present.

"Not then. I had no intention of doing it. I mean, yeah, he was hot, and who wouldn't want a dirty weekend with a guy like that? But marriage? No way. I forgot all about it and he didn't mention it again."

"So what happened? You did eventually marry him, didn't you?"

Molly nodded and looked out across the garden, now in darkness. "Yes. But he didn't push me into it in any way. It was all my doing."

Molly could see Jay shift in the chair and knew he was impatient. She didn't mean to tease him by drawing out the story but it took her a while to go back to that time and those long-forgotten memories. It had all been buried in her subconscious. Bringing it back was like rummaging in an old trunk where the mementoes of her youth had sunk to the bottom.

"So," Jay murmured. "When did you make your offer? And why?"

"It was months later," Molly said in a near whisper. "At the end of the summer. Miguel threw a party at his flat, a farewell party. One of the girls told me he was forced to go back to Argentina because his student visa had expired. 'Just at the wrong moment,' she said. 'He's just been offered a job with an American company setting up in Dublin, but he can't take it because of that stupid visa.' We talked about it, even discussing the marriage thing. She was engaged to be married, but I was still single and had just broken up after a brief fling with a medical student. She didn't say anything about me getting married to Miguel to help him stay, but it stuck in my mind. I thought, why not? I could help him out and we could get divorced once he had organised the citizenship."

"How did you break it to him?"

"I contacted him before the party to tell him I'd changed my mind."

"What did he say?"

"Nothing much. At first, he thought I was joking. We met at the pier in Dun Laoghaire. That's a long pier on the south side of Dublin. It's a lovely place for a walk with beautiful views of the sea. We sat on a bench out there, watched the boats and the view out to sea and talked about it. Jay was hesitant at first, but when he had thought about it for a while, he thanked me and kissed my cheek and said how much he appreciated what I was doing for him. 'You saved my life', he said, which made me feel quite odd. I realised that marrying me and being able to take that job *would* change his life. It was as if he was at a crossroads, and because of me, he could take the easier, more profitable path."

"That was a huge gift you gave him." Jay took her hand.

"I suppose," Molly said. "It made me happy to do that for him. I didn't think it was a big deal. Not such a high price to pay to help a friend. But…"

"But?"

Molly felt tears prick her eyes. "The price was higher than I'd anticipated."

Chapter 11

"Should we announce it?" Miguel asked. "Or keep it secret?"

They were sharing a pizza in Molly's tiny south Dublin flat, trying to work out the details of their forthcoming wedding at the registry office. It was three months after that night on the pier and they had just received the marriage registration form. They would be married the following Saturday.

Molly looked at her future husband. "Secret," she said immediately.

"Why?"

She took a bite of her pizza wedge and chewed for a while. "Because I don't want anyone to know. My mother would have a heart attack if she knew I was doing this. She's dreaming of my white wedding in a gown and veil and the whole shebang. That's never going to happen but nothing will convince her. I don't want to shatter her dream."

He nodded. "Okay. Fair enough. I don't think I'd want my parents to know until later anyway. So we'll just trot off to the registry office and get married."

"Have you organised the witnesses?"

He wiped his fingers on a paper towel. "Yes, two guys from the rugby club. Don't know them that well but I made up a story about…" He picked at his pizza, looking sheepish. "I said you were pregnant."

Molly shot up from the table. "Shit, you didn't!"

"I'm afraid I did. Sorry."

"How did we manage that, then? Immaculate conception? We haven't done as much as shake hands since we met."

"They won't know that."

"You eejit." Molly paced around the room. "How could you tell such a whopping lie? What am I going to do now? Stuff a cushion under my shirt?"

"No, of course not. You're only three months pregnant."

Molly sank down on her chair again. "Gee, that's a relief. So I'm just going through morning sickness and mood swings? Maybe I should puke on you during the ceremony to lend authenticity to your story?"

Miguel laughed nervously. "No, you don't have to do that. Just act like you hate me for getting you pregnant."

"That'll be a breeze. I won't even have to act."

"That's a relief."

"Yeah." She snatched the pizza away from him. "But we're not married yet, so you can get out of here right now. I need to be alone for a while."

He got up. "I don't know why you have to get into such snot about it. We'll just turn up, say whatever we need to say, sign on the dotted line and get the hell out of there."

"And then move into your flat and pretend we're newlyweds and in love until you can apply for citizenship. Easy-peasy, right?"

"Shit, we don't even have to act like we're in love. We can just be like a normal married couple and fight all the time."

"Yeah, right. Should I fake a miscarriage then? Or just keep stuffing bigger pillows under my jumpers?"

He shrugged. "Didn't think of that. We could say it was a false alarm?"

"Yeah, whatever." Molly folded her arms and tapped her foot. "You'd better get out fast. I feel one of those pregnancy mood swings coming on. I might even hit you. Or chuck the pizza right in your face."

"You wouldn't"

"Try me." Molly picked up the pizza "Feck off, or you'll be wearing this."

He backed away holding up his hands, his eyes full of laughter. "I'll go then. You're so scary when you're mad." Miguel ran to the door and opened it. "See you at the wedding, darlin'." He blew her a kiss. The pizza hit the door as he closed it.

Molly picked it up, put it in the bin and burst into tears.

* * *

They were married three days later. Miguel wore jeans, a white shirt, no tie and a navy blazer with the rugby club emblem. Molly had put on a blue silk dress she had worn at innumerable weddings and carried a small bouquet of flowers she got at a petrol station on the way to the registry office. Miguel had bought weddings rings at a pawnbroker's. They didn't even fit properly, as Molly discovered when she had to push it onto Miguel's finger, and the one he put on hers was too big.

When the registrar pronounced them husband and wife, Miguel grabbed Molly and pressed a hard kiss on her closed mouth. His rugby pals cheered and threw confetti at them when they emerged from the building, Miguel clutching the marriage certificate in his hand. They had lunch with the witnesses at the Marino restaurant in Dun Laoghaire, a dreary little place that served fish and chips and bad wine.

They went to the pub on the way home, neither of them wanting to face the evening ahead when they would be alone in Miguel's flat. Molly had done her best to brighten it up with new curtains, cushions and nick-knacks. But nothing could improve the dingy wall paper and the mustard-coloured walls in the kitchen. Not a place to call home but it was all they could afford until Miguel started working. He had been hired by the American firm and would do a training course before he could start. Molly worked in a jewellery shop while she finished her degree in art and design.

The flat had two bedrooms, and they had put a double bed in the largest one, should anyone have questioned their marriage. "Not likely, but you never know," Miguel said. He offered Molly the larger bed but she declined, saying Miguel, with his tall frame, would feel cramped in the smaller bed. She tried not to show him how she wished they would share that double bed. She knew he wasn't physically attracted to her, which made her own feelings for him all the more painful.

So there they sat, in the dingy pub, drinking several pints until the pub closed and they were forced to go home and start their married life. A marriage of convenience. A marriage that wasn't real but still felt like a commitment to Molly. Before their wedding, she had liked Miguel and considered him a friend. But when they started to share a home, she soon felt differently. She started to fall in love with him.

She began to regret her decision to help him with his visa problem while she tried to figure out why they didn't get on. She blamed it on a clash of personalities. They just rubbed each other up the wrong way. But being in his presence was better than not seeing him at all.

Living so close with him became more and more painful, as it was obvious he didn't have any feelings for her whatsoever. She began to think it would be better to walk away. She couldn't wait for the first year to end, when he could at last apply for Irish citizenship on the strength of being married to her. And when they split up, she would try to forget him and never get married again.

Jay looked at Molly with concern when she took a break. "So you just split up but never got divorced? Why was that?"

"Because he disappeared…the day after he got his passport."

"Disappeared?"

"Yes. He was gone when I came home from work. I never heard from him again."

"How strange." Jay poured more brandy into his glass. "And if that man I was talking to is him, why is he here now?"

"Maybe he wants that divorce. But we don't know it's the same man. Same initials, yes. And same last name, even if Hegarty is quite common Irish name. But…but…" Molly hesitated.

"What?"

"Don't say I'm crazy, but I've had the feeling lately that I'm being watched. Or followed. It could be my imagination, of course. I'm probably just a bit jumpy right now with everything going on. That man is probably someone else entirely."

Jay lifted an eyebrow. "Only one way to find out, right?"

Molly shivered. "I know."

Chapter 12

After a sleepless night, Molly lay in bed in Sophia's house, reliving those days. She hadn't thought about them for many years. She had put it all firmly to the back of her mind, telling herself there was no use crying over what never was. A rash decision that helped a friend but tore her apart when it all ended.

Maybe telling Jay about it hadn't been the best idea, but she suddenly felt like talking about it when he was so sympathetic and willing to listen. There had been a certain amount of catharsis as she told him her story, but no real closure. That was something she would probably never get. Except if he had turned up here, in Saint-Tropez. Was that man with the Irish name Miguel?

She mentally shook herself and got out of bed to face the new day. The curtains swayed gently, and a ray of golden sunshine poked a finger through a narrow slit. There was a smell of newly baked bread and coffee. Sophia was singing to herself as she worked in the garden below, getting ready for the grand tour. Molly threw back the bedclothes and got up. Life wasn't so bad after all. She had two new friends and was moving into her first home. Her new life was beginning. She had to move on and try to come to terms with what happened in her youth. But it was hard to forget the pain of loving someone who didn't love her back.

The wedding that had felt so fake and the year they lived

together such a strain, loving him, but never daring to show it. His laughing eyes, his smile, the smell of him that she loved so much she used the press her nose to his sweater when he was out. And then… that last night, just before he left, when he finally got his passport.

* * *

They had celebrated with steaks at Blooms Brasserie and drunk a lot of wine. Miguel had been ecstatic and kept hugging her and thanking her for making his Irish citizenship possible.

"A ticket to Europe and a better life," he said on the bus on the way to their flat. "All thanks to you. I'll never forget what you did for me."

She made a dismissive gesture. "Ah, shucks, it was nuttin.'"

He looked suddenly serious. "It was a great deal. I know this year hasn't been easy for you. But now you're free."

She felt a pang of sadness, but the bus arrived at their stop, and in the hustle of getting off, he didn't see her face or her eyes welling up. She had composed herself by the time they arrived at their building and managed to reply to his chatter in a cool, friendly way. Later, she would reflect on how the spark had been ignited and how it could so easily not have been there. But it was. *If only*, she thought many times afterwards.

If only he hadn't kissed her as they closed the front door, it wouldn't have happened. She wouldn't have opened her mouth and allowed him to put his tongue inside. He wouldn't have squeezed her tightly, and she wouldn't have pressed herself up against him and felt his erection. But it did happen. Maybe it was the wine or the feeling of ending something that made them suddenly so aroused. In Molly's case, it was all her pent-up emotions, the love and sexual attraction she had locked up for so long that erupted into the invitation she offered him. Miguel accepted it without a moment's hesitation. She knew he had been sleeping with other women during their year of fake marriage. But that night, he was all hers.

"Bed," he whispered against her mouth as his hands cupped her breasts inside her silk shirt that had suddenly lost all the buttons.

She nodded and whispered something that sounded like 'yes, please', and they tumbled onto the double bed in his bedroom, the marital bed they had never used. And that night, after a whole year, they finally consummated their marriage. Molly had never felt such lust, had never responded to any man's lovemaking with such fervour. They kept the light on so they could see each other, the visual impact of their entwined limbs adding to the heat. Molly would always remember how their eyes locked as they climaxed and how their bodies connected and their minds met at that final explosion of feelings. Then they were still in a silence thick with emotion, staring at each other in shock.

Still on top, Miguel touched her face. "My sweet Molly. My sweet, sweet Irish colleen. I'll never forget you."

Molly closed her eyes. She knew what he was trying to say. She had hoped, just for a moment, that this would change things, that he would tell her he shared her feelings, that maybe they could stay together and see what happened. Maybe she even hoped he would say this crazy marriage was now real. But his expression told a different story. She turned her face and closed her eyes, hiding the tears that seeped out of the corners of her eyes.

He rolled off her and lay looking at the ceiling. "Shit, we shouldn't have done it," he moaned. "What a stupid thing to do."

"We were drunk," she said.

"And you looked so cute, all flushed and your hair tousled. I just couldn't resist you. I'm really sorry."

"It's okay. Not a big deal."

He turned his head. "Are you sure?"

She slid off the bed and gathered up her underwear. "Of course. Let's have a cup of tea and forget about it."

He laughed. "What a typical Irish thing to say. A cup of tea is the great comforter in all situations, isn't it?"

Molly stopped at the door, her underwear clutched to her bare breasts. "But you want to be Irish, don't you? You have the passport, now you have to wear the colours as well. Drinking tea at times of great distress is only part of it. Or perhaps your Irishness is as fake as this marriage!" She walked out, slammed the door shut behind her, then went to her own bedroom and locked the door. She collapsed on the bed and pulled the duvet over her head, crying herself to sleep.

When she woke up the next morning, he had already gone to work. She dragged herself around and finally managed to get dressed and go to college, spending the day trying to concentrate on lectures and design classes. When she got home late that evening, she found the flat empty Miguel's clothes and personal effects gone and a note on the kitchen table.

Dear Molly,

When you get this, I'll be gone. I didn't tell you, but the firm is sending me to Germany to their affiliate company there. I'll be catching the flight the day after tomorrow. I'll get the divorce papers organised as agreed very soon, and then all you have to do is to sign them and send it all back to the solicitor. Our marriage will be dissolved in a year, and then you'll be free again and your life will be back to normal.

I can't thank you enough for what you did for me. It changed my life forever and made it possible for me to have a better future. I'm sorry about last night, but I'm sure you feel like I do, that it was just a sweet episode and a very nice way to say goodbye.

Good luck with your career and your life. I hope it will be very happy. Maybe one day, we'll meet again, share a drink and a laugh about this mad year we had together.

With very best wishes,

Miguel

Molly still had the note, tucked into an envelope, hidden at the bottom of her suitcase with her wedding ring. She couldn't bring herself to throw it away. The divorce papers never arrived, and there were no more messages of any kind from Miguel. Molly kept watching the post, but after a while other concerns put it all out of her mind. He mother was diagnosed with a rare form of cancer, and Molly had to go back to the farm to help nurse her. After her mother's death two years later, her brother, Liam, lost his young wife and was left to bring up his little boy on his own. Molly stepped in to help him, becoming a kind of mother to little Tommy, and when they moved to France and settled into the new house, she was able to get going on her career as jewellery designer, put on hold for so long. Throwing herself into her craft and helping out with Tommy was all-consuming.

The memory of the year with Miguel slowly faded into a hazy dream. That he hadn't bothered to organise a divorce didn't worry her much. It was, in a strange way, a comfort, a connection that hadn't been broken. Then she became used to it, and it worried her less and less, until it all became an indelible part of her and who she was. She didn't think she would ever see Miguel again, but she felt he was out there, somewhere, living his own life but still married to her. *And now, he might be here*, she thought. *I have to find out. If that man is him, I might finally be able to close the chapter and move on.*

* * *

The man called Michael Hegarty proved to be elusive. Molly asked Jay to call him, but there was no reply to either calls or text messages.

"How strange," Jay said after yet another attempt. "He was so eager to move into this house. He asked me to let him know when it would be possible, but now there's no reply from the number he gave me."

"Maybe he knows I'm on his case," Molly suggested. She was on her way to her new apartment, the car loaded with tins of paint, brushes, rags and a ladder. "But you left some messages, so he'll know you want him to get in touch. You didn't mention me in your messages, did you?"

"No, of course not. Are you going to drive with the back door open like that?"

"Yes, I have to. I need the ladder. But I'll take the back roads through the woods and drive slowly."

"Let me at least tie it with some twine," Jay suggested. "Just to make it more secure". He went to the greenhouse and came back with a roll of garden twine. He tied down the back hatch of the car so it stayed down, with the ladder sticking out. "There. That's more secure. You wouldn't want the wind to catch it."

"Thank you." Molly got into the car and started the engine. "See you later," she shouted through the window.

Jay slapped the roof of the car. "Drive safely. Will be you here for dinner?"

"No, I'm going to the workshop. I have to keep working on the designs, and I want to see Liam and Daisy. See you tomorrow." Molly rolled up the window and drove off.

The back road from Gigaro to Saint-Tropez was steep, narrow and full of hairpin bends. But it was the most beautiful stretch of road in this area, winding its way through woods of pine trees and cork oaks with stunning views of the sea glimmering below steep slopes. Molly had to concentrate hard to keep her eyes on the road as the beautiful vistas pulled her away from the task of driving. She passed a few big gates with fancy names—the homes of celebrities such as the aging rock star and national icon, Johnny Halliday, and the notorious but reclusive Brigitte Bardot, who hid from the public in this remote area.

Molly's mind drifted as she drove. So many things had happened since she had moved in with Sophia: the contract with H&A; the connection—or whatever it was—with Ted; finding and buying the apartment; the stranger who might have been Miguel. So much to deal with. What a relief to have Jay to talk to. He was like a solid rock of compassion and good sense. He was much older than her, but still very attractive with a kind of timeless sex appeal. So self-contained with this age-old wisdom she guessed came from his gypsy blood. Molly smiled to herself, thinking that if he were younger, she might even fall in love with him. But as he was a good ten years older and Sophia's secret lover, he was a better alternative—a wonderful friend.

With Jay still in her thoughts, Molly drove out of the wooded areas into a valley with vineyards on either side of the road, stretching all the way up the hills, dotted with pink stucco manor houses, centuries old. This was where the famous Rosé de Provence was made.

She glanced into the rear-view mirror and saw a car close behind. An electric-blue Citroen she had seen out of the corner of her eye earlier, far behind like a blue dot. It hadn't registered with her then. Now it did, coming closer, too close for comfort. The car flashed its headlights, and she could see the outline of a man with broad shoulders at the wheel. Did he want her to pull over? Molly's heart sank as she realised who he must have been: a policeman wanting to fine her for having a ladder sticking out of the boot. She sighed and pulled into the hard shoulder. The man got out of the car, and Molly rolled down the window, ready to beam him an apologetic smile and give him the helpless female act. But her smile froze as he bent down, and she was confronted by a face that was shockingly familiar.

Chapter 13

Their eyes locked while time stood still. Molly blinked. Was it really happening? Or was she dreaming and would wake up in a cold sweat?

But no, it was real and it was—him. Miguel. Older, with a few lines around his eyes and mouth, his dark hair sprinkled with grey, but with the same amazing good looks. His broad grin took her back fifteen years, and she felt that same pull at her heart, just like when they had lived together.

"It's..." she breathed. "You...Miguel." She closed her eyes and opened them again, her hands gripping the wheel and her body rigid with shock and anger. She stared wildly at him. "What are you doing here?" she demanded. "What do you want?" Then she was seized by a flaming rage. "You big shit!" she screamed.

He grinned. "Lovely to see you too, Molly."

"I mean it," she snarled. "You just disappeared without warning, without a word, except for that letter you left behind. You promised we'd get a divorce. You said we'd get together and sign the papers. You'd do it all, you said. But that was too much for you, wasn't it? Disappearing and never getting in touch was much easier, right? But it was okay. I could live with that. Eventually. So what the hell do you want now, after all these years?"

He kept staring back at her as if she was a vision. "Molly. Oh, Molly, you are exactly the same."

"Only fifteen years older."

A truck roared past them up the hill, then another, followed by a motorbike. Molly realised they were near the junction to the main coast road. "I can't talk to you here," she shouted above the roar of the traffic. "Meet me at the little bar near the old harbour in twenty minutes." She started the engine, slowly edged away from the side of the road and drove off, watching him in the rear-view mirror as he got back into his car. Her hands shaking, Molly managed to drive to the apartment building and park in the narrow lane outside the bakery on the ground floor.

The owner, a stocky man with greying hair and kind eyes, stuck his head out the door. "Do you need help?" he called to Molly in French. "I could carry that ladder up for you."

Molly shook her head. "Thanks, but not right now. I'll just leave it here for the moment while I—go to see someone. I'll let you know when I need a bit of help."

"D'accord." The man pulled his head back in.

Her knees wobbly, Molly got out of the car and walked the short distance to the little bar on the other side of the old stone wall. It was small, with just one table and two stools outside, overlooking the pier, where the water lapped against the stone steps—the oldest part of the town, where little fishing boats would have moored hundreds of years earlier with their catch to be sold at the market. Molly loved sitting there with a glass of wine after finishing her painting jobs at the apartment. At dusk, this was a heavenly spot, with the setting sun turning the old walls a golden pink and the odd seabird landing on the still water. There was a hush then, when the hustle and bustle of this busy little town slowly abated and everyone took a break before dinner.

Molly checked her watch. He would arrive soon—if he was coming at all. It was too cold to sit outside, so she went into the small bar and settled on the window seat where she could see everyone outside. She ordered a glass of red wine, which arrived at her table at the same time as the door opened, and Miguel walked in, his tall frame blocking the light from the window. He looked around the dim little bar.

"I'm here," Molly said.

He finally saw her. "Oh. All right."

"Sit down. You make the place look even smaller than it is."

He let out a laugh. "Yes. I can see that. What a tiny place."

"The smallest and oldest bar in Saint-Tropez."

"It's very quaint all right." He sat down opposite her and made a gesture to the girl behind the bar at Molly's glass. "La mème chose," he said. He turned to Molly. "We must talk."

"You bet we must." Molly took a sip from her glass, the shock of meeting him again still making her hands tremble.

The light from the dusty window fell on his face. Molly could see him clearly. The hazel eyes once so full of laughter were hard, as if they had looked at unbearable things. The tiny lines around his eyes were more from squinting against strong sunlight than laughing and there were deep furrows from his nose to that sexy mouth she would dream of kissing. It now had a bitter twist, and she didn't feel like kissing it anymore.

"Where have you been?" she asked.

He shrugged. "Here and there. Mostly there."

"That's not good enough. I want to know what you've been doing all these years. Where you've been hiding. I did try to find you, but I gave up after a while. I had to live, you know. I had to try and go forward. Move on, as they say." She drew breath.

"You certainly did, my darling. And now, here you are, doing so very well." He lifted his glass in a mock salute. "Cheers to you, Molly, and your success."

She didn't join him in his toast but kept her hands on her glass while she glared at him. "What do you know about me?"

He put down his glass without drinking. "I know more about you than you think. You've signed a very lucrative contract with H&A. You've just bought an apartment I feel will keep going up in value as you do it up. You're dating a billionaire—or someone who will be one day."

"I'm not dating anyone."

He shrugged. "Looked very much like it, but whatever. In any case, you're finally realising all your dreams and hopes and more. That's pretty impressive stuff, my dear."

"Are you stalking me?"

He laughed. "Yeah, I suppose that's what you'd call it. I've been in the area for a while, looking for—you. Then I found you, but…" he paused. "The time wasn't right. Until now."

"Why now?" She shook her head and took a swig of wine. "No, never mind. Just tell me where you've been since the last time I saw you."

He took her hand. "The last time. That was pretty special. But too heavy. I just couldn't stick around. If I did, I knew I wouldn't be able to leave."

She pulled away her hand. "Yeah, right. Don't try to pull at my heartstrings. Come on, Miguel. Let me have your story. You owe me after all I've been through."

He nodded, looking slightly shamefaced. "I suppose I do. But what you've been through is a walk in the park compared to mine." He leaned forward, his eyes boring into hers. "You want to know where I've been?"

She nodded, unable to turn away. "Yes, of course."

"Hell. That's where I've been. To hell and back."

* * *

The light outside faded while Miguel told his story. It was a sad one. It had started so well with his new job in Germany fifteen years earlier and ended in a prison in Thailand, from where he had travelled back to Europe.

"Two years in a Thai prison put manners on you," he said with a wry smile. "Makes you appreciate small comforts."

Molly listened, her back stiff. She had been riveted to the hard chair ever since Miguel started his tale. "You were arrested even though the bag wasn't yours?"

He shrugged. "Yes. It's a well-known scam. Pretty Asian girl asks you to take her very heavy bag through the security check, as she has another one. Bats eyelids and says she'll 'reward you'. Then when the coke is discovered, you're arrested and thrown into jail, no questions asked. I was lucky though. Due to my Irish passport, I managed to get in touch with the nearest Irish embassy. They got me a hot-shot lawyer. I only got three years. It could have been life—or a death sentence. That's how tough they are."

"Must have been a hell of a lawyer."

He winked. "You bet. A woman too. Asian. Cute and smarter than Einstein. I would have married her, except, well…I'm already married."

"Is that why you're here? To get me to divorce you so you can marry her?"

Miguel laughed. "No. She's married too and older than me. It was just a feeling I had, when I heard the verdict. I knew it would be five years in hell, but at least it wasn't for life. Could have been a death sentence had I been very unlucky. As it turned out, they released me after two years."

"For good behaviour?" Molly asked in a feeble attempt of a joke.

"I have no idea. But I have to tell you, another week in there, and I would have killed myself." He closed his eyes, then opened them again and stared out the window. "I'd give anything to erase the images, the sounds and smells from my mind," he mumbled. "I hate going to sleep. My dreams…" he stopped and shook his head. "I won't burden you with all this. It's not your fault, it's mine."

"Must have been horrible."

He let out a sound halfway between a laugh and a groan. "That's the understatement of the year. But during those long days and nights, I tried to think of pleasant things, of happy times and good people I met along the way." His eyes focused on Molly. "You're one of them, Molly. The more I thought of you, the more I realised that I…that *we* missed out on something that could have been special."

"Well, that can't be undone. Maybe it wouldn't have been as special as you think."

He sighed. "We'll never know, will we? And I'll never know what would have happened if I had gone on a package holiday to the Canaries, instead of going to Thailand on this luxury holiday. But I wanted to see Thailand. I had heard it was so beautiful and unique. And it was. I was on my way back, my head full of images and impressions, and then—" He sighed. "Funny how your life can change in an instant, isn't it?"

Molly nodded. "Yes. It can. Completely."

"I have to thank you though. I mean, if I didn't have my Irish passport, I wouldn't be here now. The Argentinians would not have been as helpful, I can assure you."

"Maybe not. But…" Molly hesitated. "When you got out, why did you come here? Why didn't you go back to Germany?"

He sighed. "Germany? I had nothing left there. I lost my job when I was convicted. My girlfriend didn't want to wait for me. We had been together ten years, but she wasn't the kind who'd stick around and wait for me to come back. And then…you see…" He paused. "I have no money and no job."

"So?"

He took her hand. "But then, of course, I have a very wealthy wife."

She pulled away. "What do you mean? You've been gone fifteen years. I owe you nothing."

He grinned. "Yes, well, of course not. But now that I have

no income, you have an obligation to support me, don't you? Forgive me, I might have forgotten...but did we sign a pre-nup?"

Molly blinked. "No. We didn't. I don't think we even discussed it."

"Ah. There you are then. I'm your husband, your spouse. You're the sole breadwinner. And I need bread. And other things too. A roof over my head. Clothes." He waved his hand in the air. "And maybe some pocket money."

She studied him for a moment. Even if his leather bomber jacket was scuffed and worn and his shirt wrinkly, his hair was clean and trimmed, his face clean-shaven and he smelt faintly of Savon de Marseille. A little unkempt but reasonable well groomed.

"Where are you living now?" she asked.

"At a vineyard outside Saint-Tropez. I got a job picking grapes during the harvest, which is now nearly over. Hard work but I enjoyed it. I like being outdoors. So once the work is done there, the staff quarters will no longer be available to me."

"What about your qualifications? You have a degree in engineering from Trinity College. And you must have great experience and references from the firm you were with."

He shrugged. "A degree, yes. References, no. The firm fired me when I was convicted. Don't think they'd be inclined to give me references."

"But you worked with them for over ten years," Molly exclaimed.

"Yeah, sure. But they seemed to think I was guilty, and a drug trafficker is not someone they want to admit to have had on their staff. I could go back and argue with them, but I honestly don't have the energy. I'd end up losing anyway, so what's the point?" He finished the dregs of his wine and looked out the window. "The sun is setting. The light is lovely out there. Why don't we go outside and sit on the wall? I find this bar very cramped. I hate cramped places." He looked suddenly lost and heartbreakingly lonely.

Molly felt a pang of pity. He must have been through some kind of hell during the years in a Thai prison. And now, here he was, without work or friends. She got up. "Come on, let's go and sit on the wall and look at the sea and the birds. The sun is setting behind the mountains and the light is so beautiful this time of year."

They left the bar and went out into the chilly evening, where the golden light made everything seem slightly unreal. "Like a dream," Miguel said and sat down on the low wall near the little pier. "It's like the world is holding its breath for a moment before darkness falls."

Molly joined him on the wall and looked out across the bay, where the pink clouds were reflected in the still waters. There was a faint smell of wood smoke in the air.

"Yes," she said. "That's how it feels. Then the noise and traffic starts again but in a calmer way. I love the evenings here in this town. I can't wait to move into the flat."

"Can I see it?" he asked. "I know where it is, but I'd love to see it from the inside."

"How long have you been following me?" Molly asked, wondering if it was a good idea to keep talking to him. She knew she should walk away, get a lawyer to place a restraining order or something and then start divorce proceedings. But all that seemed too big, too complicated and too—cruel. It wouldn't have been kind to kick him when he was down.

"I found you by accident," he replied. "I thought you were still in Ireland, and I was going to go there and look you up. But I googled your name and saw on your website you lived in Saint-Tropez. So I came here and got this job picking grapes. I didn't know quite where you lived, but I read about your brother's wedding, so I went to the church and stood at the back during the ceremony." He touched her face. "You were so beautiful in that pink dress. Like a vision from the past. Oh, Molly, I wish…"

She turned her face away. "Wishing won't make it so. I can't believe you were spying on me at the wedding! And then you didn't get in touch. You just hovered around, stalking me, for God's sake!"

He hung his head. "I know. Cowardly of me. But it didn't seem right to intrude. And then I saw you in Nice, in that fancy restaurant with that guy. I recognised him from an article about the family in a magazine I read on the plane. Theodore Anderson, heir to the Anderson fortune. I wanted to find out more so I pretended to be a journalist and e-mailed that woman who—"

Molly clapped a hand to her forehead. "You were the journalist from The Herald Tribune? Jesus, Miguel, you do have some nerve!"

He shrugged and smiled. "Yeah, I know. But what did I have to lose? Then I found out about the contract you had just signed. And I met that guy in the Spanish restaurant and asked a few questions. So here and there, I got all the information I wanted."

"Holy shit."

"I know. Must be a little startling all right."

She stared at him through the gloom of the twilight. "Startling? Are you kidding? I nearly had a heart attack when I saw you again."

"Sorry."

She got off the wall. "Yeah, right. 'Sorry' won't do it, I'm afraid. Look, I have to go. I was supposed to do some of the painting in the apartment. But now I'll just bring up the paints and the ladder, and then I have to go to my workshop to finish my designs."

He jumped to his feet. "Hey, I have an idea."

She backed away. "I don't want to hear your ideas."

"You'll like this one. Just shut up for a moment and listen. I have a week left at the vineyard. Just a few little jobs I promised to do. But I have plenty of time, so I could paint the flat for you, so you can move in sooner than you thought. Then I could rent the room at the house you're in now. I have a little bit of money left and I'll look for something else locally."

Molly hesitated. She knew she shouldn't trust him, shouldn't let him into her life. There must have been some way of getting a divorce from a spouse who hadn't been in touch for fifteen years. But as she looked at him in the gathering dusk, all she saw was a desperately lonely man who had come to an impasse in his life, who had no way out other than asking her for help. She also knew his offer was a good one. He had painted their little flat in Dublin and even sanded and polished the wooden floors, transforming the dingy rooms and making the whole place fresh and inviting. She cleared her throat and took a deep breath.

"Okay. I take you up on your offer. I'll even pay you for doing the work. I know you'll do a professional job."

His face brightened. "You will? You're a darling, Molly!"

"No, I'm a sucker and a fool. I should tell you to go to hell and get myself a lawyer. But right now I don't have the time for all that. So here's the deal—you do up my apartment, I pay you the going rate for the job, and then you get out and we sort out the divorce." She leaned forward and stared at him. "And you don't get any of my money, is that clear?"

"Except if we decide to get back together, of course," he said, laughing at her stern face. "I'm rapidly falling in love with you, Molly." He ran his finger down her cheek, all the way to her throat. "Don't tell me you don't feel anything for me."

"No, I don't." She backed away from his touch.

"Not even the slightest little vibe, like a gentle breeze stirring the leaves on a summer's morning?"

As if conjured up by his words, a soft wind gently lifted the curls around her hot cheeks. She got off the wall and started to walk away. "Come on, let's get going. It's too late to do any painting but you can help me get the stuff from my car and up the stairs.

"Yes, ma'am. Lead the way."

Molly walked ahead of him up the lane to her apartment building, where she came to a stop. The bakery was closed, and there was only a faint light through the shutters of the first floor apartment, where the baker and his family lived. The rest of the house was in darkness. She dug in her handbag for her keys, while behind her, Miguel was unloading tins of paint from her car. Together they climbed the stairs up to the top floor.

"Who lives on the second floor?" Miguel asked.

"I don't think it's occupied. There's only the baker's family and me in this whole building." Molly unlocked the old oak door and switched on the light in the ceiling. "It looks very worn at the moment but once it gets a lick of paint…"

Miguel stepped inside and looked in awe at the faint frescoes in the high ceiling. "What an amazing place."

"Not very big."

"Not tiny either. Much bigger than the cubby hole we had in Dublin. And I bet there's a lovely view from that terrace."

"Yes. Could you get that ladder for me and then we'll lock up. I have to get to my workshop."

But Miguel wasn't listening. He walked around the small apartment, peeking into the kitchen and the bedrooms before he came back. "This will be a true gem once we get it finished."

Molly stiffened. "There is no 'we' here. Just me. I own this place, and you'll be doing the painting and then clear off, do you hear me?"

"Yes, yes, stop nagging," Miguel said, touching the mantelpiece. "Great fireplace. Does it work?"

"I have no idea. I'm going to get the chimney cleaned, anyway."

"You should."

Molly's phone pinged. "It must be Liam wondering where I am." She fished the phone out of her bag and looked at the message. But it wasn't from Liam. Molly gasped when she saw the caller ID and the message: ***I'm here and I want to see you. Where r u?***

Chapter 14

"Bloody hell, Ted, what's going on?" Molly shouted into her phone. She had left Miguel in front of her building and driven off, only to stop in a parking lot just outside town to call Ted. Still shaken after the sudden arrival of her so-called husband, Molly tried to get her mind around Ted and what he was doing.

"I'm in a small hotel in Cavalaire. It's only twenty minutes from Saint-Tropez," Ted said.

"Yeah, yeah, I know where it is. What the hell are you doing there?"

"I had to hide somewhere for a while, and this was the only place I could think of. Please, don't tell anyone. They think I went to our chalet in Colorado. That's what I said to my sisters anyway, after…" He paused. "You see…the wedding…it didn't go ahead after all."

"I know that. I saw it all on TV. I had no idea you were even getting married before I heard it from your sister. You know, it would have been *nice* if you had shared that little snippet of information with me the last time we met."

Ted breathed noisily before he replied. "I know. I'm sorry. It was just that I didn't want to ruin that day by even thinking about the wedding. I was feeling very uneasy about it."

"I figured that out when I saw what happened. Why did you let it get that far? I mean…" Molly stopped. She knew it was useless asking these questions. Ted would tell her in his own time. He obviously needed help in some way. "Are you okay?" she asked.

"Yes. No, I'm not. But I think I need to be on my own for a while. I just thought I'd tell you I was here in case…in case you were worried about me."

"Thanks. I wasn't really," Molly said, realising Ted and the wedding that never was had completely slipped her mind when she was confronted by Miguel. "I have a lot going on right now, you know. I mean, yeah, when I saw what happened I was quite shocked. But then you hadn't told me about it and I thought…shit, I'm sorry. I'm so confused right now."

"It's okay. I understand. Not fair to lean on you like this."

"Not really, no. We hardly know each other."

"That's true. But you know, I felt so close to you when we were out walking. As if something new and really great was happening. And that's partly why I couldn't go through with it. The wedding, I mean. I kept thinking…" He paused for breath.

"Me too," Molly cut in. "I felt a very strong connection to you. But let's leave that aside for now. If you're okay, I'll keep going and catch up with you later."

"Good. Thanks for…being there, Molly. For being *you*."

"No problem," Molly said and hung up. She sat there for a while, staring out the window, at the traffic and people without really seeing them. *Here I go again*, she thought, *helping people. But what's wrong with that? They need me. Ted, so desperate and so alone. And Miguel…*

She put her forehead on the steering wheel and closed her eyes, while images of those days so long ago crowded into her mind: the strange wedding; living together but apart at the same time; painting the flat and flicking paint at each other. Laughing with him; teasing him; loving him and having to hide it; dreams of him finally loving her back, of him kissing her, of him *staying*. And their night together before he left. She knew she shouldn't go there, shouldn't allow herself to fall into that black hole of despair—of futile hopes and dreams she knew would never come true. *Why didn't I try to get him declared dead*, she asked herself, as she had over and over again. *Why did I not go and see a lawyer? Because you never let go of the dream, didn't want to close the door completely,* she answered back. *And now you're going to pay for that stupidity.*

Her phoned pinged with a text message from Daisy. ***Where r u? Dinner getting cold.***

On my way, Molly replied and started the engine.

* * *

"What's wrong with you?" Tommy asked, peering at Molly over his plate of lamb Provençal. "You're not listening."

They were in Daisy's kitchen, sitting at the round table where the glow of the lamplight and the smell of herbs and garlic created a cosy cocoon against the cold, dark evening.

Molly's eyes focused on Tommy. "I'm sorry. I was thinking about something—a bit of a problem. But I heard you say you were swimming, right?"

Tommy nodded and stuck his fork into a piece of meat. "Yes. I can swim now, I swam and swam, didn't I, Daisy?"

"You sure did," Daisy said. "You'll be on the Olympic team one day. "You're a very good swimmer."

"A problem?" Liam cut in. "Something wrong?"

Daisy put down her fork. "What's going on, Molly? You look tired and stressed. Is it the deadline for the designs?"

"No, not really. That's under control."

"Then what?" Liam said. "You look like you've seen a ghost."

Molly looked at the little family around the kitchen table, still glowing with health and happiness after their long honeymoon in Corsica. Daisy, all blonde and tanned and sparkly, Liam so at peace with himself and Tommy secure with parents who loved him. She didn't want to drag them into her mess. How could she tell them about Miguel? Liam didn't know about the fake marriage…she had never told him about it. Now it was too late. How could she break the news to him that she had married someone she didn't love? No. She couldn't bring herself to do it.

But later, when Tommy had gone to bed, and they were having coffee in the living room, that's exactly what she did.

* * *

Liam stared at Molly when she had finished her story. "Jesus, Molly, why didn't you tell me?"

Molly looked into her cup. "I was ashamed."

Liam shot up. "I bet you were!" He started to pace around the room. "What a stupid thing to do! Marrying some foreigner to get him a passport. Were you out of your mind?"

"I…well, I didn't think."

"I bet you didn't, you moron!" He stopped in front of her, his face like thunder. "I suppose you just wanted to help out, in your usual way. You felt sorry for him, right? You felt he needed your help?"

Molly shrank from Liam's blazing eyes. "Yes, I did. He would have had to leave the country and miss out on a great job opportunity. Nobody else wanted to help him."

"Of course they didn't," Liam growled. "Who'd be that stupid?"

Daisy got up and put her hand on Liam's shoulder. "Calm down, sweetheart. Losing your temper isn't going to help Molly."

Liam shook off her hand. "Why didn't you tell me? Why have you never said a word about it to me? I understand why you didn't want to say anything to Mam. She was so ill and it would have upset her. And Dad would have blown a fuse. But why not me?"

"Why do you think?" Molly suddenly shouted. "Look at you now. You're apoplectic. Back then you'd have killed me."

"You bet I would," Liam shouted back. "But back then there was so much going on. Mam dying, Dad in such a poor state of health. But after that…"

Molly felt tears sting her eyes. "But then Maureen got sick and…"

Liam's face softened. He sat down beside her on the sofa and put his arm around her. "I know. You stepped in and saved my life. And Tommy's. You put your life on hold for us."

"So then I was too worried about you to even think about that stupid marriage," Molly continued. "I forgot about it. Put it away in a box I never opened again. Got on with my life—and yours."

"But when things settled down," Daisy cut in. "Why didn't you do something about it? I mean, had it been me, no matter what else happened, in fifteen years, I would have found the time to walk into a lawyer or paralegal's office and divorce that guy's ass."

"Sounds like it would be a breeze in America." Molly let out a raucous laugh. "But not in Ireland. Divorce was made legal only twenty years ago. But it's still very difficult and complicated to get a divorce."

Daisy stared at Molly. "Seriously? Before the mid-nineteen nineties, there was no way you could get a divorce in Ireland?"

"That's right. The last bastion of the Catholic church," Liam muttered and got up from the sofa. "I suppose you don't want me to beat that gobshite to a pulp to make him get that divorce?"

"No," Molly said. "I'll deal with it. I'll finally face him and tell him we have to get it done.

Liam nodded. "Okay. You must. But enough of this. I'm going to get some writing down."

Molly nodded. "Good idea. I suppose I should go to the workshop and look over the designs. I'm sorry if I upset you, Liam."

He paused at the door. "There you go, apologising again. No need. All I want you to do is sort this out. Get a lawyer, go to the European Court, or whatever you need to do, and get rid of this guy for good. I can't imagine a judge would grant him any rights to your property whatsoever."

"I will," Molly promised. "I'll talk to Marianne's lawyer tomorrow and see what's to be done."

"Good."

When Liam had gone, Daisy closed the shutters and pulled the curtains while Molly put the screen in front of the fire.

"It's cold tonight," Daisy remarked. "But I turned on the heating in your workshop."

"Thanks. I know it's late, but working on the drawings will help take my mind off things."

Daisy hesitated. "I know this is none of my business, but I want to tell you I understand why you did it and why you let that marriage drag on without doing anything about it."

Molly stared at Daisy. "You do? I hardly understand it myself, to be honest."

"But I do. It's a bit like that abusive relationship I allowed to continue for years. I was always hoping that one day, things would change and that Bruno would love me as much as I loved him. And maybe you kept hoping he—whatshis-name—would come back and want to have a real marriage?"

Molly nodded. "Yes, I think I did. It was a foolish dream I hung onto. But now that he has come back, I'm not so sure. I don't feel like that for him anymore. But I want to help him. He's been through a lot."

"I can see that. I felt the same for Bruno. I was sorry

for him and knew he was deeply unhappy. But I learnt one important lesson during the time I was stuck in that relationship."

"What was that?"

"Don't confuse pity with love."

* * *

The apartment was beautiful. As Miguel worked on the renovations, the rooms sprang to life. He was astonished at how the freshly painted walls and window trims transformed the worn, slightly forlorn space into a warm, inviting set of rooms that would soon be Molly's home. He hadn't held a paint brush in years, but the skills were still there, he discovered, as he started to prime the walls and then apply the paints she had bought. He liked her choice of colours: off-white with a hint of pink for the living room, pale primrose for her bedroom with the wardrobes in pure white. The bathroom would be painted a pale sea-green to match the deeper green of the tiles, and the smaller bedroom would be papered with a floral print in a delicate pink. She hadn't yet decided on the kitchen. The shutters would be painted sage green to match the others in the house. It was perfect with the pale-pink stucco façade.

As he worked from early morning until darkness fell, he thought of Molly. She had been in his mind all through the torturous years of imprisonment in Thailand. During those years in hell, he had spent most of his days looking back on his life and the choices he had made: his childhood in Argentina, living in a dysfunctional family where his parents were constantly at war with each other; the student years in Dublin, the happiest years of his life; his adult life in Germany; his difficult relationships with women; his achievements and choices. And then—the regrets, the greatest of which was leaving Molly and never getting in touch. A cold, cowardly act. What a shit he had been to her. She didn't deserve it. But he felt then she cared too much for him and would slow him down, make him stay and commit to a marriage he didn't want, didn't dare to believe in.

He should have stayed and at least gone through with the divorce. But in those days in Ireland, a divorce was both costly and slow, so he had taken the easy option. Not because he didn't have any feelings for Molly—but because he did, and that felt like entrapment. But what man wouldn't be seduced by that cute freckly face and red curls? The blue eyes, full lips and dimply smile. The shapely figure and the melodious voice that would break into a lilting Irish song when she was feeling wistful or romantic. And her kooky, quirky character that never failed to make him laugh. All of that had been suddenly so fresh in his mind, and it had kept him sane, like a mirage, during his incarceration. Where was she? What was she doing with her life?

He had been trying to find her ever since returning to Europe, reading about her success story in The Sunday Times and then little snippets here and there in the press. He realised she was now successful and comfortably off. Maybe she would have been willing to at least give him a little financial help? He had been following her around for weeks, familiarising himself with her life and her surroundings, planning what he would do and how appeal to her kind and generous nature. That wouldn't be too hard. She was a sucker for sad stories.

But when they finally were face to face, she didn't match the dreams. She wasn't quite the girl he had left behind but a woman with confidence and style, which was both intriguing and intimidating—and even quite seductive. She had been sympathetic and helpful, but he didn't want her pity. He wanted her to love him again. Then, and only then would she be pliable enough to share some of her newfound wealth.

As he finished for the day, cleaned the brushes and put them away, he realised there was only one way to get around her. He heard her key in the lock, and she stepped inside. His stomach churned as their eyes met.

He cleared his throat. "I have something to tell you."

Chapter 15

"Me too." Molly clenched her fists by her sides to keep her from being softened by his sad eyes. "What I want to say is, I've been in touch with a lawyer."

He looked startled. "But I was going to—"

"Please let me finish." Molly pulled her dark green corduroy jacket tighter around her against the chilly air in the unheated apartment. "I want to start divorce proceedings. He—the lawyer—said he'd get me the papers and file for divorce at once. In our case, it shouldn't take long, except if you contest it and ask for support or something."

Miguel wiped his hands on a rag. "I have no intention of asking for anything. I was going to tell you that I have looked into divorce proceedings myself, and it doesn't seem that complicated."

Molly stared at him. "You have? But yesterday you said you needed money and that I, as your wife..."

He took a step forward. "I know what I said. But I didn't mean it. Did you really believe I'd come back like this just to get money from you?"

Molly let out a long sigh. "I don't know you. We never really got to know each other, did we? In any case, we're both different, both older, and hopefully wiser, than we were back then."

"Yes, that's true."

Molly went across the room to sit on the edge of the

window seat, not because she was tired, but because she wanted to put a little distance between them. It was unnerving to be so close to him, to feel the warmth of his body and the faint smell of paint mingled with aftershave. "Why did you come back?" she asked. "Why did you want to find me?"

He shrugged, avoiding her gaze. "I wanted to see the real you, instead of that image I had in my mind. I think I felt we both needed to finally close the chapter."

Molly crossed her arms. "About bloody time."

He laughed. "Sure is. But that's my fault and I want you to know how sorry I am. I hope it hasn't wrecked your life. I mean, if you wanted to get married…"

"I never did."

"Or have children?"

"No."

He leaned against the wall, peering at her in a way that made her blush. "You didn't fall in love during all those years?"

"Yes. Twice. But it never lasted. I always felt—trapped. I don't believe in marriage. Never have. And children…well, I had Tommy and that was enough for me. Motherhood scares me."

He nodded. "Me too. All of what you just said. That's why I never felt sorting out the divorce was that important."

"Exactly. I kind of forgot about it," Molly added, knowing it was a lie.

"Yes, I did too. Life and work took over."

Unable to meet his gaze, Molly looked at her feet. "So it will all be okay in the end," she mumbled. She looked around the room. "You've done a good job."

"The ceiling needs to be retouched. Those angels should be redone. But they're very old, could be from the sixteenth century, so you need an expert to restore it."

"I like them like that. They're soft, like in a dream. Or a vision."

He looked up. "Yes, I see what you mean. You could be right. I'll be finished in a couple of days. You can move in once the paint dries. Do you want me to hang the wallpaper in the small bedroom?"

She got off the window seat. "No. I can do that. You go on home. I'll lock up."

He put his hand out to stop her when she walked past. "There's something you're not telling me. I can see it in your eyes."

She turned to face him. "What do you see?"

"Grief."

She looked at him and suddenly grabbed his arms, pressing her face to his chest. "Yes. There is—was—grief. When you left, I felt as if you had suddenly died," she whispered into his tee shirt. Tears suddenly welled out of her eyes, wetting his shirt. "I loved you, you see. And I never stopped hoping that you would love me too."

He hugged her tightly. "I didn't know." He put his cheek to her hair. "What can I say? I felt something similar, but I was afraid to show it. God, Molly, I'm so sorry. But you did get over it, didn't you? Eventually?"

She lifted her tearstained face to his. "Yes. And no. Grief isn't something you 'get over'. You learn to live with it. You heal and build your life around the loss. You're whole again after a while, but you're never the same. And you don't want to be." She slowly detached herself from his arms. "And that's why I didn't want to get a divorce. Can you understand that?"

"Yes," he said in a voice so hoarse it was like a whisper. "Yes, I can." He touched her face. "And now? After all these years? How do you feel?"

She broke away from him, took a tissue from her pocket and wiped her eyes. "I want to be free."

* * *

Free, Molly thought as she drove back to Sophia's house. *Yes, that's what I want to be. Free from dreams and false hopes.* She drove through the gate and parked in front of the house, in darkness except for the light on the porch and a faint glimmer from the kitchen. Jay must still be up. But when she walked in, she found Sophia sitting at the table with a glass of wine and a deck of cards. The kitchen was dim and smelled faintly of Moroccan lamb stew and lavender from a scented candle on the table.

"You're up late," Molly remarked.

"I couldn't sleep. Long day and lots going on. How about you? Same story?"

"Yes. Very long day and a great deal going on."

Sophia picked up the wine bottle. "How about a glass of wine?"

"No, thank you. I'll make myself some of that calming tea you have."

Sophia rubbed her eyes. "Oh yes, make some for me too."

"Have you and Jay been playing cards?" Molly asked, eyeing the deck.

"No. These are tarot cards. I just got them. I wanted to see if I can find out things about people. Or what might be happening to them. I thought I'd use my intuition and turn it into a business. But Jay doesn't like them. He says it's all evil mumbo-jumbo."

Molly sat down while she waited for the kettle to boil. "What kind of things can you find out?"

Sophia's eyes lit up. She quickly spread all the cards face down in front of her on the table. "Go on, pick a card and we'll see what it says."

Molly hesitated. "Oh, well, what harm can it do?" She put her finger on one of the cards. "This one."

Sophia turned it around. "Aha. The Fool. Interesting."

"Beautiful card. But what is that figure? A man dressed in a tunic standing on a cliff. Looks like some kind of jester. Does that mean I'm a fool?"

"No, not at all. The card is called The Fool, but in the upright position like this it means a dreamer, an idealist. The fool desires to do great things but their goals are often unrealistic." Sophia leaned closer. "The fool—in this case, you—must be careful in the choices you make. This card also means a new beginning, but you must look at all your options before you make important choices in your life."

"Oh." Molly jumped as the kettle came to a boil and realised she had been holding her breath. "That's amazing."

"Really?" Sophia studied Molly. "Does it fit?"

"Perfectly." Molly got up to make the tea.

"That's splendid." Sophia pushed the cards around. "You're an excellent subject. I can feel there are some interesting vibes here. Let's see if we can find out some more."

Molly carried two steaming mugs to the table. "Why not? It's kind of fun."

"Take another card."

Molly turned a card with the figure of a woman dressed in white. "The High Priestess. What does that mean?"

"Ooh," Sophia said. "It's upside down. That means…hang on, I'll get the booklet. She rummaged around in a pile of papers on the table and pulled out a small brochure.

"You don't know this by heart?"

"No, I just got these in the post. I thought I'd study to be a medium. Good ones make a lot of money, you know." She flicked through the booklet. "So, The High Priestess. Oh, this is interesting."

"What? Come on, tell me," Molly urged.

"In the reversed position, The High Priestess card can signify a hidden agenda, a lack of compassion or selfishness. Not you, but someone you know. There could be someone close to you trying to harm you. 'Beware of false prophets,' it says." Sophia shook her head. "Could be just a warning."

Molly shivered. "Scary."

Sophia nodded. "Could be."

"Gosh." Molly pulled another card out of the pack. "A naked woman with a star over her head, pouring water into a lake from a jug. The Star, it says. Looks nice."

"But again, it came out upside down." Sophia peered at the card and consulted her book. "The Star, reversed, can signify despair, crushed dreams, gloom and an unwillingness to adapt. Your own self-doubt may be getting in the way of courage. And it says this could be a sign that now's the time to take a look at past failures and mistakes and learn from them. And then, finally, it says that there is always hope and that rest and a positive outlook are important." She drew breath. "That was quite encouraging, don't you think?"

"Yes." Molly sipped her tea. "And eerily true."

Sophia's face lit up. "Really? Goodness, I might have hit on something big here. I could be a terrific medium and make a lot of money. You must let me know what happens and if any of this comes true." She mixed the cards around again. "Go on, one last card."

"No. You take one. Let's see if the cards can say something about you and your future."

"Oh, gosh. I suppose I should." Sophia's hand hovered over the deck before she turned one of the cards in the top row. She peered at it. "Aha. The Empress. She looks good. And she's the right way up. What does it say about her?"

Molly picked up the booklet. "Okay…yes, here it is. The Empress. It says that in the upright position, it symbolises fruitfulness, fertility or the beginning of a new venture." Molly giggled. "Could you be having a baby?"

Sophia laughed. "That would be fun. But no, it's a little too late for that. A new venture sounds promising. Go on, what else does it say?"

"The Empress understands that life's simple pleasures bring you joy, although you also enjoy the finer things," Molly read. "You're sensual and earthy and generous. It also signifies creativity and a broadening of horizons. Growth, prosperity and joy are in your future. You will have good health, domestic stability and happiness. You will reap the benefits of your efforts. Your rewards will be greater than your expectations."

Sophia beamed. "That was an absolutely superb card!"

"And spot on."

"Incredible." Sophia shook her head. "I never imagined I could be this good. I must see if I can set up a business or maybe train with another medium or something."

"I think you should. I didn't believe in that nonsense until now." Molly's fingers hovered over the cards. "I'm going to pull out one more, just to see if it was all a fluke or real."

"Yes, do."

Molly turned over a card with a naked man and a woman holding hands with a kind of angel hovering over them. "The Love card," she whispered. "I'm afraid to ask what it says."

"But it's upright," Sophia soothed. "The upright cards are mostly good. This one, I know by heart."

"Tell me what it means."

"Well," Sophia said. "The Lover's card in the upright position signifies the most powerful of unions but also the most challenging of conflicts. It could mean love between two people that will never end. Or it could be that you have to choose between two paths in your relationship. You have to choose carefully and follow your intuition and your heart. It might also mean your true love is right under your nose, but you can't see him." She gazed at Molly. "Does that ring true?"

"Yes." Molly hesitated. Should she reveal the secret of her marriage and the impending divorce? Better not—the less people who knew the better. But what about the true love she couldn't see? Who could that be? Ted? Or...Miguel? "I don't want to go into details, but have come to a kind of crossroads in my emotional life," she explained.

"I see. Hmm, in that case I would do what it said. Be very careful in your choices." Sophia picked up her mug and drank her tea. "I'm exhausted. Being a medium demands a lot of concentration. I'm going to bed. I have to bone up on seances too. That will be a huge challenge."

Molly rinsed the mugs at the sink. "I'll be in bed very soon, too. Thanks for the readings. Very interesting."

"Yes. And very revealing." Sophia stopped in the door and looked darkly at Molly. "Don't forget the most important message you got there."

"Message? What message?"

"Beware of false prophets. Someone's out to harm you."

Chapter 16

Molly had forgotten about Ted and his problems, but he came hurtling back into her life the next day. Literally. She had woken up early to a morning of baby-blue skies and sunshine and decided to take her coffee and croissant to the beach and enjoy some fresh air before she set off to the workshop and the final work on the designs. Jay had done an early dash to the local boulangerie so he could surprise Sophia with breakfast in the garden, not forgetting Molly and her love of croissants for breakfast.

Molly sat down on a rock, sipping coffee and taking a bite out of the warm flaky pastry. She closed her eyes to the sun while she chewed, but was suddenly jolted out of the early morning peace by someone pushing her so hard the croissant was knocked out of her hand.

"What the—?"Molly gasped.

"Damn." Ted bent to pick up the croissant and blew the sand off it. "I was running and didn't see you until the last minute."

"Can't you watch where you're going, you eejit? Now you've ruined my breakfast."

"Sorry," Ted panted. He handed Molly the croissant. "It should be okay…just a little more crunchy than before."

"Gee thanks." Molly stuffed it into her mouth and swallowed, chasing it down with a mouthful of coffee. "What are you doing here, anyway?"

"Running." Ted breathed hard, his back bent, hands on his knees. "It's a great running beach. And then I thought I'd call in to see you afterwards. But here you are."

"Right, smack in your path."

"Yeah." Ted wiped the sweat off his forehead with the edge of his tee shirt, revealing tight abs. "Didn't mean to knock into you like that."

"I should hope not." Molly shuffled over on the rock. "Sit down."

"Okay." Ted joined her, his hands on his thighs, looking out at sea. "Lovely morning."

"Gorgeous." Molly knocked back the last of her coffee. "So, how's tricks? Other than standing that gorgeous girl up at the altar, then flying across the Atlantic and hiding in some grotty hotel in Cavalaire?"

He looked at her sideways. "You sound annoyed."

"Me? Annoyed?" Molly quipped. "Not at all. It's just that life seems to be piling one thing after another on me right now. But whatever. If you've come to talk, so talk. But this time, don't leave anything out. Tell me the whole story, okay?"

"Okay." Ted was silent for a moment while he kept looking at Molly as if gauging her mood. "I don't know if this makes sense, but when I sat there at that dinner and looked at Cindy—my—the girl who was going to be my wife—I saw that I was about to marry…my mother."

"What? Oh. Okay." Molly suddenly giggled. "Sorry, but the image of your mother in a wedding dress just popped into my mind."

Ted snorted a laugh. "Yeah, that would have been some freak show." He shoved her with his elbow. "Could you be serious for a minute?"

Molly pulled herself together. "Yes, of course. It's not something to laugh about. I understand exactly how you must have felt."

Ted brightened. "You do? Do you also see I couldn't go through with it? Nobody else does. How could I walk out on such a stunning woman? And yes, she is. Stunning. At first, I thought marrying Cindy would be a way of getting away from my mother, but then I realised it was the other way around. Cindy and Mother are very close, which I didn't realise until just before the wedding. All through our relationship, Cindy manipulated and cajoled me to do what my mother wanted. I saw that like a flash from above, right there, at the dinner table. The two of them, heads together, whispering, smiling, looking at me as if I was on the menu and they were going to dissect me and eat me. And then I knew I had to run if I was to save myself. I saw it like a dream—or a nightmare really. The life I would have with her, would have been like…" he stopped. "I can't describe it."

"A kind of death?" Molly took his hand. "I've had this feeling ever since we met, that you're trapped in a bubble. I wanted to prick that bubble and get you out, but I didn't know how."

Ted pushed his hair out of his eyes. "But you did. If not for you, I'd never have had the courage. That day, when we were walking in the mountains, I suddenly saw, knew I must—had to—break free. I had to save my life. I felt it was my last chance to—"

"To what?"

"Escape," Ted mumbled. He looked wildly at Molly. "I saw the trap closing. I saw those women getting their teeth into me. Then I thought of my dad and how he was slowly crushed by her—my mother, even though he had started the business and was the brain behind it. And I remembered how he had made all his children take dual citizenship—Swedish and American—when we were born. Both my parents were born in Sweden, so we qualified for citizenship. Dad told me to always keep both passports valid. Then, just before he died, he told me he had put money into a bank account in Sweden for me and made me promise not to tell anyone. Running-away money he called it and laughed. I don't think he did that for the girls. He might have noticed how my mother was beginning to manipulate and abuse me. Not physically, but mentally."

"So you used your Swedish passport when you left?"

"Yes. I left the other one on my desk. I wanted them to think I was still in the US. Hope they do."

"Oh Lord, what a story," Molly sighed. "What are you going to do now?"

Ted looked at her long and hard. Then he suddenly put his arm around her and pulled her close. His green eyes glittered with something wild, something new and very strong. "I've felt like a kind of Peter Pan for many years—the boy who never grew up. And maybe I never will. But now I want to fly, go somewhere else."

"Where would that be?" Molly asked, startled by the fire in his eyes.

"The second star to the right and then right on 'til' morning. Do you know what I mean?"

Molly touched his face. "Oh. Yes. That's exactly where you have to go—where everyone should go."

He nodded. "I knew you'd understand. Will you…come with me?"

Molly pulled away from his touch. This was getting to hot. She felt such a strong attraction to him at that moment, and she would have done anything he asked. But a little voice inside told her to resist. It was too much, too soon.

"No. I can't. Not right now. I have to go on my own journey first. Break away from something hard and painful. Deal with my feelings and try to figure out who I really am."

He took her hand and looked at her, his hair tousled by the wind, his eyes tender. "I'm sorry. That was selfish of me. I should've realised you might have your own issues."

"Everyone does," Molly said, resisting an urge to put her

arms around him. She wanted to comfort him, help him and protect him from harm. But that wouldn't have been right. She picked up her mug that had fallen onto the sand. "I have to go. I have a deadline for those designs, remember."

"I know. I saw the drawings. I loved them. They'll be a huge hit. So unusual."

"Thank you."

He got up. "I'd better get back to my jog. I'm trying to get fit for the skiing season. It's starting up very soon. It's already snowed in the Alps. Thought I'd go there and see if I can get a job as a ski instructor. I have a diploma from Aspen I did just for fun. But it's one qualification I'm very proud of. Not that my mother would approve of me being a ski bum, but who gives a shit?"

Molly laughed. "Sounds like a great idea."

"Will you come and see me? It's only a couple of hours by car. I'll let you know which resort I'm at."

"I don't know how to ski."

"I'll teach you. Free lessons, how about that?"

"Yeah, right. You just want to watch me break my ass."

"You're so suspicious." Ted looked past her and started to walk away. "Someone's coming. I'm out of here. See you." He broke into a sprint and disappeared around the rocks so fast Molly wondered if he had been there at all.

"Look at this," a voice said in her ear. Molly turned and discovered Marianne holding her phone up for Molly to see.

Molly squinted at the phone. "What? I can't see the screen properly in this glare."

Marianne cupped her hand over the screen. "Try it now."

Molly twisted her head and looked at the picture of a woman. "That's—Monica Verucci, isn't it? The film star?"

"Yes. And what is she wearing?"

Molly took a closer look and realised what she was looking at. "A necklace—oh shit!" She stared uncomprehendingly at Marianne. "It's my necklace," she stammered.

"For the Anderson collection. Did they make a prototype for her?"

"Nope," Marianne snapped. "It's says in the caption that it's from the spring range by Bloom & Smith."

"The lingerie firm?"

"That's the one. They're getting into jewellery to go with their new range in evening wear."

"But…I mean…they're mine. How is this possible?"

Marianne's face was grim. "Your designs were nicked, darling. Someone stole the drawings. Or copied them"

"Who would do that? And how?"

"I'd say it was an inside job. Someone at Harlow & Anderson maybe. Who has access to those designs?"

Molly thought for a moment. "Only me and Karen. As far as I know, anyway. But I have no idea who she showed them to at the New York office. She said she'd lock them in the safe and the designs wouldn't be revealed until the launch just after Christmas. I haven't sent her the final drawings and specifications yet either."

"How about Ted?" Marianne suggested. "Could he have nicked them and sold them off before he left that girl at the altar? I've heard his mother has cut him off without a cent and thrown him off the board. I wouldn't say he has much to live on wherever he is hiding."

"No," Molly exclaimed. "He'd never do a thing like that. Not Ted."

Marianne sat down beside Molly on the rock. "I know you like him. But you never know with people in that kind of situation."

"I still don't think it could have been Ted," Molly declared.

"Yeah, you're probably right." Marianne looked at her feet, deep in thought. "But who? Maybe a leak in the New York office? In any case, I'm sure you'll hear from them very soon."

"I'm sure I will," Molly said glumly and got off the rock.

"I'd better get back to the house and get on my computer." She started to walk away.

Marianne fell into step with her. "What are you going to do? They might think it was you who sold out to the Bloom people."

"Why would I do something so stupid?"

"I know. Why would you? But you never know with that Anderson woman. She might be looking for a reason to break the contract. You have to consider all possibilities, even the craziest ones."

"I intend to be a step ahead. When they call me, I'll present them with a plan."

"You have a plan?"

Molly stopped and stared out to sea, the wind whipping her hair around her face. "No. But I will. A whole new design, a new concept." She laughed and looked at Marianne. "This could be a very happy accident."

"I don't have a clue what you're talking about."

Molly turned her face to the sky. "Neither do I. But I have this feeling…this germ of an idea.

* * *

The idea became clearer, and by midday Molly was sketching up a whole new design concept. It was completely different and much bolder and dramatic than the first one that was now out there with another fashion house.

Karen Anderson called just after lunch. "I suppose you know what happened."

Molly stuck the phone between her ear and her shoulder while she filled in the outline of an earring. "Yes. Marianne, my business manager, told me. I thought you'd have been in touch as soon as you knew."

"We've been rather busy lately. My brother…well, he

went missing at his own wedding. I'm sure you heard about that little event too."

"Yes. It was all over the news." Molly put down her pencil and sat up on her stool. "Do you know where he went?" she asked, trying to sound casual.

"No. We thought he was in Aspen but that trail went cold. We're trying to find out where he went. It's been pretty rough around here since he disappeared. Finding out about the theft of your designs was the cherry on the cake, so to speak. My mother isn't very happy."

"I can imagine. I'm sure she's upset."

"Upset?" Karen let out a laugh. "She's spitting nails. First she tried to blame you, but nobody in the boardroom could believe that, so now there's an investigation, and everyone's a suspect, and they're all looking sideways at each other. Talk about tension city."

"You have no idea who might have done it?"

Karen sighed. "No. I secretly believe it was Ted, but I wouldn't say that aloud."

Molly nearly dropped the phone. "Ted? Why would he do that?"

"To get back at Mother."

"But that would have hurt me as well," Molly said. "We don't know each other well, but we've had some nice chats. I don't think he has it in him to be that vindictive. As far as I could gather in such a short time, anyway."

"Really? Hmm." Karen was quiet for such a long time, Molly thought she had hung up.

"You're not trying to hide something from me, are you?" Karen enquired with a slight edge in her voice.

"Like what?"

"Like a closer relationship with my brother than you're willing to admit?"

"As I said, we only met a couple of times. I hardly know him."

"Of course," Karen drawled. "But hey, whatever. None of my beeswax, anyway. But back to your work. What did you say you were doing? You've ditched the old concept?"

"Completely." Molly looked at the drawings in front of her on the workbench. "This is very different. Better too. I think you'll like them. But I won't give them to you until I've finished and made up a template. Then I want to hand it to you in person, right here at my workshop. That way we eliminate the risk of anyone—and I mean *anyone*—getting their hands on them before they get to the manufacturers in China."

"Not even Mother?"

"Not even her. This will be between you and me."

"She won't like it."

"I don't care if she likes it or not."

Karen was silent again.

"Hello?" Molly said. "Did you hear what I said?"

"Yes."

"And?"

"I like it." Karen suddenly laughed. "In fact, I love it."

"You haven't seen the designs."

"I know I'll love them too. Your designs are always fantastic. I agree with your plan. The fewer people who see the new line, the better. But," Karen paused, "before I go, a word of warning."

"Yes? Please make it brief, I have to get back to work."

"Be very careful. Mother's network reaches far and wide. She is vindictive, and if there is *anything* between you and Ted, or if you know where he is, she'll be out to get you."

"I'm not scared of her," Molly said with false bravado.

"Maybe not, but now she has a powerful ally."

"An ally? Who?"

"Do I need to paint a picture? You know what they say about a woman scorned?"

Chapter 17

Molly put her head down during the following two weeks and worked furiously on the new designs. She had decided to do fewer pieces, cutting the collection down to five different necklaces and two bracelets. There would be assorted earrings in shapes and colours to go with practically everything but worn, preferably, with the line of denim jeans and cotton tops planned for the spring collection. She worked late into the night in her workshop, the wood-burning stove glowing and all the lights on. She was beyond tired by the time she had finished, but happy with the results of her labours. She was finally able to hand the drawings and the prototypes over to Karen, who had flown across the Atlantic to collect it all in person. They had lunch in a small bistro in the old town of Saint-Tropez to celebrate.

Karen mopped the last of the salad dressing off her plate with a piece of bread. "Delicious. I was starving even if I would have preferred breakfast."

Molly waved at the waiter for the bill. "You must have terrible jet lag."

"Yes. But I'll be on the next plane back tomorrow morning, so I won't bother trying to get used to this time zone." Karen patted the bag at her feet. "This baby is not leaving my side until I can get it despatched to our manufacturer in China." She pushed the last of the bread into her mouth. "I can't tell you how happy I am with your work and the way you dealt with this crisis so quickly."

"Thank you." Molly gave the waiter her credit card. "I hope your mother wasn't too annoyed about us keeping it secret."

"No, she wasn't." Karen giggled. "Because I didn't tell her. I will break it to her when I get back but not before the stuff is in the hands of the Chinese. Then it'll be too late for her do anything about it. The launch after the New Year will be even better now that there's a bit of mystery." Karen dug in her handbag. "Hey, you shouldn't be paying. Let me get my credit card."

"This is on me."

"What? But I should really pay the bill from our expense account."

Molly punched in the pin number on the machine the waiter held out. "I know, but you can pay me back some other time. Or add it to my royalties or something. You're tired and need to get some rest before you go back."

Karen sighed, sat back and closed her eyes. "You're right. I'll go and have a rest at our apartment in Nice…when I get the energy to drive back."

Molly suddenly felt sorry for her. Karen's hair was flat and lifeless, her eyes puffy and her navy suit crumpled. "Do you want to go back to my place and have a nap?"

Karen opened her eyes. "Could I? I'd sleep anywhere right now."

"My apartment is just around the corner. I haven't moved in yet, but there's a sofa and a few chairs. You could lie down for an hour or two while I get going on papering the small bedroom. There's a guy coming in to finish some painting, but the living room will be quiet, and I'll light a fire. Not ideal, but better than falling asleep here."

Karen slowly got to her feet. "Any couch in any space would be heaven, even if it was in a railway station." She stopped as the door to the restaurant opened and a man stepped inside.

Not just any man. Miguel, who smiled when he saw Molly. "Hi there. I'm taking a break," he called across the restaurant.

"Okay," Molly called back.

"Who is that divine man?" Karen muttered.

"My…uh, a friend, who's doing some work on my apartment."

"Nice friend." Karen's face had suddenly come to life and her cheeks turned pink. "Introduce me, please."

Molly waved at Miguel to come closer. "Karen, this is Miguel. And Miguel, may I introduce my sort of boss, Karen."

"Boss?" Miguel's eyes lit up. "You mean—"

"That's right. I'm one of the infamous Andersons." Karen held out her hand and showed her dimples in a warm smile. "Hi, Miguel. Nice to meet you."

"The pleasure's all mine." Miguel looked deep into Karen's eyes and shook her hand. "Meeting an attractive woman on such a dull day in the middle of winter is a real treat. Do you live around here?"

"No, I'm just here to see Molly, and then I'm flying back to New York," Karen purred. "But I visit this part of the world quite often."

"That's very good news," Miguel replied with a wink.

Molly looked from Miguel to Karen. What was happening? The two of them looked like they were going to either fall into each other's arms or burst into song. Miguel was a practiced flirt, but Karen had never seemed the type who fell easily for a pair of melting brown eyes and a handsome face. But here she was, practically throwing her knickers at him.

Miguel suddenly noticed Molly's puzzled look. He turned to her, his face more sober. "I signed those papers and sent them back to your lawyer."

"Thank you," Molly said curtly. "We should be…I mean it'll all be finalised soon."

"Wonderful," Miguel said in a flat voice. "All sorted out, finally."

"Yes." Molly pulled at Karen's sleeve. "We'd better get going. Don't forget the bag."

"I have it right here." Karen shot a lingering look at Miguel as she followed Molly out the door. "Nice to meet you, Miguel."

Miguel smiled. "See you very soon, I hope, Karen."

"Who is he?" Karen said when they were walking across the square. "What was that you had to finalise with him?"

"That? Oh nothing serious. Just an old business arrangement we never sorted out."

"You did business with that divine man? What kind of—" She stopped. "God, I'm sorry. Please tell me to shut up."

"Shut up, Karen."

"Thanks. I needed that. I'm not usually this nosy." She looked up at the pale-pink building. "What a beautiful house. Is this where you're going to live?"

"Yes." Molly pointed at the top floor. "Up there."

"Fabulous."

"It's not finished yet," Molly explained as they climbed the stairs. "And the place reeks of paint and turpentine." They reached the top floor and Molly opened the sage-green door.

"It's incredible." Karen looked around the big living room, the walls now painted white and the terracotta floor tiles polished. She gazed up at the frescos in the ceiling. "Magical. Angels and butterflies." She kicked off her shoes and sank down on the sofa, still looking up. "I'm going to lie here and look at them until I fall asleep."

Molly crouched in front of the fireplace and set a match to the logs and kindling she had put there earlier. "This should warm you up a bit."

Karen lay back, put up her feet and closed her eyes. "I think it's working."

Molly put a fleece blanket on Karen and tiptoed out.

While Karen slept, Molly started the work in the small bedroom, applying glue on rolls of wallpaper and hanging each roll, standing on a ladder. Then she evened it all out with a wallpaper brush, and stepped back to check it was all smooth, the pattern matched and the joints invisible. She took a break when she had done a whole wall, sitting down on a paint splattered stool, catching her breath. The flat was nearly ready. Some of the furniture would be delivered later that day, and after a trip to IKEA, she could move out of Sophia's house and into her new home. A flash of joy suddenly hit Molly. The first place she could truly call home. How incredible. And the divorce being sorted out at practically the same time. Everything was falling into place all at once. Even the hiccup with the designs had been a happy accident. The new collection would be even better.

Her thoughts drifted to Karen, asleep on the sofa. She was a thoroughly honest, nice woman who now felt more like a friend than a boss. It was strange how she had seemed to fall for Miguel. And maybe he for Karen? It was hard to gauge, as he flirted like that with most women. But she wasn't exactly his type. He had sneered at larger women all those years ago. But maybe he had changed? Maybe he was able to see how attractive Karen was despite or even because of her generous curves. Molly tried to analyse her own feelings, but failed. It was all so confusing—Miguel turning up like that out of the blue and the divorce suddenly imminent. Everything was changing so fast.

A gust of wind rattled the shutters. Molly went to secure them. She opened the window and reached out for the bracket on the wall outside. As she found it, she noticed a woman looking up at her in the square below. Their eyes met and the woman turned quickly and disappeared around the corner. Molly stared down at the now empty square. Who was that woman? Blonde, tall and elegant, she was faintly familiar. Molly knew she had seen her before. But where? She racked her brains but couldn't remember where she had seen that face and that shiny blonde hair. She secured the shutter and returned to the living room, still trying to figure out who the woman was.

* * *

"Butterflies," Karen mumbled on the sofa, looking up at the ceiling. She turned to Molly. "Why don't you do a summer theme like that? Tiny enamelled butterflies in those pastel colours on silver chains."

Molly sat down on the edge of the sofa and followed Karen's gaze up to the ceiling and the faded frescoes. "Oh, yes. Why didn't I think of that? They're so ethereal, like something from a fairy tale." She turned to Karen. "It could go with a whole line of summer clothes. Gossamer-light Indian cotton in soft pink, blue, green and grey. Linen skirts and palazzo pants. Light tunics for the beach. I can see it now on tanned skin. Gorgeous."

Karen sat up and grabbed her bag. "I'm going to write that down. Sounds awesome. I love it." She pulled a notepad and pen from the bag and started scribbling furiously. "I'm thinking Edwardian and floaty muslin, like in those nineteen sixties movies; Death in Venice, Elvira Madigan. Oh wow, this will be so different from the sexy stuff the others are doing. The spring range you just gave me is bold and punchy. This will be a great contrast. I have to get this idea to the designers as soon as I can. We've already finished the summer collection, but we could add this as the resort collection or something."

"Don't you have to run it past your mother first?" Molly asked.

Karen stopped scribbling, her pen frozen in mid-air. "You

have a point there." She thought for a moment, and then a mischievous smile lit up her face. "No, not this time. I'll just get the ball rolling and tell her when it's finished. Then she can't argue." Karen let out a giggle. "I've never done anything without asking Mother before. This feels a bit scary, but very good." She looked at Molly. "It's all your fault, of course. You make us do things we never dared before. First Ted did a bunk at his wedding and refused to marry that barracuda in Louboutin shoes and now you've got me to do something really sneaky."

"I didn't make you do anything," Molly protested.

"Yes, you did, you gorgeous wild woman. You do your own thing and have that devil-may-care look. That makes us feel like trained monkeys, which is exactly what we are. It's time we grew up and became adults."

"Don't tell me you're going to run away, too."

"Absolutely not," Karen said with feeling. "I'm going to stay. I plan to run the company one day. My sisters are clones of my mother. Real yes-men, I mean women. But I'm not." She paused and shot Molly a stern look. "All this is between us, of course."

"Holy shit, woman, of course it is."

Karen laughed. "I love the Irish turn of phrase. I take it we don't have sign a pact in our own blood or anything."

"Yuck, no." Molly got off the sofa. "I'd rather have a cup of tea. Of the Irish kind. Industrial strength."

Karen sat up and stretched. "Lovely. And then I'll go back and start this mini revolution. You can tell Ted things will get a little ugly before they settle into a new grove."

Molly froze on her way to the kitchen. "Tell Ted? But I don't know where he is."

Karen laughed. "Sure you do. But don't tell me. I don't want to know. Just that he's okay."

Molly let out a sigh. "He's fine and he's very happy. Landed on his feet, he said, when last I spoke to him."

"So he's not here, then?"

"No he's—" Molly started, but stopped when Karen held up her hand. "Okay. I won't say any more."

Karen nodded. "Thank you. If I knew, I might tell Mother at a weak moment. Like when she applies the thumbscrews — metaphorically speaking."

Molly was about to reply when there was a noise in the hall, followed by the arrival of Miguel. Karen sat up straighter and pushed at her hair. "Hello there. This is a nice surprise. What are you doing here?"

Miguel stopped in the door and stared at the two women. "I didn't know there was anyone here."

"We're just about to leave," Molly said. "Karen needed a break before she drives back to Nice."

Miguel nodded. "I was just going to add a last coat to the walls in the kitchen and paint the window frames, and then it's all finished."

"You've done a great job," Molly said. "I was just about to make a cup of tea. Will you join us?"

Miguel took off his leather jacket and dropped it at the end of the sofa. "No, I think I'll get going on the painting while we still have daylight."

"Okay. Let me just make the tea and we'll be out of your way." Molly walked into the kitchen, and Miguel sat down beside Karen. She could hear them talking in dulcet tones while she made the tea. She strained her ears to hear what they were talking about.

"Nice scarf," Miguel said. "Is it from your fashion house?"

Karen giggled. "Fashion house? Gimme a break. It's a chain-store operation. But thanks. This scarf comes from Chanel, I'm ashamed to say."

"It's lovely. Matches your eyes."

More giggles from Karen. "Yeah, blue goes so well with red eyes."

"Yes, you look a little tired but I can see past that."

The sofa creaked. Karen must be moving closer. "What can you see?" she purred.

Miguel lowered his voice. "I can see a very attractive, interesting woman. Someone I'd like to see more of one day."

Karen let out a chuckle. "You're a real smoothie, aren't you?

"I take that as a compliment."

"And a conceited bastard too."

Now it was Miguel's turn to laugh. Then they lowered their voices to a murmur, too soft for Molly to hear.

Shit, why can't they stop cooing to each other? Molly's hands shook as she poured boiling water on the teabags. The obvious attraction between them troubled her more than she cared to admit. She still wasn't quite sure of her feelings for him. The divorce finally going through was a relief, but she was left with a feeling of loss, as if she was forced to let go of a hope, a dream that had been part of her for so long. Had she been hoping his feelings for her would be different, now that they were both more mature? Or was it more a sense of ownership? Confused and bewildered, Molly picked up the two mugs. She cleared her throat before she walked. "I didn't know how you take your tea, so I just put milk in it. Do you want sugar?"

Karen moved away from Miguel and took one of the mugs. "No, this is perfect."

Miguel got up. "I'll get started, then."

Karen took a careful sip of tea. "I'd better leave. Must get back to Nice with the designs, and then I'll contact my assistant in New York about that other thing we discussed." She shot a coy look at Miguel over the rim of her mug. "See you later, Miguel."

"I'm looking forward to seeing more of you, guapa." Miguel smiled and disappeared into the kitchen, where they could hear him putting up the ladder and opening a tin of paint.

"Guapa?" Karen said. "What does that mean?"

"No idea." Molly put on her jacket. "Google it."

Karen picked up her phone and turned it on. "Ooh," she said, blushing. "It means beautiful in Spanish. Gosh."

"Are you seeing him before going back?"

"Yes. I invited him to join me for dinner tonight." She looked at Molly. "Do you want to come?"

"You really want me?"

Karen laughed. "Hell, no. Oh God, Molly this is weird. And I'm sorry if there is something between you two. If you feel…"

Molly shook her head. "No, absolutely not. We're old… acquaintances or whatever you might call it. Old student pals. But that's in the past. I want to forget all that and move on. So, please…" She lowered her voice. "Go ahead. He's all yours."

Karen's eyes twinkled. "Terrific." She shot a look at the closed door and lowered her voice. "I'll be pulling out all the stops. Hey, just one question. Why is he doing all this painting for you?"

"He's paying back an old debt. Believe me, he owes me."

"Oh? Why?"

"It's complicated."

"Ah." Karen nodded. "You just told me to shut up again, right?"

Molly laughed. "You got it. I'll just go and say goodbye, and then we'll get out of here and let him finish." Molly opened the door to the kitchen and stuck her head in. "We're off now. When you've finished, e-mail me your bank details, and I'll send the money to your account."

Miguel looked down at her from the top of the ladder, a roller loaded with paint in his hand. "Okay." He paused and lowered his voice. "That cute woman…your boss, you said?"

"Yes."

"So she is one of the Anderson daughters?"

"That's right. Didn't she tell you?"

"She did, but I just wanted to have it confirmed." He turned back to his painting. "See you around then, Molly."

"Bye for now." Molly closed the door, trying not to worry about the calculating glint she had seen in his eyes when he asked about Karen.

Chapter 18

Chantal called the following day with some disturbing news.

"I'm afraid a problem has cropped up with the deeds of your apartment."

Molly coughed as her morning tea went the wrong way. "The deeds? But I got them yesterday."

"Yes, and the sale should be all sealed and finished. But the notaire handling the sale just e-mailed me to tell me the apartment is subject to probate, which hasn't been sorted out yet. There are two more heirs to this estate who haven't agreed to sell."

"How did this happen?"

"They got an e-mail from a lawyer representing the heirs. It will be followed up by a letter. I thought you should know what's going on, so you can decide what to do."

Molly's stomach churned. "Shit. I don't believe this. Are you saying I don't own the apartment after handing over the full asking price?"

"Technically, yes. They will pay you back at once, of course."

"Of course," Molly said in a flat tone, trying her best not to burst into tears. The gorgeous apartment that she had been thinking of as home wasn't hers after all. She stared out the kitchen window at Sophia's garden, the late roses glittering with early morning dew and the sparrows fluttering around in the birdbath. The lovely morning had suddenly turned dark and dreary.

"I'm sure we can find something else just as nice," Chantal soothed. "I have a place in Sainte-Maxime, a little bit up the hill with lovely—"

"I don't want anything else," Molly interrupted. "I want *my* apartment. I'm sure it isn't legal to sell something and then back out of it. The deeds have my name on it, so I must own it. And in any case, if the one of heirs wants to sell, isn't everyone else forced to agree? You know, this sounds very strange."

Chantal didn't reply.

"Hello? Are you still there?" Molly called.

"Yes. I'm thinking."

"And?"

"You're right. I'm going to call the notaire. I smell a very big rat."

Molly felt a tiny flutter of hope. "You think he's making it up? Or someone is out to get their hands on the apartment?"

"Or maybe someone is out to get *you*," Chantal suggested.

"Why would anyone..." Molly paused, remembering what Sophia had said during that Tarot reading. "Someone is out to get you..." But who? Did it have something to do with the blonde woman staring up at her from the square that day? Had Charlotte Anderson twigged there was a connection between Molly and Ted? She shivered as the words 'Her net reaches far and wide.' echoed in her head. That's what Ted had said as a joke, but it was probably true.

Chantal's voice cut into Molly's thoughts. "I'll get back to you as soon as I've talked to the notaire." There was a click as she hung up.

The phone rang twenty nerve-racking minutes later. Her heart beating, Molly picked up on the first ring. "Chantal? Have you—?"

"It's Miguel. I have heard from your lawyer. Did he call you?"

"I have a voicemail message. Could be him. What about?"

Molly asked, trying not to be affected by Miguel's deep voice. In the past, talking to him on the phone used to do strange things to her libido. It still did, she found.

"It's about the divorce. It appears that one of the spouses has to be resident in Ireland for a year before you can apply for a divorce. So we'll be married for a bit longer, my sweet wife."

Molly winced at the teasing note in his voice. "Shit. So what do we do?"

"Would you be willing to go and live in Ireland for a year?"

"Right now I'd go and live in the Outer Hebrides not to be married to you," she snapped.

He laughed. "That won't be necessary. And I'm suddenly just as keen to have this thing finished once and for all. I'm going to Ireland next week, and I'll establish residency there. I'll see if I can get some legal advice too. Maybe this thing can be speeded up, considering the circumstances. I might even get a job."

"Oh." Molly was taken aback at his sudden compliance. "Well, that's…very decent of you."

"Least I can do after all the years I didn't keep in touch."

"That's for sure," she said with feeling. She breathed in, then out very slowly. It suddenly felt so good to know she would be out of the emotional limbo she had been in for fifteen years.

"But I'll be back here regularly," Miguel continued. "I can go away for holidays and so on during that time, of course."

"Of course," Molly said, confused. Why would he be coming back? Then it dawned on her. Karen. They were probably dating or something, and she was often in Nice.

"I take it you won't say anything about this to anyone?" Miguel cut in. "I mean, no need, now that it'll soon be all over, right?"

"Right." *You bastard*, she thought. *You want to be free so you can marry Karen and get your hands on her millions.* Those thoughts instantly cured her of any remaining attraction she had felt. He had used her, and now he was about to use Karen as well. "I'm not going to shout it from the rooftops. I don't want anyone to know how stupid I was."

"Good. I have to arrange a few things. Thanks for the money. I hope you'll be happy in your new apartment. Good luck, Molly."

"Thanks. Goodbye," Molly said flatly. She hung up and immediately burst into tears. It was all too much. Losing the apartment and then finding out what kind of man Miguel was. She had held a candle to him all these years, ruining any potential relationship, as every man she met had been unfavourably compared to Miguel. So many broken relationships, so many lost opportunities, and it was all his fault.

The phone rang again. Molly picked up after blowing her nose. "Yes?"

"Do you have a cold?" Chantal asked.

"No. I'm crying."

"Oh, I'm sorry," Chantal soothed. "I can imagine you're very upset."

"Yes, I am. I'm already miserable, so give me the bad news. I've lost the apartment?"

"No. You were right. It was a scam. The notaire told me it wasn't true. The legal firm supposed to have sent this e-mail knew nothing about it and said they hadn't sent it. So it was some kind of prank to get at you, we think."

Molly let out her breath in a long sigh. "That's wonderful news. But what a stupid thing to do. Didn't they realise that this wouldn't work?"

"Seems more malicious than an actual attack. Like someone played a trick to frighten you."

"It worked." Molly pulled a Kleenex from the box on the windowsill and blew her nose.

"Only for a while. But now you can relax and move in."

"Finally."

"I'm sorry this happened. I should have realised it was a hoax and checked it before I called you. How stupid of me."

"Don't worry about it, Chantal. I'll be all right."

When she had said goodbye to Chantal and hung up, Molly pulled herself together and tidied up the breakfast dishes. She could see Sophia walking around the garden, dead-heading roses and picking up twigs from the lawn. She noticed Molly and waved. Such a sweet woman, even if a little eccentric. But it was that quirkiness that made her so attractive. She seemed to be able to see right into your soul. Molly had never believed in auras before, but now she was beginning to come around to the idea. Not that she saw them herself, but some people had a special talent or spirituality that made them more perceptive. What would Sophia make of Miguel? It would be interesting to get her to meet him.

As Molly started to pack her things to take to the apartment and look up IKEA and other furniture stores online, she found her thoughts drifting to Karen. Should she be warned about Miguel? But then their marriage and what had happened would come out. Molly wasn't sure she was ready to talk about it to Karen. The only person she confided in was Jay.

* * *

They were in the garden picking the last of the apples, not talking about anything in particular, when Molly suddenly found herself telling Jay about Miguel and how he had appeared out of the blue.

Jay put down his nearly full basket. "How did that feel?"

"Shocking beyond belief. Imagine coming face to face with someone you thought was dead."

"Someone you cared about deeply for a long time, too."

"Yes." Molly bent down to pick up a few windfalls. "I felt so confused. Didn't know if I was happy to see him or not. He's so different from the man of my dreams."

Jay studied her for a moment, while the wind whipped at their hair and the clouds rushed across the sky. "I suppose you both changed and evolved. How did he behave with you?"

Molly put the apples in Jay's basket. "He was quite cocky at first. He told me he had spent some time in jail in Thailand. He got caught at the airport with drugs in a bag some girl asked him to mind for her. He seems quite shaken by it all, I have to say. He said he had been thinking about me all through the time in prison. I thought it sounded very romantic, until he started talking about money and how, as we're still married, he can demand financial support."

"How crass. But maybe it was a good thing you found out who he really is?"

"I suppose. But I feel sorry for him at the same time. I worry about the way he is. He has now agreed to a divorce and went to Ireland to help speed things up. He said he'll waive any support or money from me. I thought that was nice of him until I found out he wants to be free so he can marry someone else—a rich woman who happens to be a friend. So now I don't know what to do. Should I warn her? But then it would sound like sour grapes. She's such a good person. I don't want her to get hurt."

Jay put his hands on Molly's shoulders and looked into her eyes. "Do you want to know what I think you should do?"

"Yes."

"You should stop carrying other people's burdens. Stop letting them lean on you. You seem to have done that for most of your life. You told me you looked after your mother until her death. Then your dad, then your brother and his little boy. You married Miguel because you wanted to help him. He treated you like dirt and now you still worry about him? And that other woman—the friend he's hitting on? I presume she's an adult and has had this happen to her before. Leave her alone. Maybe she's aware of why he's flirting with her but doesn't care? Maybe she's using him as well but in a different way"

Molly stared at Jay. "Oh. I never thought of it that way. I suppose I think I can save her or something. Like I think I can stop everyone being hurt if I'm there for them."

He nodded. "And who gets hurt instead? You. Why don't you take a break from worrying and caring and start thinking about yourself for a change? Move into that flat. Go out. Have fun. Be selfish."

"Selfish?"

"Yes. Just like everyone else. It would be a relief to us all if Saint Molly let her hair down and told the world to fuck off."

Molly gasped and then burst out laughing. "You're right. What a pain I've been, doing good deeds and being helpful."

Jay let go of her. "People like you can be very annoying, not to mention boring."

"Shit, yes, they—I mean we—can." She stood on tiptoe and kissed his cheek. "Thank you."

"For what?"

"For telling me off. I needed that. I'll be off now." She skipped away across the garden.

"But what about the rest of the apples?" he called. "There are lots more to be picked."

"Pick them yourself, big boy. I'm off to be a bad girl."

"Where are you going?"

"I don't know yet. I'll send you a postcard—from the edge."

* * *

The road wound its way up the mountainside through snow-covered pine forests. Molly had been driving since early morning, eager to reach her destination before lunchtime. She would make that easily, as the resort was less than two hours' drive from the coast. A weekend in the Maritime Alps would be a welcome break after the past week of work and moving house. She had booked a yoga retreat at a hotel in Isola 2000, a ski resort well known for its good snow cover and nearly constant sunshine. She wouldn't do any skiing—she was going for the scenery and the crisp, clean Alpine air. And Ted. He had sent her a message telling her he was at the resort and it would be a terrific place for her to take break. He suggested she book into a spa hotel just outside the resort, a short walk from bars and restaurants, but far enough away from the village and noisy tourists.

"They do yoga and all kinds of relaxing stuff. You'll love it," he said in his message.

Molly tried to push the stressful events of the past week to the back of her mind, but bits and pieces kept popping up: the hard work of moving into the apartment; Miguel offering to move to Ireland for a year, and leaving for Dublin, only to be back a week later, saying that he could 'commute' between the two countries. The reason for this was Karen. She had announced she would be based in Nice for the coming year in order to look after the affairs of the company in Europe and their flagship store in Paris.

"It's really a way of getting away from Mother," she said and laughed. "If she knew I was dating an out-of-work Irish-Argentinian, she'd go berserk."

"Dating?" Molly said, trying to hide the panic she felt. Was Karen being fooled by Miguel and his flirting? Should she warn her? Then she restrained herself from wading in to offer advice. Jay was right. She had to stop trying to help people all the time. She had to live her own life. Let them sort it out. "Good for you," she said instead, cringing as Karen chatted on about Miguel and what an amazing man he was.

Turning her mind away, Molly relaxed as she drove further into winter wonderland. This early in the season, there was little traffic, and the silent white world gave her an inner peace she had been craving for a long time. She pulled up at a clearing and got out of the car to breathe in the thin mountain air and look out over the white slopes and the Alps rising majestically against the blue sky. Shivering in her thin cotton top, she wrapped her arms around herself and closed her eyes. The intense cold, the pine-scented air and the complete silence made her feel as she was on another planet, about to enter a higher plane and a different mind-set. Energised and hopeful, she got back into the car and continued her journey, driving around hairpin bends like a rally driver, until she reached the entrance to the resort and spotted the signs pointing to a side road that lead to Hotel Paisible, where she would spend the weekend.

The car rounded the last bend and came to a screeching halt at the entrance. A tall figure bent to open her door.

Molly jumped out of the car. "Ted!"

Ted's tanned face broke into a huge grin and he held out his arms. "Hey, Molly." He pulled her into a warm hug, pressing her face into his down ski jacket.

"Stop, you're smothering me." Molly pulled away and laughed. "I'm happy to see you too, you ski bum."

"Not a ski bum, a chalet girl."

She blinked. "What?"

He laughed at her confusion. "I didn't get a job as a ski instructor after all, but there was this luxury chalet company looking for a chef for one of their chalets. I have no professional training, but I love cooking. I had to cook them a dinner and then they hired me on the spot. A good salary and free accommodation for the whole season. Howzat?"

"Incredible," Molly laughed and hugged him again, only to feel his arms around her. "I didn't know you could cook."

"Why would you? I never told you. There's a lot you don't know about me." Ted winked, a mischievous glint in his eyes. "I don't know much about you either. But this weekend, we'll catch up and really find out everything about each other."

"I'd like that," Molly said, feasting her eyes on this new Ted. Gone were the slicked back hair and clean-shaven face. His new look included short cropped hair, dark stubble on his chin and a determined look in his amazing green eyes. "Your eyes look different," she remarked.

"I had laser surgery. Mother never approved of it, so I wasn't allowed to do it. But I had it done in Nice last week. It was a very easy operation that took ten minutes. No more contact lenses. Now I have laser vision, ha ha."

"That's brilliant. It must be a lot easier."

"Yes, especially for skiing, cooking and sex. Not that I've had much of that lately, but I'm working on it."

"I bet you are," Molly laughed, slightly startled. "I'd say there would be a lot of pretty girls around here dying to—"

He pulled her close again. "Yes, I'm getting a little attention from some hot babes."

Molly smiled into his eyes. "I bet you are."

"All thanks to you," Ted murmured into her ear. "But you must go and check in."

"I will." Molly pulled her fleece out of the car and put it on. "There's a yoga class this afternoon, but after that, I'll be free. How about you? Do you have to cook or something?"

"Nope. Not until next week. The season has barely started despite this amazing early snow, so I'm free. I would take you out to dinner, but I can actually cook you something much better in my own little flat." His eyes flashed. "Would you dare go to a man's apartment all alone at night?"

"I never thought you'd ask."

He pulled her close again. "I can't promise to behave."

"Neither can I." Molly laughed, suddenly carried away by a wave of attraction for him. She stepped away and looked at him while he took her weekend bag out of the car. What was happening? Why did she suddenly feel so drawn to him? Was it his newfound confidence and change in looks? Or his obvious attraction to her? Or simply her own determination to cast off and do exactly what came into her mind? But why try to analyse it? Whatever would happen was meant to be, just as her response to Ted's e-mail earlier in the week had led to her going to this place.

"Karma," she whispered to herself, while she followed Ted into the hotel reception.

Chapter 19

"Namaste," the teacher said and bowed.

"Namaste," the class murmured in unison, sitting cross-legged with their hands in the prayer position.

Everyone started to get on their feet, rolling up their mats and putting back the blocks and bolsters they had used. But Molly remained on her mat, looking out at the snow-covered landscape through the large windows. Even though it was dusk with just a strip of pink at the horizon, there was a faint glow from the snow and the lights outside. The room itself smelt of incense and scented candles and there was a hush of peace after the long class.

Molly had done the odd yoga class now and then, but it had never been like this—working every muscle in her body to screaming point, followed by a relaxation so deep she had drifted into a light sleep, during which her body and mind connected, giving her a sense of inner peace and joy. And that word: Namaste, meaning *the divine in me bows to the divine in you.* It had such a humble ring to it. It was true. There is something divine in everyone, and nobody is better than anyone else. What a beautiful thought.

Molly slowly rose and rolled up her mat. She smiled at the teacher and left, looking forward to the next yoga session. While she had a long hot shower, her thoughts drifted to Ted and his amazing transformation. It was as if he had suddenly grown up and was giving the finger to his family and his old life. That took a lot of courage and strength. It would be interesting to see what he would do with his life.

Molly dressed casually in jeans, a silk shirt and an Irish fisherman's sweater, adding a pair of gold hoop earrings and the jade heart she always wore. It wasn't a real date, just dinner in Ted's room. No need to dress up or try to impress him, although she put on a little more makeup than usual, outlining her eyes with dark grey kohl and applying deep red lipstick. *I might as well make a little bit of an effort, just in case. Just in case—of what?* she asked herself, but she couldn't answer. Except that the yoga session had freed something inside her, and she felt whatever that was float away into the dark star-studded sky as she walked towards Ted's chalet and the evening ahead.

* * *

"Voilà, madame," Ted said and put a plate in front of Molly. "The starter."

Molly leant forward and looked at the bright- green soup studded with bits of crisp bacon. "What is it?"

"Avocado soup. My own invention." He put a plate at his own place opposite Molly at the small table tucked in between the sofa and the window in his cosy studio. "Go on, taste it."

Molly picked up her spoon and put a mouthful of soup in her mouth, not expecting to taste more than avocado and bacon. But there were other things hitting her taste buds, and she closed her eyes. "Mmm. Like green velvet…" She opened her eyes and took another spoonful. "It's delicious. What's in it?"

"Avocado, chicken stock and a few other things. I didn't want it to taste like guacamole, so I tried to get that lovely mild avocado flavour without a strong hit. The bacon adds a salty contrast, don't you think?"

Molly took another spoonful. "It certainly does. Gosh, you're such a good cook. I'm truly impressed."

"That was just the starter. Wait till you've tasted my chicken cooked in white wine and herbs."

Molly sniffed. "Is that what I can smell?"

"Yes. It's simmering in that casserole on the hob."

"Wow." Molly looked at Ted with new respect. "I'm always in awe of good cooks."

Ted grinned. "I hit on the right way to impress you, then."

"You certainly did. Not sure I'll be as impressed with my waistline after this, though."

Ted let his gaze wander down her body. "I'm sure your waist will keep its shape."

"I hope so." Molly spooned some more of the soup into her mouth, enjoying the blend of flavours and the little bits of bacon crunching between her teeth. When she looked up again, her eyes met Ted's. "What's the matter?" she asked, startled by the expression in his eyes.

"Nothing." He took her hand. "Are you still hungry?"

"Not really," she whispered, suddenly carried away by a wave of lust, so hot she thought she might burst into flames. She peeled off her heavy sweater. "It's quite warm, don't you think?"

"It certainly is." He pulled her to her feet, his mouth hovering over hers. "I've wanted to do this for so long," he muttered, and kissed her.

The kiss lasted a long time, during which they made serious efforts to remove each other's clothes. Molly backed away, her mouth throbbing, her silk shirt open and the zip of her jeans half undone.

"Let's strip and get to bed," she panted, removing her shirt and stepping out of her jeans. She couldn't take her eyes off Ted, as he peeled off his clothes, revealing a very male, very toned body. "Shit, you're hot," she said. "Why did we wait so long?"

"I don't know. Oh, Molly, you're beautiful," Ted whispered, pulling her close, cupping her buttocks while he licked a trail from her breasts all the way to her crotch. They sank onto the bed, kissing, licking, touching and murmuring words that didn't make much sense, the sound of their voices adding to the sensuality. Ted rolled Molly over on her back. She closed her eyes and met his thrusts with her hips, ready for him, when he suddenly froze.

"Who the hell is that?"

"What?" Molly stared at him. Then she heard it: a pounding on the door, followed by shouting. "There's someone at the door."

"We'll ignore them."

"How? Someone is trying to break down the door."

Ted jumped up, grabbed a towel from the chair beside the bed and tied it around his waist. "Stay here."

Molly wrapped the sheet tightly around her, hesitating for a moment before she got out of bed. She gave a start as the door burst open, and a blonde woman dressed in a black ski jacket, boots and pants nearly fell into the room.

"I knew it!" the woman screeched.

Ted stared at the woman. "Jesus, it's Cindy. What the hell are you doing here?"

"I followed *her*." Cindy pointed at Molly. "That…that Irish tart! You were screwing her! I could hear you doing it through the door."

Ted folded his arms and leaned against the wall, managing, despite the skimpy towel, to look unperturbed. "Doing what?"

The blonde pointed at the bed. "What do you think, yoga?"

"Whatever we were doing is none of your business," Ted retorted. "But you snuck up on me and stood there eavesdropping? Jesus, Cindy, I knew you were a bitch but you've hit an all-time low."

"Cindy?" Molly said, holding on to the sheet as tightly as she could. "Oh my God, yes. I recognise you now. You were outside my apartment a couple of weeks ago."

Cindy looked at Molly. "Sure I was," she sneered. "I was following Karen and then I saw who she was with." Cindy turned to Ted, pointing a shaking finger at Molly. "I know something about her that might surprise you."

"And what would that be?" Ted enquired.

"She's married!" Cindy spat.

Ted didn't blink. "I know, sweetie," he drawled. "Anything else you'd care to tell me?"

Molly gasped. "You know?"

Ted turned and looked at Molly. "Yes."

"How? When did you find out?" Molly stammered.

Ted's eyes lost their warmth. "Mother told me when I went back to New York."

"How did she know?" Molly demanded.

"She can find out anything about anyone," Ted replied.

"You mean she's been trying to dig up some dirt on me? Why?"

Ted shrugged. "Who knows? She does that sometimes when she wants to vet people she's working with. Maybe she found out about me spending that day with you up in the mountains? I wasn't sure, but I had a feeling someone was following me when I drove from Nice. But I lost them when I left Grasse, so I forgot about it. But whatever, she told me about your marriage, maybe to stop me liking you. I…" he hesitated. "I came back to New York determined to break my engagement to Cindy, but when I found out about you, I lost my nerve. I thought I'd have to try to forget you. So I went through with it all, until…."

"Until you chickened out and dumped me in front of everyone," Cindy sneered. "What a class act, Ted."

Ted sighed. "Yeah, I know. Didn't handle that too well."

Cindy let out a sarcastic laugh. "You totally fucked it up."

"I'm getting a divorce," Molly announced. "Ted, my marriage was a scam. It didn't mean anything."

Ted looked at Molly. "I'm glad to hear it. It would have been nice if you had told me in the first place."

"I was going to tell you, but…"

"But what?" Cindy cut in. "You wanted to fuck him first?"

"No." Molly turned to Ted. "All this time you knew and never said a word?"

Ted looked at the floor. "Yeah, well…"

"Hey, Ted here's another bit of information for you," Cindy interrupted, as if she had noticed the focus was no longer on her. "Karen is dating the man she's married to."

Ted lifted an eyebrow. "Really? That's a weird coincidence. But hey, whatever. If that makes Karen happy, I'm all for it."

"He's after her money, of course," Cindy remarked.

"That's her problem." Ted pushed away from the wall. "If you've finished, I'd appreciate it if you'd leave. I invited Molly to dinner, but we got a little distracted."

"I'm going to tell your mother what you're up to," Cindy snapped. "It won't take her long to find you."

"Tell her what you like," Ted drawled. "It's no longer in her power to hurt me."

"Or yours, Cindy," Molly cut in. "It was you who sent that e-mail to the notaire, wasn't it? You tried to stop me buying my new apartment. Nice try, but I suspect you just wanted to piss me off, right?"

"I don't know what you're talking about," Cindy sniffed.

"If there was some kind of fooling around with someone's e-mail account, I'm pretty sure Cindy did it," Ted remarked. "She used to do that kind of stuff for fun, I remember. Cindy's a whiz with computers. She could make a fortune with that kind of fraud."

"Not to mention the little detail of the designs that got stolen," Molly continued, feeling she was on a roll.

"Nothing to do with me," Cindy replied.

"Of course that was you as well," Ted cut in. "Just the kind of thing you'd do."

"Shut up!" Cindy screeched.

"I will if you get the hell out of here."

"Why should I?"

"Because if you don't, I'll call the cops and say you broke into my room."

"Yeah, right," Cindy sniffed. "You wouldn't dare."

"Try me." Ted glanced around the room and picked up his phone from the bookshelf. "Either you leave or—"

"Jesus Christ," Cindy muttered, and walked to the door. She stopped suddenly and started to pull something off her finger. A ring with a huge heart-shaped diamond, Molly noticed, at least three carats. "Take this and shove it up your ass," Cindy shouted and threw the ring across the room. It landed with a plop in the casserole that was still simmering on the stove. "I hope it chokes you," she sobbed and left, slamming the door shut.

Ted stared at Molly. "Not exactly the kind of evening I had planned."

"No."

"Can we forget about it and pick up where we left off?"

Molly looked at Ted, standing there so sure of himself. Where was the vulnerability and sensibility that had drawn her to him? Of course, Cindy was a bitch, but why hadn't he told Molly he knew about her marriage? Why hadn't she told him herself? Because she was afraid it would make him think less of her, she answered herself. "I don't think so," she replied. "I need to be by myself for a while."

"But…" Ted made a pleading gesture, nearly dropping his towel

"No, Ted, I can't stay." Molly tore her eyes away from his body and quickly gathered up her clothes. She slipped into the bathroom and wriggled into her underwear and jeans. Buttoning the wrinkly silk shirt she pushed away the memory of Ted's hands on her skin, his mouth on her breasts, his—*stop it,* she whispered to herself as she tried to tame her wild curls. *Stop thinking about him that way.* But how could she not? They had nearly made love less than twenty minutes earlier and shared a sweet moment of intimacy, shattered by Cindy's sudden arrival. And then doubts and fears had crept into Molly's mind as Cindy spewed her hatred and Ted revealed he knew about Molly all along and never said anything. It was dishonest and sneaky. How could she trust him after that?

When she came out of the bathroom, she found Ted, having pulled on his jeans, fishing the ring out of the casserole with a spoon. He looked up. "Don't know what I'll do with it."

"With what?"

"The ring. A four-carat diamond. Cindy picked it out herself. Not something I would have chosen." He dropped the ring on a towel. "Molly, please don't go. I…we need to talk."

Molly hid her face by pulling on her fisherman's sweater. "Not now," she mumbled into the thick wool.

Ted pulled the sweater off her face and forced her to look into his troubled eyes. "I know I should have been more honest with you. But I was scared. I wanted to see how we were together first. If we could trust each other. But then you said nothing about the most important thing in your life. So I thought, when you couldn't share that with me, you didn't have strong feelings and maybe you just wanted to fool around without strings and…stuff." He pulled her close. "Come on, Molly, let's pick up where we left off."

For a split second, Molly was tempted to strip off her clothes and sink into bed next to that hot body. But then she pulled away. "No. I think the spell was broken just there and I woke up. I should have told you about my marriage but I was scared. I didn't know how you'd react. And you didn't tell me that you knew about it. It seems wrong to...do what we were doing under the circumstances."

"I see." Ted's eyes narrowed. "You're just as cold and calculating as Cindy. Go on, then. Get out of here."

"I will." Molly picked up her bag and shrugged on her jacket. "Bye, Ted. I'm really sorry about—"

"Fuck off, okay?" Ted snapped.

Without another word, Molly walked out of the room and banged the door shut behind her. She ran through the falling snow, tears streaming, her heart aching, confused and bewildered. But as she saw the lights of the hotel ahead of her, she suddenly knew, as if hit by lightning, exactly where she was going.

Chapter 20

The drive back seemed to take twice as long, hampered by the dark and the whirling snow. Molly was relieved when the snow turned to rain and she reached the main coast road. Not wanting to stay around in the ski resort, despite having paid for the whole weekend, she had packed her bag and loaded it into the car. She needed to get as far away from Ted as she could. She longed to reach her destination and the one person she knew could give her comfort. But was it too late? She checked the time on the dashboard. Eleven o'clock. She would drive by and see if the lights were on. If not, she would just go to her own apartment and get some sleep. In its half-furnished state, it didn't seem like the best place to relax after what had happened, but still, it was home.

She reached the crossroad. Left, then right and on to the house. With a sigh of relief, she arrived at the gate and drove inside. She could see a light glimmer in the kitchen and someone moving around. Molly heaved a sigh of relief. She got out of the car and walked swiftly around the house to the back door, ducking her head against the driving rain. As usual, the door was open, and she nearly fell into the warm, bright kitchen, where Jay was drinking a glass of wine and checking his phone at the kitchen table.

He looked up. "Hello! What are you doing here so late? I thought you were practicing yoga in the mountains."

Molly breathed in the scent of apples and cinnamon. "I was. But then, things happened and I had to leave."

Jay got up. "What happened? You look upset."

"Not so much upset as confused," Molly sighed. "I needed to talk. To…a friend."

"You look more like you need a hug." Jays held out his arms.

Molly sank into his warm embrace, closed her eyes and pressed her face into the soft wool of his sweater.

"Oooh, yes," she murmured. "That's exactly what I need right now." She wrapped her arms around his waist and breathed in the smell of verbena soap and spices. "You smell nice. Have you been making an apple pie?"

"I made about twenty of them with the last of the apples. I put all of them in the freezer, except the last one. Do you want a slice?"

"I can't think of anything I'd like more."

He laughed. "If you let go of me I'll get it for you."

"Okay," Molly said, still holding on to him. He felt so good, so safe and comforting, like a rock in a stormy sea. Then she laughed and stepped back. "Sorry. I needed a little comfort. But I'm okay now."

"Do you want to talk about it?"

"Give me that pie first."

"You drive a hard bargain. Sit down and I'll get the pie. How about a glass of wine? Or maybe a cup of Sophia's herbal tea? Very soothing."

"Tea sounds good. I have to drive home soon." Molly sat down at the kitchen table. "Where's Sophia?"

Jay waggled his eyebrows. "Out on a hot date."

Molly stared at him. "What? A hot date? Sophia?"

"Yes." Jay busied himself with cutting a slice of pie and putting it on a plate. "She was very excited about it. She met this man at a dinner in Sainte-Maxime a couple of weeks ago. British. A newly arrived expat. I think he's going to live here permanently. Very charming. Sophia is madly in love with him but trying not to show it. She spent hours getting ready. You should have seen her when she left." Jay kissed his fingers. "Magnifica."

"What?" Molly said again, her mind whirling. "But I thought…I mean…you and her…"

Jay pushed the plate in front of Molly. "You thought what? That Sophia and I are…in love?"

Molly felt her face flush. "Yes. It seemed quite obvious to me. I'm sorry if I drew the wrong conclusions."

Jay burst out laughing. "Sophia and me? Can you imagine the rows? Or her trying to explain to her posh relatives that she's dating a Spanish gypsy?"

Molly giggled. "Now you mention it, it does seem a little unbelievable. It was just that you two seem so close. And then I heard something one night…"

Jay looked at her quizzically. "What did you hear?"

"Noises coming from Sophia's room. And her shouting 'Jesus' very loudly. So I thought…"

"That we were having hot sex?" Jay chuckled.

Molly blushed. "Uh, yes."

Jay shook his head. "I'm afraid not. She woke up one night and thought someone was moving around in her room. She got an awful fright and shouted for me to come and help her. It turned out to be a stray cat that had jumped up on her balcony and got in through the open door."

Molly put her hand to her mouth. "Oh no, how stupid of me. I peeped out and saw you leaving her room. So I put two and two together and got five, I suppose. Sorry."

"Quite understandable." Jay put a steaming mug in front of Molly. "Here. Tea. It'll calm you down." He sat down again and picked up his glass of wine. "Maybe I should fill you in about Sophia and me. Before Sophia's husband died, I promised to look after her and make sure she was never lonely or afraid. He was my best friend, despite the age difference. I'm very fond of Sophia and she of me, but there's nothing more than that between us. She offered me a place to stay after my divorce and I'm still here. I suppose I should have left, but I was too comfortable and Sophia needed me. We get on quite well, but as for any romance between us, not possible. Not just because of her being quite a lot older. There just isn't the right chemistry. She says there's something wrong with my aura, but I suspect it's just snobbery." He sighed and shook his head. "That's just the way it is. I hope you're not disappointed."

"Not at all," Molly replied. "I'm only sorry if I embarrassed you."

He laughed again and touched her cheek. "It would take a lot to embarrass me, my dear."

Molly joined in, and they laughed together at the ridiculous idea of Sophia and Jay as lovers. Molly met his eyes as they laughed. What an attractive man he was, with his black curly hair sprinkled with grey, his flashing brown eyes so full of humour and compassion. The broken nose, the scar on his cheek and the earring made him look slightly dangerous, but she knew that was a false image.

"Are you really a gypsy?" she asked when they stopped laughing.

"There's Gypsy blood on my mother's side. But my father was from a very ordinary Spanish family. They ran a small business in Andalucía, where I grew up. I think my nomadic streak comes from my mother, though."

"How old are you?"

"You're very inquisitive tonight."

Molly smiled. "I know. Cheeky of me. Don't reply if you don't want to."

Jay drained his glass. "I don't mind. I'm forty-six. Not old enough to be your father, but maybe I could be your older brother?"

"Sounds nice," Molly replied. But the way he looked at her was not the slightest bit brotherly. "How did you break your nose?" she asked, hungry for more information. "And the scar?"

He winked. "I have a very interesting past. Are you sure you want to know?"

"Incredibly sure."

He touched his cheek. "I got the scar when I fell down a ravine in the Pyrenees doing some very foolish rock climbing at the age of sixteen. I broke my collar bone as well. It could have been worse."

"And the broken nose? Bull fighting?"

He snorted a laugh. "No. I got that in a tube station in London. Two guys were beating up a young boy. I intervened and they turned on me. Beat me to a pulp. I didn't look too pretty afterwards."

"That was very brave of you."

"Not really. I have a hot temper and can't stand bullies. But enough about me." He leaned forward and studied her. "So, why were you so troubled when you came in?"

"Oh," Molly looked into her mug, "just some stuff." She raised her eyes and looked Jay, speaking very fast. "I nearly had sex with the wrong man. I thought I was falling in love with him, and we were both so hot for each other. We were close to…to having full-on sex when we got interrupted by his ex-girlfriend bursting in through the door at the last moment."

Jay's mouth quivered. "So it was a case of coitus interruptus that turned into a saved by the belle? With an e at the end," he added, laughing.

"Exactly. Then there was a huge row and we all traded insults until she left."

"And after all that, did you—"

"Pick up where we left off? No. He wanted to, but I just couldn't."

"Poor guy."

Molly sighed. "I suppose that makes me a prick teaser, right?"

Jay nodded. "Absolutely. But you know what? Those are the kind of women I like—much more of a challenge."

"He didn't seem to want to rise to it. He told me to fuck off."

"What a wimp. But he must have been crippled with frustration."

Molly couldn't help laughing. "I know. He was visibly in pain."

"What about you?"

"I was frustrated too, of course. He is so hot. I wanted him like crazy before that spoiled little bitch burst in on us. But then…I just couldn't do it. Not after all that was said. I was upset about it, but now I realise it was a lucky escape."

"It wasn't the guy you married, was it? You told me he turned up here out of the blue."

"Miguel? No, he has gone to Ireland to fix the divorce." Molly sighed and laughed at the same time. "What a moron I must seem to you. My love life is like something out of The Rocky Horror Show."

He put his hand on hers. "It's a little topsy-turvy all right. Here's my advice. Step away from those men. Neither of them will make you happy."

The warmth of his hand spread to the rest of her body and made her eyes sting. She blinked away the tears. "I know I should." She looked up at him. "But at the same time I feel sorry for them both. For Miguel who is so lost, and for Ted who is so damaged by his abusive mother. I don't know how to help them."

"Stop it!" Jay suddenly shouted so loudly Molly jumped. "Stop all this caring for other people. What did I tell you about that?"

Molly got up and walked to the sink with her mug. "I know, I know. You said I should think of myself first. But how can I when they need someone to help them?"

"Ha. I bet pity was the last thing on your mind when you were falling into bed with…Ted, was it?"

Molly turned her back on him while she rinsed her mug.

"Okay, no. There wasn't much in my head except sex at that moment."

"I'm glad to hear it." Jay joined her at the sink and took the mug from her. "I think it's clean enough by now. Go on, Molly, go home, go to bed and sleep. Let people fix their own problems. Everything will look better in the morning."

"I know. Thank you, Jay." She picked up her bag from the table. "I feel better now."

"Good. I'll walk you to the car."

"Thanks."

When she had settled in the front seat and started the engine, Jay looked in through the window. "Send me a text when you get there. I'm worried about you driving in the dark. Especially after all you've been through tonight."

"I promise." Molly started the engine, waved to Jay and drove off into the dark night, her stomach full of apple pie and her head full of—Jay.

* * *

Molly tried to concentrate on sorting out immediate problems the next day. She took a trip to the IKEA store outside Toulon, midway between Nice and Marseille, which made a nice outing. The weather had improved, and the drive along the coast in the winter sunshine provided a welcome distraction from the turmoil in her mind..

While she enjoyed the wonderful scenery, the sun shining on the sea and the French ballad wafting from the car radio, her thoughts turned to Jay. Such a cuddly bear kind of man. A friend, someone to lean on. But was that all? The night before, there had been a spark of something new between them. All that talk about sex must have ignited some kind of feeling that had been smouldering under the surface. And when they hugged, she had felt more than comfort. When she was with Ted, she had mixed up sexual attraction with love. She had wanted to have sex with him, but when the feeling wore off, there was nothing left except a sense of pity. But with Jay, the feeling was different. Deeper, more complex.

The feel of him, the smell of him had been nearly sensual. Had he felt the same? Yes. She knew he had. Molly sighed happily. If it was meant to happen, it would. She had felt a sense of security with him when he had said he worried about her driving in the dark. Nobody had worried about her before. The worrying had always been left to her. But there he was, saying he wanted to know she was safe. That had to mean something. Oh, Jay, so self-contained and confident. Happy in his own skin. Mature and strong, with a palpable charm and that spark of humour in his dark eyes. The French song of love and kisses from the radio made Molly long to see him again, to look into his eyes and ask questions he might answer to her satisfaction.

Her head full of romance, Molly drove into the centre of Toulon and enjoyed a bowl of fragrant bouillabaisse with warm crusty bread in a tiny restaurant, while she chatted with the girl behind the counter. Then she walked around the city, looking at old buildings. A naval base for many years, Toulon had not sunk into the winter sleep like all the other tourist towns along the coast. Molly found herself in a bustling city with busy streets and shops packed with locals doing their Christmas shopping.

As she walked into the main square, she saw the big Christmas tree and was suddenly struck by the thought that Christmas was only ten days away. How time had flown since she bought her flat. High time to get it finished.

Molly returned to her car and drove to IKEA, where she spent a few hours picking out basic furniture, crockery, bed linen and lamps. She would add a quirky touch with pieces from the flea market later. Satisfied with her purchases,

Molly organised to have her order delivered the next day, and drove home as the setting sun streaked the sky with orange and pink.

Back at the apartment, Molly looked around the rooms, making plans for the rest of the refurbishments. All she had was an antique sleigh bed, known in France as a 'lit Napoleon', the couch she had picked up at a furniture shop in Sainte-Maxime and an old table from Liam's house with two mismatched chairs. The IKEA furniture would improve things and make the apartment more functional.

As there was no TV or radio and the internet hadn't been connected yet, Molly found herself at a loose end. She didn't want to drop in on Jay unannounced. Not then. It would be too soon. Let him come to her. There was only one other option: Liam and Daisy. Great idea. She hadn't been there for over two weeks and had heard nothing from them, so it was a good opportunity to catch up. Not bothering to call, Molly set off to join Liam, Daisy and Tommy for dinner and a good long chat.

Before she got into her car, she decided to buy something for dessert. The bakery on the ground floor was closed, but she knew the patisserie in the main square was open late. Their famous tarte Tropézienne, a sponge cake with gooey vanilla cream, would be the perfect treat.

As she left the patisserie with the tart in a box, she spotted Jay coming out of a café across the street. She was about to call out to him, when she noticed he wasn't alone. A young, beautiful woman with black hair appeared beside him, putting her arm around his waist. Molly stared as Jay pulled her close and planted a kiss on her cheek. The woman looked up at him with an expression of pure love, matched by the delight in Jay's eyes. He didn't see Molly, as his attention was focused on the young woman by his side. The sight cut through Molly like a blade. She kept staring at them, rooted to the spot.

The couple reached a small red car. The woman's car. She clicked her key to open the door and then turned to Jay. Molly watched as he enveloped the woman in one of his bear hugs before she got into the car and drove off.

Chapter 21

"I'm glad you got that sorted at last," Liam said when Molly had finished telling him about Miguel. "You can close that chapter in your life now."

"And you can put away the shotgun, Liam," Daisy laughed. "The guy is safe from you now."

"Phew," Molly sighed. "I wasn't looking forward to visiting my brother in prison."

"You're kinder than I am," Daisy remarked. "I'd have left him to rot."

"Be quiet woman, and serve the food." Liam sat down at the kitchen table beside Molly. "That's the way to treat 'em, you know. Otherwise women think they can rule the world."

Daisy banged a platter with sliced roast beef and vegetables on the table. "We already do, darlin'. But we make you think you're the boss while we silently run things when you're busy fighting."

"Ah, come on," Molly pleaded. "Stop the aggro. It's nearly Christmas."

"You're right," Daisy said. "Shut up, Liam."

"We're going to America for Christmas," Tommy interrupted.

Molly's forkful of beef froze in mid-air. "What?"

Liam nodded. "Yes. We just made the reservations. I should have told you, but you haven't been around much lately."

"Yes, well…I've been busy," Molly explained. "Lots of work and stuff. I had no idea you were going away. I thought we'd be doing the usual Christmas, like last year."

"Not this year. My mother invited us to the inn she runs in Vermont," Daisy explained. "But there's a special occasion. She has finally decided to marry her Italian boyfriend. She only just told me about it. They'll be married in this gorgeous church there."

"I'm going to carry the ring again," Tommy cut in.

Daisy ruffled his hair. "You're so good at that. The best ring bearer in the world." She turned to Molly. "But you're going to spend Christmas with Sophia and her boyfriend, isn't that what you said?"

Molly frowned. "Did I? When did I say that?"

"Last time you were here," Daisy replied.

"Oh." Molly put down her fork and thought for a moment. Yes she had said that. Sophia mentioned Christmas dinner a few weeks earlier. But it had been just chat, not a firm offer. That seemed so long ago when she had still assumed Sophia and Jay were a couple. Now she knew the truth. Sophia had fallen in love with some elderly Englishman, and Jay had a young and beautiful girlfriend. And Molly had nobody.

She looked at Liam, Daisy and Tommy, and saw, as if for the first time, that they were a real family. A family that would make their own traditions which didn't include her. In the past, before Liam and Daisy had been together, Molly had organised Christmas for them, bought the presents, baked the Christmas cake and the pudding, bought the tree and decorated it, cooked the dinner and provided Christmas cheer for a man without a wife and a little boy without a mother. How things had changed.

"You'll be all right?" Liam asked, looking worried. "You'll have your friends, won't you?"

"Of course," Molly assured him, beaming him a bright smile. "I'll have a ball. It'll be such a relief not to have all that work and pressure. This will be the best Christmas ever for me."

Liam let out a long sigh. "Of course it will. You'll have fun. No more hard work or stress. I believe a French Christmas is amazing."

Molly nodded. "I've heard so much about it. Now I get to experience it for real."

"What is a real French Christmas?" Tommy asked.

"I'll tell you about it when we're having the tart."

Molly got up from the table and helped Daisy put the plates in the dishwasher. Then she eased the tart out of its box onto a plate and cut it up into slices. Once they were all enjoying the light sponge, and the vanilla cream melted in their mouths, Molly told Tommy how French people celebrated Christmas.

"They get all dressed up, some of the men in tuxedo and the women in their prettiest dresses and then they go to midnight mass. After that, they either go to a restaurant or to their own home, where they drink champagne and eat a fancy meal, lobster, oyster, steak, that kind of thing. Dessert is something called 'bûche de Noël', which is a chocolate log."

"When do they get their presents?" Tommy asked.

"After dinner. That can turn out to be pretty late, but the children get to stay up with the grownups."

"Then they'll have waited all day to get their presents," Tommy sighed and stuffed a spoonful of tart into his mouth.

"Pure torture," Molly laughed. "But the French like to challenge their children."

"So you're all organised then?" Daisy asked.

Molly finished the last morsel of cake. "Oh, yes. I'll be fine. You'll have a wonderful time in Vermont."

"It's already snowing there," Tommy said. "My new grandma told me when she called. I'm going to learn to ski."

"Won't that be fun?" Molly kissed his cheek. "But now I'll be off. I have to get up in the morning for deliveries to the apartment. I'll be organised in my new home at last."

Liam held out her jacket. "Everything is falling into place for you, sis. I'm really happy for you."

Molly took the jacket and picked up her bag. "Yes," she said brightly. "Everything is pretty perfect." She hugged Liam and Daisy. "Have a wonderful Christmas, guys. Give me a shout when you get back and I'll invite you to dinner in my new place."

Molly held back the tears while she drove the short distance to her apartment, choked back the sobs as she climbed the stairs and opened the door. Once inside, she slammed the door shut, stumbled to the couch where she threw herself among the cushions, finally succumbing to pain and sorrow.

* * *

"Hello, Molly," Sophia twittered on the phone early next morning. "How are you this fine morning?"

"Fide," Molly mumbled through a nose all stuffed up from crying. "I have a bit of a cold."

"Sorry about that, my dear. I hope it clears up before Christmas Eve."

"Why?"

"Because we're going to a party."

"You are? With—sorry, can't remember his name."

"Peter. Peter McDougal. He's Scottish. Retired RAF pilot and ever so dashing. You'll see when you meet him. But you're coming with us, too. It's going to be a wonderful evening. A French Christmas with a dash of Spain."

"How do you mean?" Molly said and crawled out of the sofa, where she had fallen asleep after crying for hours. "What time is it?" she croaked.

"Eight o'clock. Sorry if I woke you."

"That's okay." Molly blinked in the bright sunlight that streamed in through the tall French window. "But tell me about Christmas Eve."

"We're going to mass first in La Croix Valmer up the hill—lovely church. Peter's a Catholic, so that's where he wants to go. I have no objections, even though I'm not really that into religion and my family is Anglican. It'll probably be a beautiful mass in that French old fashioned way with incense and lovely hymns, which to me is very spiritual." Sophia drew breath. "Anyway, to cut a long story short, we'll be going to Jay's restaurant for the Christmas réveillon. That's French for a late night party. So it should be fun and quite glamorous as the dress code is black tie and long dress for the ladies."

"Long dress?" Molly asked. "Is that what you said?"

"Yes—or short with some bling. Everyone will be pulling out all the stops." Sophia laughed. "Including me. Peter will be wearing a kilt. He has the most wonderful legs."

"I can imagine."

"So that was what I was going to tell you. We'll be setting off from my house at around eleven p.m. after a glass of champagne. I have invited a nice man to escort you, a relative of Peter. See you then," Sophia said and hung up.

* * *

"Cheers." Marianne held up her glass of chilled white wine.

"Chin, chin." Molly clinked her glass with Marianne's. They were having lunch on the terrace of Marianne's villa. "Thanks for inviting me over."

"I thought we'd get together before I disappear to Sweden for Christmas. I wanted to do a traditional Swedish lunch, but meatballs, ham and red cabbage don't really go with the warm sunshine of the Mediterranean."

"It's a gorgeous day." Molly looked at the view across the blue waters of the bay, where sailing boats dotted the horizon and warm winds ruffled the fronds of the palm trees and the tall Pampas grass in the middle of the immaculate lawn. She closed her eyes and turned her face to the sun, feeling its calming effect.

"You look tired, sweetie. What's up? Work?"

Molly opened her eyes and looked at Marianne's sweet face so full of concern. "Not really. I mean yes, partly. Karen had this idea of a special boutique collection for the summer, so I'm trying to get that ready. But it's only a few pieces and the first collection is already being made in China, so that's all okay."

Marianne nodded. "Brilliant. You were a star to turn around and do a new one when the first designs ended up in Walmart."

Molly laughed. "And it turned out that it was that little bitch's fault all along. She wanted to get back at Ted. And at me. She thought we were—"

"But you weren't?" Marianne prodded. "You haven't told me much about that, about you and…him."

"Nothing much to tell." Molly squirmed under Marianne's probing gaze. "Okay, so we did have a hot date that could have been even hotter had Cindy not broken the door down and interrupted. But, in hindsight, I know it was a good thing."

"Hindsight is a bitch, isn't it?" Marianne took a slice of smoked salmon from a large platter with an array of salads and cold cuts.

Molly laughed. "Yeah. I missed out on some great sex by being sensible. So now I'm telling myself it was a lucky break."

"Is that why you're looking so miserable?"

Molly let out a long sigh. "No. God, it's all so complicated. You don't want to know."

"Try me. I love complicated stories."

"Okay, you asked for it. When I left Ted up there at the ski station, I went back to Sophia's, hoping to have a chat with Jay. I thought he, as a friend, would provide a shoulder to cry on."

"Jay? You mean Sophia's boyfriend? Now there's a gorgeous man. Lucky Sophia." Marianne picked up a slice of cured ham from the serving dish. "Don't know why I'm so hungry today," she muttered. "But go on, what happened?"

Molly took a swig of wine. "Jay was there, in the kitchen. Sophia was out with, it appeared, another man. So I felt a little sorry for Jay, thinking he had been jilted, but that made him laugh. He and Sophia have never been involved in that way. And when we had cleared that up, I told him about what happened with Ted. It was during that conversation it suddenly dawned on me..."

"What?" Marianne exclaimed. "Please stop pausing like that. What the hell dawned on you? That you were there with this hot man, who is also actually nice? And that you're hugely attracted to him and you might be falling in real true love with him? I could have told you that weeks ago."

"What do you mean?" Molly stared at Marianne. "Weeks ago?"

Marianne nodded several times. "Yes! Remember when we were at Sophia's house that time just after we signed the contract? Jay came in and hugged you and seemed so happy for you. There was something between you then, I felt. But I wasn't sure. Now, of course, I realise I was right all along." Marianne beamed from ear to ear. "How romantic. You finally found true love. And he was there, right under your nose all this time. Am I right?"

"No. Wrong," Molly said and burst into tears. "Wrong, wrong, wrong," she sobbed.

Marianne ran to Molly's side and put her arm around her. "What's the matter, Molly? Has he done or said anything to hurt you?"

"No," Molly cried into Marianne's slim shoulder. "He hasn't done anything—other than smooching a gorgeous young woman in the street right in front of me."

"In front of you?"

"I mean across the street when I came out of the patisserie. I nearly dropped a huge tarte Tropézienne when I saw them."

"Maybe she was a dear friend or relative?"

"It wasn't that kind of smooching."

"How odd." Marianne pulled back and handed Molly a paper napkin. "Gosh. That's really bad."

"Yeah, and now I have to go to his restaurant on Christmas Eve, where he's throwing one of those French Christmas parties. Sophia invited me, and she wants me to go with some stuffy old Scotsman in…in a kilt!" Molly started to cry again.

"Jesus, what a mess." Marianne went back to her seat. She propped her chin in her hand and looked thoughtfully at Molly. "You know what? You have nothing to lose. You should go out there and fight for him."

"Fight? How? Give that woman a sock on the jaw?"

Marianne rolled her eyes. "Don't be silly. There are other, more subtle ways."

Chapter 22

After a full day of yoga, massage, cleansing and detoxing at Marianne's favourite spa hotel, Molly slept all night and woke up full of energy and nervous anticipation of the day ahead. As she caught sight of herself in the mirror on her way to the bathroom, she stopped and stared. What a miracle. Her skin glowed, her eyes sparkled, and her hair no longer looked like a brillo pad. The glossy curls framing her face were a tribute to the hairdresser, who had given her an intense hair mask followed by an expert cut. She smiled at herself and whispered a silent thank you to Marianne who had treated Molly to a full day's beauty treatment, bullying the hotel staff to fit her into their already packed schedule. The violet silk dress Marianne had found for Molly in a small boutique hung on the back of the wardrobe, ready to be slipped on before the party. *Ready for battle*, Molly said to herself.

In her pink fleece dressing gown, Molly stepped over the boxes with furniture from IKEA, waiting to be assembled, and walked into the sunlit kitchen. She turned on the radio, and made herself a big bowl of café au lait while she listened to Christmas songs. Then she walked to the front door to take the bag with fresh bread the bakery delivered each day. That morning, she found not the usual healthy sour-dough bread, but two fresh, fragrant croissants, dripping with butter. Oh well, it was Christmas. A little indulgence was a good thing. Molly was about to close the door, when she heard someone coming up the stairs. Molly looked down the stairwell and spotted a familiar figure. Karen. What was she doing here?

"Hi," Karen panted.

"Hi, Karen. I thought you were in New York for the holidays."

"I was, but the flight was cancelled due to a snowstorm in New York. So now I'm stranded here until it clears."

"I'm sorry. That must be disappointing."

Karen reached the landing and paused to catch her breath. "It sucks big time."

Molly opened the door wide. "Come in. As it happens, I have two freshly baked croissants in this bag. I'll make some more coffee. Excuse the mess, but I haven't had the energy to put together the flat-pack furniture."

Karen followed Molly into the kitchen and stopped at the table, glaring at Molly. "I didn't come here for breakfast."

Molly turned from the coffee machine. "Why did you come then? Is it about the boutique collection? It'll be on time, don't worry."

Karen eased off her trench coat and hung it on the back of a chair. "It's not about that. It's about Miguel."

"What about him? Is he back?"

"No, but I spoke to him on the phone last night, and he confirmed the story."

Molly flicked the switch on the coffee machine and faced Karen. "What story?"

Karen sighed. "This will sound weird, but it all started with Cindy, who turned up out of the blue at the office in Nice the other day. She's been here for a while, following Ted, and trying to make all sorts of trouble."

Molly nodded. "I know. I was with Ted at the ski station last week. She burst in on us and started making all kinds of accusations."

"Yeah. She told me. I bet her story is not very close to

what actually happened. But I won't go into that. Or whatever is going on with you and Ted—or isn't."

"Isn't," Molly interrupted. "It was all a mistake. But let's not go there, okay?"

"Nah, let's not," Karen agreed.

The coffee machine gurgled. Molly turned it off. "Okay, so give me the reason you're here. Is it about me being married to Miguel?"

Karen blinked. "Yes. Is it true?"

"I'm afraid it is." Molly picked up her bowl and took a sip of the now tepid coffee. "He didn't tell you?"

"No. He just said he had to organise residency in Ireland to sort out some citizenship issues. But…" Karen leaned forward and stared at Molly. "Then Cindy told me and it all fell into place. So I've been having an affair with a married man, who happens to be your husband? Nice."

"The big shit. He should have told you." Molly said. "Or I should have, really. But I wanted to keep this as quiet as possible." She nipped a bit off her croissant and put it into her mouth. "It's not a big deal, you know. Yes, we're married, but the divorce will go through in about a year. The thing is that this marriage was not real. We got married to get him an Irish passport, years ago when we were both students. Then he just took off after that, and I didn't see him again until a few weeks ago."

"And you did nothing about it during all this time?"

"No."

Karen shook her head. "Weird." She eyed the bag with the croissants and hesitated for a moment before she sat down. "Okay, then, I guess it's not that big a deal. Except why the hell didn't you sort this out a long time ago instead of letting it fester?"

Molly sighed. "I know. We should have. Long story. Let's not go there either if it's all right with you."

Karen shrugged "Yeah, sure. Whatever. I'm glad we

straightened this out. But I will let him know what I think of it when we meet up in New York. We're supposed to celebrate the New Year there together."

"You should give him hell. He deserves it."

Karen shot Molly a probing look. "Were you in love with him? Back then, I mean."

Molly nodded. "Yes," she mumbled. "I was."

"Of course you were. Look at him now, at forty. He must have been even hotter at—what—twenty five?"

"Yes, he was gorgeous. Sexy, fun, charming too. I was taken in by all of that. Who wouldn't be? But that was then. Now I feel differently," Molly said, realising it was true. The dream she had held onto for so long was fading into the past. A stupid obsession, a fantasy that had nothing to do with the real world. She blinked and looked at Karen. "Are you in love with him?"

Karen blushed and looked down. "I don't know. I think so. I've never felt like this before." She looked bleakly at Molly. "Do you think he's just after my money?"

Molly didn't reply but turned back to the coffee machine and made them two bowls of fresh coffee with hot milk. She put one of the bowls in front of Karen. "Here…coffee. You need it. Grab one of the croissants before I eat them all. I always stuff myself when I'm stressed."

"Me too," Karen said, pulling a croissant out of the bag. She broke off a piece, stuffed it into her mouth and washed it down with a huge gulp of coffee. "God, that's good," she sighed and picked up her coffee. "I love drinking café au lait out of these big bowls. Makes me feel French."

Molly joined her at the table. "They sure know how to live in this country."

"You didn't answer my question."

"That's because I don't know. I have no idea what goes on in that man's head. When we met again, it was such a shock, and for a moment I thought—hoped—he had some feelings for me. He said he thought about me every day during his time in that Thai prison. But I suspect I was more like a lifeline, someone who could help him get back on his feet once he got out. He'd read about my work, so he must have figured out I wasn't exactly poor."

"And then he met me and saw an even bigger fish, you mean?"

"Possibly. He's a bit of an opportunist. Always looking out for himself first."

Karen drained her bowl. "Yeah. A lot of people are. Not a federal offense, but not a very attractive feature either. Good to know, though." She got up from the table. "I have to get back to Nice. I've been invited to one of those mad parties the French throw on Christmas Eve."

"Me too." Molly got up and tidied away the bowls. "I'm going with a group of Scotsmen in kilts. Don't ask."

Karen laughed. "Sounds like fun." She put on her trench coat and picked up her bag. "Thanks for breakfast and the chat. And for being so honest."

"I'm glad I told you."

Karen suddenly looked wistful. "I was hoping you'd tell me something different, but hey, forewarned is forearmed and all that. I know how to handle him now."

"How?" Molly asked, intrigued.

"With an iron fist inside a silk glove."

"I'd just tell him to get lost."

Karen shook her head. "Are you nuts? And give up the best sex I've ever had?" She suddenly looked wistful. "You know what? You can't look at people like an à la carte menu and pick out the best bits. Everyone has flaws."

"Of course," Molly agreed. "But some are worse than others."

Karen stuck out her chin. "I know what I want." She counted on her fingers. "One, I want to take charge of the company, two, I want that man. Don't tell me I can't have both."

Molly laughed. "I wouldn't dare. But I'm beginning to feel sorry for him."

Karen snorted. "Sorry? Save your pity. He'll get what he wants and so will I. It'll be a win-win for us both." She paused on her way to the door and looked at Molly. "Sometimes you have to be sneaky to make a man love you. Isn't that what you're up to yourself?"

Molly blinked. "How do you mean?"

"Look at you. All shiny and beautified. And that spectacular dress I can see through the bedroom door. Don't tell me you're not on the warpath."

Molly couldn't help laughing. "Are you psychic?"

Karen winked. "Of course. Merry Christmas, Molly. Go get that man."

* * *

In the warm glow of a thousand candles, Molly listened to the choir singing Silent Night in French. The priests were dressed in robes embroidered with gold and red, and the altar boys wore short red capes over white floor-length surplices. The readings were entirely in Latin, taking her back to ancient times, when the mediaeval church would have been built. It was as if the stones of the walls still echoed with the prayers of people who must have worshipped there centuries ago. Molly shivered and wrapped herself in her cashmere cape. There was a rustle around her of silk and fur. Expensive perfume and a slight whiff of aftershave mingled with the smell of incense. Everyone was in full gala dress. It was the chicest congregation Molly had ever seen. The French took Christmas seriously; her own dress was no exception.

Not the conventional silver lamé or little black dress, the dark-violet velvet dress with lace sleeves was the perfect fit for Molly. Demure at the front but plunging to the base of her spine at the back, it had a daring touch she liked. Her only jewellery was a pair of pendant gold earrings with large amethysts the same shade as the dress. The colour made her eyes darker and brought out their violet hue. Black strappy sandals and a matching handbag completed the outfit.

Sophia had clapped her hands as Molly walked into the living room. "Magnifique," she exclaimed and handed Molly a glass of champagne. She introduced Molly to the two Scotsmen in kilts, black jackets and frilly shirts. Peter Mc Dougal was a stocky, handsome man with dark hair and beard sprinkled with grey. The fat man standing beside him had a shock of white hair and a matching moustache.

He took Molly's hand and squeezed it so hard she winced. "Hamish Mc Alpine is my name," he said with a distinct Scottish burr. "Nice to meet you, Molly."

Molly eased her hand out of his grip and backed away from his beery breath. "Hello, Hamish. Merry Christmas."

"Hamish is my cousin," Peter said when they had shaken hands. "He's here to escape the Scottish winter."

Hamish nodded. "Call me a wimp, but sleet and snow begin to lose their appeal after the age of sixty."

"I never liked it much," Sophia laughed. In a red silk brocade jacket, black, ankle-length, taffeta skirt and her dark curls tumbling down her back, she looked sexy and sultry. At least, Peter seemed to think so.

Hamish, on the other hand, didn't take his eyes off Molly, despite her efforts not to encourage him. Sophia, noticing Molly's discomfort, tried her best to distract him with a plate of canapés.

"Here, Hamish, try some of these little snacks," she said, waving the plate under his nose. "We won't get anything to eat until after midnight."

"Thank you, lovely lass." Hamish stuffed smoked salmon and cured ham with pickled cucumber into his mouth while still ogling Molly. “Very tasty,” he spluttered through his mouthful while Molly squirmed under his gaze.

Sophia pulled her aside. “I’m sorry about Hamish,” she whispered. “I’ll tell Peter to keep him away from you. You should be able to get away in the church. I’ll make sure we sit apart.”

“If you don’t, I’m going home,” Molly hissed back. “He’s leering at me.”

“I know. Very annoying. How about Peter? Isn’t he handsome?”

“Very good-looking,” Molly agreed. “Pity about the cousin.”

“A huge pain. But he lives in the Highlands. Probably hasn’t seen a good-looking woman in years. But leave it to me. I’ll get him off your back.” Sophia winked and went back to the two men, announcing it was time to get to church. “We’ll walk up the hill. Molly, why don’t you set off with Peter and Hamish, and I’ll follow. Right, Hamish? You don’t mind escorting me to church?”

Hamish shot a lingering look at Molly. “Of course not, lass. It’ll be my pleasure.”

Peter offered Molly his arm. “Let’s get going then, my dear.”

Walking up the hill, they were both silent. Peter possibly thinking about Sophia and Molly’s thoughts on Jay and the evening ahead. She suddenly felt foolish in her sexy dress. Was it a mistake to try to get Jay to notice her? She looked good, but she was no match for that beautiful young woman with the flashing dark eyes and stunning body. If she was at the party, Jay would only have eyes for her. But there would be other people there, and going was better than staying at home alone on Christmas Eve. It might be fun if she could forget her heartache and newfound feelings for Jay. *Stay cool. Don’t wear your heart on your sleeve.*

As the choir sang the Gloria and then eased into Adeste

Videtis, Molly gave herself up to the spirituality of the mass, the heavenly voices of the choir and the light shining on the little crib at the altar, where Mary and Joseph stood beside the pink baby in the crib. All her childhood memories came flooding back, and she blinked back tears as she remembered Christmas in a small village in the south of Ireland. The good days, the happy days of being safe and loved and tucked up in bed looking forward to presents Santa had brought during the night. Her childhood on the farm had been a stark contrast to the rollercoaster of her adult life. But it was there, deep down, giving her strength and courage to face whatever would come, even if it would bring a lot of sadness. Molly sat up straighter and joined in with the congregation as they broke into *Joy to the World* in English as a friendly gesture to foreign visitors.

As they filed out of the church, Molly spotted a familiar figure in the crowd. Jay. With that woman beside him. He saw Molly and his face lit up. She tried to push through the throng in the opposite direction, but it was impossible. Jay was suddenly at her side. He put his arm around her and planted a kiss on her cheek. "Molly. Merry Christmas. How wonderful you look."

Molly pulled away. "Hello," she said flatly.

Jay pulled at the woman beside her. "I want you to meet Marie-Christine, my—"

"Molly," The woman said with a dimply smile before Jay had a chance to finish. "Bonsoir. I've heard so much about you."

"Really?" Molly said, bewildered. She stared coldly at the woman. "I've heard nothing about you." She started to walk faster, ahead of them. "See you at the restaurant," she said over her shoulder.

Chapter 23

"What's the matter?" Marie-Christine put her arm through Jay's. "Why was that woman so rude?"

He patted her hand. "She's had some upsets lately. I'll go and talk to her later."

"She's very pretty."

"She's nice too. Not like her to be rude. I'm sorry about that."

Marie-Christine shrugged. "Never mind. Let's just enjoy the evening. It's Christmas, after all."

As they walked up the hill, Jay stared at Molly's receding form, walking as swiftly as she could in those high heels. She had been rude and dismissive. What was wrong? She looked a little tearful coming out of the church. Maybe the Christmas mass had reminded her of her family, of loved ones she had lost? Despite her honesty and openness about her relationship with the man she had foolishly married, he didn't know much about her childhood or youth. He was sure of his own feelings for her but not if they were reciprocated.

When she had walked into the kitchen that first evening in October looking for Sophia, he had been struck by that bolt of lightning the French call 'coup de foudre'. Love at first sight. Having lived the life of a near hermit since his painful divorce ten years earlier, this had shaken him to the core. Falling in love with a woman like that at first sight frightened him. He was no longer in control, no longer aloof, no longer Jay the wise, world-weary man.

As she sat there that first night and talked to him, joking, laughing, with her bright-blue eyes, red curls and upturned little nose covered in freckles, he became even more smitten. Her throaty laugh and slightly hoarse voice with that Irish lilt and her gentle self-deprecating humour all made him fall even more deeply in love. And weeks later, when he had given her a hug, the smell of her, the feel of her, the pale, flawless Irish skin…

He had pulled back, tried to curb his feelings. She deserved someone better, younger, more successful. Not this old Spaniard with a scarred soul and jaded outlook on life. But then, that night when she had stumbled into the kitchen, all confused and bewildered, looking for help and comfort, he had sensed her feelings for him had deepened. As she drove off into the darkness, he had looked at the lights of her car disappear up the winding road knowing he loved her. Marie-Christine had, until now, been the only woman in his life. But that was a different love, a different relationship. Could he have both?

* * *

After a short walk, they reached the edge of the village and the restaurant, where light flooded through open doors. There was already a stream of guests going inside and musicians were tuning their instruments.

"Live music?" Molly said to Jay when he caught up with her.

"Yes. They'll be playing during the meal, and then we'll be dancing."

"Jay will play his guitar later," Marie-Christine announced. She clicked her fingers over her head. "Flamenco, olé!"

"I might try an Irish tune," Jay said. "But I'd need some assistance. Can you sing, Molly?"

"No. I have no ear for music whatsoever." Molly pulled her hand out of Jay's grip and went into the warm, bright restaurant. Inside, she looked around with interest. So this was Jay's patch. The interior was done in Spanish style, with oak floors, wall panelling and a bar with intricate woodwork. The windows were swathed in deep red velvet. It was like a set for Carmen at the Paris opera. The perfect place to enjoy a plate of tapas and a glass of Rioja while listening to Spanish music and watching Flamenco dancing. A bit over the top, but in a nice way. The mouth-watering smell of spices and grilled meat made Molly's stomach rumble. She realised she hadn't eaten more than a few bites of toast and an apple since morning. The prospect of some good food brightened her mood.

Molly took off her cape and walked across the floor to find Sophia's table, where Hamish pulled out a chair while he let his eyes wander over her body.

"Sit here, bonny lass," he wheezed. "I could do with some company."

Molly grabbed the glass of champagne a waiter was offering her and downed it in one go. It was going to be a long night.

* * *

It started off quite well, with good food, excellent wines and fun conversation around the tables. Jay was darting in and out of the kitchen, supervising and snapping orders at the waiters. Molly forgot her sorrow and began to enjoy herself, ignoring Hamish's drunken advances. But as the musicians struck up a fast tune, he put his warm, moist hand on Molly's thigh. "How about a twirl on the dance floor?"

Molly pushed his hand away. "No thanks. I think you're a little, eh, overtired."

"I'm in great form," he protested, leaning over her, his bright red lips pursed. "How about a wee kiss?"

As his moustache tickled her cheek, Molly looked around for help. But the table was deserted. Everyone was dancing, including Sophia and Peter, who were doing a hot salsa, their arms and legs entwined, eyes only for each other. She could see Jay and Marie-Christine doing some kind of two-step, not touching but laughing together at their silly dancing, oblivious of everyone else. She got up and took her evening bag and cape. "If you'll excuse me, I'll go and, uh, powder my nose."

Hamish nodded and waved his hand drunkenly. "Sure, me lovely lass. I'll be here when you come back, and we'll do the fandango, eh?"

Molly supressed a giggle. "Of course." She walked swiftly along the edge of the dance floor and the dancing, laughing crowd to the French window and groped around the curtain until she could open the doors and step outside, onto the starlit terrace overlooking the village with all the twinkling lights and the Christmas tree in the square beyond. Out there, it was blissfully cool, and once she had closed the door behind her, there was suddenly peace with a whisper of a wind stirring her hair. Molly swept the cape around her shoulders and stood there, breathing in the air and the peace. She saw the crescent of a new moon rise above the rooftops, and felt, just for a second, as if time stood still.

There was a movement behind her as someone stepped onto the terrace. A hand on her shoulder. Molly pulled away. *Oh, please, not that drunken eejit.* A voice in her ear told her something different.

"Molly?"

She turned. "Jay. I thought you were dancing."

"I was. But then I saw you go outside, so I followed you. I want to talk to you, ask you..." He paused.

"Ask me what?" she snapped and pulled her cape tighter.

"Why are you so angry with me? I thought we were at least friends and maybe something more."

She stared at him in the dim light. "Something more? But…but—" She gestured wildly at the window. "What about her in there? How do you feel about her, then?"

"I love her more than my own life."

"You do? But…"

"Yes. Just like any parent."

"Parent?" Molly asked. "What do you mean—" Then his words slowly dawned on her and she let out a long 'oooohhh', while a wave of embarrassment washed over her. "She's your daughter."

Jay nodded. "Yes. I thought you knew. I talk about her often enough."

"Yes, but, but...oh God, how stupid I've been. You never told me her name. You kept saying 'my daughter', or 'my little girl.' I thought she was about ten. How old is she?"

"Twenty-four. I was twenty-two when she was born."

"I see. I had no idea. God, how stupid of me. My fault for being so self-centred. All I ever talked about was me and my own problems. "

"Stop." Jay put his hands on her shoulders and looked into her eyes. "You needed someone to talk to. I was happy to help, to be a friend. But then…"

"Yes?" Molly breathed.

Jay took a deep breath. "Then I started to feel differently. I began to fall in love with you. Slowly at first, so slowly I didn't realise it was happening. All I knew was that I wanted to be with you, to be in your space. I wasn't quite sure what all that meant. I only knew that everything seemed brighter when you were around. Then that last evening, when you arrived all confused and bewildered, it suddenly dawned on me how I felt."

"Why didn't you say anything?"

"It wasn't the right moment. You were still trying to figure out your feelings for Ted. I didn't want to stumble into that. You needed time and space."

"That's why you didn't call me?"

"Yes. I thought…I was hoping you'd come to your own conclusions about how you felt about me. I was prepared to wait. I thought I'd step back a little, so you wouldn't take me for granted. You might even miss me a little," he added wistfully.

Molly laughed softly. "A kind of Little Bo Peep approach?"

"How do you mean?"

"It's an old English nursery rhyme. It goes like this… Little Bo Peep has lost her sheep, blah, blah, and then…leave them alone, they will come home, wagging their tails behind them." Molly drew breath. "So that's what you did—you left me alone. In other words, you made me sweat."

His mouth quivered. "Did it work?"

Molly grabbed the front of Jay's jacket. "It worked," she growled. "I missed you like crazy." She put her face against his chest. "I felt something going on between us before I left that night. You said you worried about me and that was so sweet. But you didn't get in touch. I told myself you were busy with the restaurant. Then I saw you with Marie-Christine in the street in Saint-Tropez, hugging her."

He put his arms around her. "So you were jealous?" he mumbled into her hair.

"Yes," she sobbed, pulling back to thump his chest. "I wanted to kill you both. And that's why I was so rude to Marie-Christine earlier. It's all your fault, you beast." She relaxed and put her cheek against him, closing her eyes. "It's funny, but I feel I've known you all my life, as if I have been waiting for you."

"Me too," Jay said and rocked her in his arms. "I was afraid I wouldn't be right for you. Too old and too worn by life."

"Oh," Molly sighed. "Aren't we all worn?"

"We are."

"We should go back to the party. Weren't you supposed to play the guitar in there or something?"

"Yes, but I think I'll skip it. Let them dance till they drop." Jay let go of Molly and took her hand. "Let's find a room with a nice, soft bed."

Molly laughed. "Best suggestion I've heard all day." She started down the steps. "Come on."

He pulled her back. "Where? Your flat? But we've both been drinking and there aren't any taxis."

"Sophia's house? I'm supposed to be staying there tonight for that very reason."

"Too public. Marie-Christine's sleeping in the guest room next door to mine tonight."

"Shit," Molly groaned. "And I should apologise to her too. And you probably need to be here until the end of the party."

"You're right. I have to stay." Jay sighed and let go of her hand. "We'll have to put us on hold for a while. Can you do that?"

"Can you?"

"With difficulty." He came closer and kissed her, his mouth soft and tender. She responded slowly, wanting the kiss to last forever. His kissed her harder, running his hands down her back and around the swell of her breasts and then down to the curve of her hips.

She pulled away, putting a finger to his lips. "That's enough for now. I can't take any more and neither can you."

He laughed softly. "No, I can't."

"You're good at kissing."

"I'm even better at making love."

She pushed at him. "Stop it. Go on, go in there and do your duty. We'll pick up where we left off very soon."

"I'll hold you to that." He touched her cheek. "Bye for now, querida."

"See you soon."

"As soon as possible."

As he disappeared through the French windows, Molly turned away from the din inside and carefully made her way down the steep steps in her high heels. She couldn't go back in and face that drunken fool or sit at the table pretending she was enjoying herself. Bed and sleep, dreaming about Jay, was a better prospect. Walking down the hill past the church to Sophia's house, her mind full of what had just happened, Molly found herself smiling. She looked up at the stars and said a silent thank you to the heavens, God, her guardian angel, or whoever had made this happen. They hadn't been able to make love but that would happen. In an odd way, being forced to wait was a good thing. She needed a little space first before she could settle into a new relationship so she could finally put Miguel and her love for him in the past. Closure. That final farewell to the love of her youth.

It happened sooner than she had anticipated.

Chapter 24

"Dammit," Molly grunted. "Who invented flat-pack furniture anyway?" Kneeling on the living room carpet, she struggled to push a peg into what should be the right hole when the doorbell rang. She threw down the bits of chair she was trying to put together and went to open the door.

She gasped as she saw who it was. "Miguel! What on earth? I thought you were going to New York. With Karen."

He stepped inside. "We're flying out the day before New Year's Eve. But I had to stay in Ireland over Christmas to get the papers. And then I came here to give them to you in person." Carrying a folder, Miguel walked into the living room and looked at the bits of chair on the floor. "Flat-pack hell, is it?"

"Yeah. But I'll take a break. What papers?"

He held out the folder. "The divorce papers. My Irish solicitor found a judge willing to get the divorce through faster than we thought. He decided the circumstances of us not living together for all those years proved our intent or whatever. Sign these and we'll be all sorted in about four months. If we could do this before I go to New York."

"Oh, brilliant." Molly took the folder and opened it. "Where do I sign?"

Miguel took a pen from the pocket of his leather jacket and pointed at the bottom of the document. "Here—and—at the bottom of the next one."

"Okay." Molly went to the sofa and sat down, putting the papers on the coffee table. She glanced at the text and flinched at the words and their names, but skimmed past them and swiftly scribbled her name at the bottom. Trying to look cheerful, she handed back the papers. "There. All done. One marriage dissolved. Yippee, we're free."

"Soon, anyway." Miguel stuffed the documents back in the file. "Thanks. And thanks for filling in the forms earlier and have them sent on so promptly."

"You're welcome." Molly crossed her arms and sat back on the sofa. "Thanks for not claiming any of my assets."

Miguel shot her a crooked smile. "I had no right to them. End of this relationship, then."

"What relationship?" Molly glared at him. "We never had one." Why couldn't he just leave? His presence in her flat was uncomfortable. This was the end of all those dreams and silly fantasies, the end of her hopeless love for him. She still felt a fleeting attraction and there was some kind of chemistry between them that would never disappear. But she needed to close the door on all that and never see him again.

"How about a cup of coffee?"

She got off the couch. "Okay. I'll make you a cup. But then you'll have to leave. I'm very busy, and I want to get everything put together before New Year's Eve."

He raised an eyebrow. "Oh? You're throwing a party?"

"Yes," she said over her shoulder as she walked into the kitchen. "A party for two."

"Two, eh? You have someone new in your life?"

Molly put water, a filter and coffee in the machine and switched it on. Then she turned and looked at Michel. "Yes, I do. Someone very special."

"That's wonderful. I'm happy for you."

"Thank you," she said, her back to him. Then she turned and looked at him. "Miguel, just one thing—be nice to Karen."

He met her stare with an innocent look. "Why wouldn't I be nice to her?"

Molly rolled her eyes. "Of course you'll be *nice* to her in the conventional sense. I meant, don't let her down. Don't hurt her. Don't pretend you're in love with her if you're not. She's a very good person. She should to be treated with a lot of care and attention. She doesn't deserve to be lied to or cheated on."

He didn't reply for a long time. Instead he looked at her with a strange expression. "Well," he started, "aren't we being all moral and suspicious? Not very flattering to Karen, I have to say. Why don't you think I'd have fallen for her big time even if she had nothing? Is it because she isn't a conventional beauty? Or that she is rather, um, big? I must say, you're showing terrible prejudice here."

Molly kept staring at him. "You know what I mean. I like her a lot, and she's very attractive but not at all your type. Even if she were a stunning beauty, I'd still be suspicious."

He avoided her eyes and looked at his nails. "You don't trust me?"

"No."

He laughed and went to pour himself a cup of coffee. Bringing it to his lips, he looked at her over the rim. "Okay. I'll be honest. Of course her money is fabulously attractive. It's what drew me to her in the first place. I'm poor, but not stupid. I knew I could get her to like me if I tried hard enough. But then…" He took a sip and looked straight at Molly for the first time. "Then I got to know her. We spent a lot of time together and started to talk. And I discovered what a fun, intelligent woman she is. I began to love hearing her laugh, to discuss things, to discover mutual interests. Very slowly, I discovered the person behind the money, the power and the ambition. I like being in her company. I love her voice, the way her eyes sparkle when I make her laugh. I even love her rather generous curves. It's nice to cuddle up to that bosom, if you get my meaning. And sexy? Hell, yes, she can be. And you're right. She is a very good person—intelligent, compassionate, generous and kind—but tough as nails and determined to get what she wants. Okay, so she isn't what I used to think of as my type. But what is that, anyway? I find her attractive and I love being with her. Is there something wrong with that?" He drew breath.

"No, of course not." How strange. He really was falling in love with Karen. He had the imagination to see her great qualities, and he didn't care that she didn't fit into the mould of the perfect female shape. "Kudos, to you, I have to say. You looked and found the real person behind the façade." She paused for a moment. "May I ask you something and get an honest answer?"

"I'll do my best."

"Why couldn't you love me? I don't mean now, I mean back then when I was so in love with you. Didn't you notice how I felt?"

He put the cup on the table and folded his arms, leaning against the counter. "Of course I did. And you were so lovely. But…hell, Molly, you were so bloody *needy*. I felt trapped. I just wanted to get out and be free."

Molly rubbed her arms, as if seeking comfort from her own touch. "But you didn't hesitate to get into bed with me that last night before you left," she murmured.

"I was drunk."

"How flattering." She looked up at him. "And then you pissed off the next day, just leaving that note."

He looked away from her accusing eyes. "Like a real shit, I know. No excuse for that, is there?"

"No."

They were both silent.

He pushed away from the counter. "I'd better go."

"Yes."

"Okay."

She stayed in the kitchen while he walked through to the front door, picking up the folder with the divorce papers on his way. Molly stiffened as she heard his footsteps recede. She couldn't let him leave like that. She ran to the hall just as the door was closing, and pulled it open. "I just want to say something," she panted.

He stopped halfway down the stairs. "What?"

"Just that I'm glad you and Karen found each other. I think you'll make her very happy."

"Really?"

"Really."

His face broke into a smile as he came back up to the landing. "Thank you, Molly. Thank you for trusting me despite all I did to you."

"I just want to forget it and move on."

"Don't we all?" He put his hand on her arm. "Bye, Molly. I hope you'll be happy, too. Thank you for your generosity and kindness. I know you probably don't want to see me for a long time, but I hope that one day, we can be friends."

"Maybe sometime in the future," Molly said, wishing him gone. "But right now I want to put a lot of time and distance between us."

He patted her arm. "I understand. Happy New Year, Molly."

"Thanks. To you too."

He leaned forward and planted a light kiss on her cheek before he ran down the stairs.

Molly stood on the landing, listening to his footsteps until the heavy entrance door creaked and banged shut. It sounded symbolic, as if the door to her past had finally been closed never to be opened again. Miguel had finally set her free.

Molly returned to the living room, where the bits of furniture were still littering the carpet. It was time to put it all together. And to build herself a new life.

* * *

As she waited for Jay, on New Year's Eve, Molly's stomach was full of butterflies. She had made up the bed with Egyptian cotton sheets she had bought for a small fortune at Galeries Lafayette in Nice, splurging on some sexy underwear at the same time. She was wearing a sheer silk blouse and a short skirt, which left little to the imagination. But looking at herself in the hall mirror, she suddenly had cold feet. Did she look too sexy? Too cheap, even? Was it too much? Too soon? Should she play hard to get? This was their first real date...he might feel he wanted to wait before they went any further.

But when he came up the stairs carrying a bottle of champagne and a bunch of red roses, she relaxed instantly and sank into his warm embrace with a sigh of relief.

He pulled back and smiled. "Was that a sigh?"

"Yes. A happy sigh. But come in, I'm trying to cook you something."

He sniffed. "What? Smells nice. But you look even more delicious."

Molly pulled at the neckline of the blouse and tried to pull down the skirt at the same time. His eyes wandering up and down her body made her suddenly feel self-conscious. "Thank you," she murmured, feeling her face flush.

He pulled her close again. "Don't be nervous," he whispered. "It'll be okay. Whatever happens will happen because we both want it. And if not, no big deal. Okay?"

"Okay," Molly breathed. "Are you hungry?"

"Starving."

"That's good. Come on, then. Let's eat." She led the way to the kitchen, where a delicious smell emanated from a pot simmering on the stove. "It's Irish stew."

"I thought you said you couldn't cook." Jay put away the

champagne and the roses, spooned up some of the gravy and took a tentative sip. "Mmm. That's wonderful. Lamb, onions, herbs and carrots. I'm impressed."

"Very easy to make. You just brown some lamb and throw in the rest and let it simmer for a day or two."

"There isn't that much to any kind of cooking," Jay remarked. "But chefs have to pretend it's very difficult."

"I won't tell anyone."

"Good."

Molly shivered.

"What?" Jay asked. "Are you okay?"

"No. What *is* all this small talk?" she exclaimed. "I'm standing here looking at you and just wanting you to kiss me. And all you can do is talk about cooking. I made a huge effort to be…well, you know."

"What?" Jay looked confused.

"Sexy!" Molly shouted. "I was worried you'd think I was easy or cheap or something, but now I'm feeling so hot, and I want to get into bed and just bloody do it. What's the matter? Don't I turn you on?"

Jay didn't reply. His eyes darkened. Then he swept her into his arms. "Where's the bedroom?"

"Through the living room," Molly laughed. "The door is open."

Without saying anything further, Jay carried Molly into the bedroom and threw her on the bed. "I was going to be all romantic and open the champagne. But as you can't wait, and frankly, neither can I, we'll do what we've both been waiting for ever since I kissed you a week ago."

Molly lay there, laughing as she watched him throw off his sweater, quickly followed by his shirt, trousers and the rest of his clothes. His chest was covered in black hair, his body strong with just a small roll of fat around his waist. She liked the look of him naked. He was solid, strong, but not intimidating.

When he was naked, he lay down beside Molly and slowly stripped her to her underwear. "Lovely stuff," he said as he slid the strap of her cream silk bra over her shoulder.

"Careful, it cost a fortune."

"Waste of good money," he muttered as he unclasped it and threw it on the floor. "You'd be gorgeous in a cotton vest."

"I wanted to seduce you." Molly eased off her knickers.

"Be quiet, woman."

"Okay." Her breathing quickened as Jay cupped her breasts and kissed her throat. "Are you going to be masterful?"

"You bet," he murmured as his mouth travelled further down.

"Good. I like masterful men." She laughed out loud and threw her arms and legs around him, giving herself up to the pleasure he gave her, trying her best to please him in return. He rolled onto his back, Molly on top and they made love like that without speaking, their eyes locked. Then Molly collapsed onto Jay, letting out a long throaty sound. He shifted to his side, his arms around her and lay there, looking at her, his eyes tender.

Molly traced his profile with her finger, then down the scar on his cheek. "I love you, Jay."

"*Mi amor*," he whispered. "My love. *Te adoro*."

Molly smiled. "I love it when you speak Spanish. I want to learn it so I can say things like that back to you." She pulled out of his arms. "I'm going to have a shower. Then I want to eat and drink champagne, and eat chocolates and stand on the terrace and look at the fireworks with you and talk about us and what we're going to do."

"Sounds perfect." He propped himself on his elbow and watched her walk away. "What are we going to do?" he called as she stepped into the shower.

"You're going to move in here with me," she said when she came out.

"Yes, ma'am."

"Sorry. I'm being bossy." Molly put on her pink dressing gown. "I meant, would you like to live here with me? Please?"

Jay got out of bed. "I'll answer when I've had a shower. I need to think."

"Okay." While Jay was in the shower, Molly quickly dressed in black pants and her green cashmere top, the one she knew he liked. She put her sexy underwear in a drawer for another occasion. He might have said it was a waste of money, but she had seen the glint in his eyes as he undressed her.

When Jay came out of the bathroom, a towel around his waist, she had tidied the bed and put two pillows side by side.

"Are you reading my mind?" he asked.

"No, it's just wishful thinking."

"I see."

"Are you going to tell me what you want to do?"

"Yes. But let's eat, and we'll talk."

Molly served the stew with a salad, some crusty bread and bottle of Burgundy on the table in front of the sofa. Jay lit the fire, and while they ate, he told Molly his plan.

"Don't misunderstand me when I say this," he started. "Just listen. I don't think we should live together just yet."

Molly stopped eating and stared at him. "Why?"

He took a last mouthful and put his plate on the table. "Let me explain. First of all, I think we need to take it nice and slow. We both have a lot of baggage, and we're both adults and independent with our own careers. We shouldn't rush into something we might regret. And look at you, just moved into your own home with all your things around you. I can't push in here with all my stuff and my kitchen equipment. I need more space than that. And a room for Marie-Christine when she comes for a visit."

"But…"

"Shh. Let me finish." He took a swig of wine. "I have a plan that will mean we can be together but still live apart. I was going to tell you when I arrived, but then you made me forget all about it. And I'm glad you did." He kissed her nose. "But here it is—I've enquired about the apartment below you, the one that's been empty for many years. It belongs to an old woman who found the stairs too much for her. She's now moving into a nursing home and needs the money, so she's selling it—to me. I've been looking for somewhere to live for a while now, and when I saw your building, I began to wonder who owned that empty apartment. So I asked around and managed to track down the owner. It turned out to be perfect timing. I have some money put by that I wanted to invest, and this would be perfect. I'll finally have my own place and can move out now that Sophia has found someone at last." He drew breath.

"Oh," Molly said, while it slowly sank in. "So you'll be living there, just below me and…"

"Yes. But here's the best part. There's a staircase leading from the apartment below to your terrace. You can't see it from here, but if you look at the tiles, you'll see the mark of the old opening."

Molly nodded. "I noticed that. I thought someone had put new tiles where the old ones cracked."

"The opening was blocked off years ago, when the owner wanted to let your apartment." He leaned back. "What do you think?"

"What do I think?" Molly laughed. "It's absolutely amazingly, bloody perfect."

His face brightened. "I was worried you might feel I was making all the decisions without asking you first."

Molly took his hand. "You have no idea how wonderful it is to have someone make the decisions. I didn't quite know it straight away, but I think that all this time, I've been looking for a rock. And now I found it." She looked into his eyes. "Jay, do you want to be my rock?"

He smiled, but there were tears in his eyes. He touched her cheek. "With all my heart, querida."

Then they went to bed and made love again before they pulled up the duvet and went to sleep, their arms around each other, forgetting about the dirty dishes, the champagne, the fireworks, the New Year or anything else except the two of them together at last.

* * *

When Molly woke up the next morning, Jay was still asleep. She went out to the living room, opened the door to the terrace, and stepped outside to watch the sunrise. As the light turned from pink to gold, she felt as if she had been on a long journey and come back a different person, with a new outlook on life and a new soul. Her thoughts drifted to her family and friends. Liam, Daisy and Tommy. Ted. Miguel and Karen. She wasn't responsible for their lives. They were all on their own journeys, and she had to concentrate on hers. Let them sink or swim on their own. She took a deep breath of the cold, clean morning air and went inside to start her new life as a completely different person.

The girl who had once cared too much about everyone and everything found she no longer cared at all.

THE END

Please turn the page to read the final part of this series.

Marianne's Christmas

1

Two years later

Marianne sat on her terrace overlooking the azure sea, a glass of champagne at her elbow. The sky was baby-blue, the turquoise water of the pool glittered below the terrace, and a soft breeze caressed her cheeks and cooled her eyes—sore from weeping. She sighed and sipped the champagne, but the festive drink failed to raise her spirits. She pushed away the glass. She shouldn't be drinking so much. But it helped to soften the edges and dull the pain, even if just for a moment.

She had been prepared for the death and even for the sorrow that followed—but not for this empty feeling. After his stroke, she had nursed Klaus day and night until he finally slipped away early one morning three weeks later. "A relief," her friends had said. "Now you're free." But what kind of freedom was this? Klaus had been her rock. Now she was in freefall with nobody to catch her. Freedom wasn't a good thing if it meant being this lost and lonely.

A phone rang deep inside the villa. Marianne didn't stir. One of the staff would pick it up and tell whoever called she wasn't home. She didn't want pretend sympathy. The funeral had attracted a lot of media attention—simply because of the vast fortune Klaus had left, split between Marianne and her two stepdaughters. Yes, she was a rich widow and would possibly get a lot of invitations once the year of mourning was over. But, right now, she wanted peace and quiet. And time.

Marianne turned around as she heard a voice behind her and squinted at the figure outlined against the bright sunlight. "Maria? I said no calls and no visitors."

"It's not a visitor," a voice snapped. "It's me. Daisy. I've been calling and calling and then been told some story that 'Madame is resting,' or 'She can't take any calls.' This has been going on for months. What the hell is that? You no longer want to see your friends?"

"No." Marianne turned back to the view.

Daisy sat down on the chair at the other side of the table. "Okay. I see. Is this going to be a permanent situation?"

Marianne shrugged. "Don't know."

"Right." Daisy reached across the table, picked up Marianne's champagne glass, and drained it. "Nice. Moët et Chandon?"

"Yes."

"Klaus' favourite, wasn't it?"

"That's right. It was."

"His wine cellar was the best in town."

"I know. I'm nearly halfway through it." Marianne turned and looked at Daisy. "It's good to see you. I've missed you."

Daisy brightened. "Oh yes, me too! You have no idea how much. I have no one to talk to anymore, no one to giggle with or sit at the café in the square and ogle men or bitch about badly dressed women."

"What about Molly?"

"Molly's my sister-in-law. I love her to bits, but she doesn't have that bitchy edge I love about you." Daisy leaned forward and peered at Marianne. "You still have that?"

Marianne managed a weak smile. "Yes. It's awful, but I do. Even at the funeral, I kept looking at women and noticed fashion mistakes and botched plastic surgery. It was as if it helped me keep my sanity."

"Good for you. Those vultures don't deserve sympathy."

Marianne sighed and topped up the glass from the bottle in the cooler. "No, they don't. They were only there because, to them, it was a social occasion."

Daisy snorted. "I bet. I saw them. I'd say a lot of them thought they'd look good in black. They were all in designer mourning clothes, down to the little lace hanky they produced from their Prada handbags to delicately dab at pretend tears."

Marianne giggled. "Daisy, you're a tonic. That's exactly what I thought. Oh, shit, where have you been?"

"Right here. Only you didn't answer my calls."

"I know. I'm sorry. But I fell into this black hole after the funeral. I can't get out of it." Marianne reached across the table and grabbed Daisy's hand. "I need help. I need someone to pull me out of the darkness."

Daisy squeezed Marianne's hand with both of hers. "I'll do my best. But maybe you need someone else? A professional who knows how to handle the trauma of bereavement?"

"No! I don't want some therapist telling me how I should feel. I'm Swedish, remember? We don't do therapy. We're supposed to be strong enough to cope on our own."

Daisy rolled her eyes. "That's a load of garbage. If you need help you must try to get it. I'm sure we could find someone who—"

Marianne pulled her hand out of Daisy's grip. "No. Absolutely not. I only want you."

"I'm here. I always will be. And you for me, I hope."

"Of course. Sorry I've been such a wet blanket all these months." Marianne blinked away tears that threatened to well up. "But grief is so hard to get over. I'm trying to push through it and get to the other side, but I can't."

"I know. That's how I felt when my dad died." Daisy clasped her hands in her lap. "But grief is not something you 'push through' or 'get over.' There is no closure either. It will always be there. But it gets better with time. What you must do is accept what happened. Klaus is gone, but he will live on in our hearts and minds." Daisy looked into Marianne's eyes, as if willing her to take in and accept these wise words.

Marianne looked out to sea again. They were quiet for a long time until Marianne finally spoke. "I like that. It's a great help. Thank you."

Daisy nodded. "Glad to help in any way I can. But it's been nearly ten months: isn't it time you started living again? Sitting here feeling sorry for yourself isn't good for you. Get a grip, will ya, hon? What would Klaus say if he saw you, eh?"

"He'd think I had no guts." Marianne's eyes brightened. She looked at Daisy and smiled. "You're right. Enough moping. Let's talk about you. Come on, tell me what's been going on in your life since... since I've been away."

Daisy shrugged. "Not much. You know, looking after the baby, driving Tommy back and forth to school and all kinds of activities. All that parenting stuff." Daisy smiled and winked. "Don't tell anyone, but I love it."

"I know you do. Baby Clodagh must be getting big."

"Eleven months. God, it seems her christening in this house was only yesterday."

Marianne looked wistful. "It was just before Klaus had that stroke. Happy times ... before it all ended."

"And now it's nearly Christmas," Daisy remarked. "Not that the weather is very Christmassy, I have to say. It feels nearly hot today. I'm going to the beach for a swim later. Liam's looking after the kids today, so I have the day off. I need to get back in shape. I feel frumpy and flabby."

"You can swim here." Marianne gestured at the pool, its water shimmering in the sunlight. "I keep it heated until the end of the year."

"I will. Why don't you join me?"

Marianne jumped up from her chair. "Yes, why not? Did you bring a swimsuit?"

"No. Do we need them? The place is deserted. There's only Maria, but she won't mind."

"True. She won't. Come on, let's go."

"That's the spirit." Daisy got up. "Let's float around and talk like we used to. And I can tell you about an idea I have."

"An idea? About what?"

"You'll see," Daisy laughed and ran down the steps to the pool.

It didn't take them long to strip off and slide into the cool water of the infinity pool, perched on the hill, with stunning views of the coastline below.

Daisy propped her elbows on the edge and looked at the view. "This reminds me of when I was living in that villa down the road. The pool there is similar to this one."

"Mmm ..." Marianne closed her eyes to the sun as she enjoyed the feeling of the water and the calming effect of Daisy's presence. It was good to be with someone who cared. Especially Daisy, always so practical and honest, even if a bit raucous at times. As she floated on her back, she heard Daisy's voice as if in a dream.

"Klaus left you a huge gift, you know."

"What gift?" Marianne murmured.

"He died. He didn't linger after that stroke and make you look after a cripple. He just went. And now you're free."

"To do what?" Marianne asked, looking up at the clouds floating by.

"Everything!" Daisy said with passion. "You're young, beautiful, and rich. You don't have to suck up to those bitches anymore, you don't have to throw huge parties for those leeches who were only after Klaus' influence and money, and you don't have to worry about how you look, what you say, or what you do. The world is your oyster, Marianne!"

Marianne opened her eyes and touched the bottom of the pool with her feet. "What?"

"You heard. Think about it, darling," Daisy said softly. "And consider the alternative."

"I suppose," Marianne mumbled and tried to imagine what it would have been like to nurse a man who might have been a cripple in both body and mind. How horrible. Klaus would have hated that.

"Christmas," Daisy said.

Marianne blinked the water out of her eyes. "What about it?"

"It's going to be very hard."

"I know. I thought I might go away. Maybe to the Seychelles or something. Some place where Christmas isn't a big deal."

"Or you could stay here and have everyone around."

Marianne stared at Daisy. "What?"

Daisy flicked water at Marianne. "That's my idea. Just listen for a minute. You have this big house with all these bedrooms and staff and everything. Plus, you're loaded. So why not throw a party and invite everyone?"

"Who do you mean by 'everyone'?"

Daisy counted on her fingers. "Liam and me and the kids. And Molly and Jesus—I mean Jay—and Flora and Philippe and their kids and even Chantal and her gorgeous lover. And—" Daisy paused: "Ross."

"Ross?" Marianne stared at Daisy. "But he's about to sail around the world in his new catamaran. I thought he'd be in Hawaii by now."

"He never got there. He tore a tendon in his shoulder when he was out windsurfing. So he had to have surgery in Nice. He's only just back from hospital and staying in his house in Antibes. His new boat isn't ready yet either. I thought you knew."

"No. I had no idea. I lost touch with nearly everyone since Klaus passed away. God, I'm so stupid," Marianne wailed. "Why didn't I stay in touch with Ross instead of wallowing in self-pity? What kind of friend am I?"

Daisy put her hand on Marianne's arm. "Come on. Don't

feel guilty. It's perfectly normal that you should have forgotten about other people for a while. But now you can do something for him. You can invite him for Christmas. I'm sure he's lonely and frustrated now that his round-the-world trip was postponed."

Marianne smiled. "So that was your goal all along? Getting me to invite Ross for Christmas?"

Daisy laughed. "Yeah. But then I thought, why not include everyone else, too? No better way to stop thinking than having the house full of guests. Can you imagine a more perfect way to do Christmas this year?"

Marianne considered the scenario of a full house for Christmas. She took a deep breath and swam under water to the other end of the pool while she thought. All those people, some of whom she didn't know well. All the children and babies and even that dog Tommy loved so much. Then she thought of the alternative: spending the holidays alone in this beautiful-but-now-so-empty villa. Or going to some hotel in the tropics, looking at other lonely and lost people. Sweden? Christmas in the snow? But what little family she had left had all forgotten about her at best or at worst hated her for her wealth. When she emerged, she squinted against the sunlight and looked at Daisy across the expanse of turquoise water.

"Okay. You win. I'll do Christmas your way."

2

"She's doing it," Daisy chanted to Ross on the phone. "Christmas at Marianne's, and you're invited."

"Are you sure?" Ross asked. "I mean, she's still mourning her husband."

"It's been nearly a year. Time she joined the land of the living. It'll be good for her. You know how she used to love doing parties and events? This will be a masterpiece of organisation, and it'll take her mind off her sorrows."

"And you're doing the inviting?"

"Yes. We agreed on the guest list, and then I said I'd phone everyone and write the cards. Least I can do." Daisy pricked up her ears as she heard a faint wailing from the nursery upstairs. "Got to go. Madam is awake."

Ross laughed. "I'm looking forward to meeting this young lady. I bet she's like her mother, wild and beautiful."

"I'm not so wild these days." Daisy stood up and smoothed her hair. "Babies are very good at taking your mind off your appearance. But *she's* very beautiful, yes. Just ask her dad, and he'll give you a half-hour speech about his gorgeous daughter."

"I can imagine. Anyway, looking forward to seeing you. Thanks for calling."

"You'll be well enough to come for Christmas, then?"

Ross laughed. "I'd come even if my arm had been chopped off. Being a hermit is all very well, but not at Christmastime. See you then, my darling Daisy."

Daisy felt her face flush as she hung up. Oh, God, Ross... There was still that 'thing' between them. The attraction would never disappear completely. How would she react when they met again after two years? They had been in touch only by e-mail and phone and never met up physically. She pushed her hair away from her face. She was a mess. It was time to get out of the baby slump and smarten up a bit. Gym, swimming, then hair and make-up, not to mention clothes. She listened again. Clodagh had stopped crying. She could hear Liam cooing at her. Daisy smiled and picked up the phone again. Next on the list: Flora.

* * *

"Get back here and say sorry!" Flora yelled from the terrace.

Kieran stopped in the middle of the lawn and glared at her under his fringe of black hair. "I didn't do it. It was Pierre."

"No, it wasn't," Flora snapped. "He's still having his nap. I know it was you."

Kieran dropped his ball and burst into tears. "I couldn't help it," he wailed. "I was running and tripped, and then the bowl just fell over and smashed."

"What have I said about running in the living room?"

Kieran hung his head. "Sorry," he mumbled. "Will you tell Papa?"

Flora sighed. "No. Not if you promise not to do it again." She padded down the steps to the lawn and took Kieran's little hand in hers. "Come on, we'll go for a swim, okay? It's warm today. Too warm for December, really." She looked across the lawn at the view of the mountains and the blue sea below bathing in hazy sunshine and suddenly felt a pang of homesickness. Oh, to be in Ireland at Christmas. Cold, crisp air with a smell of turf fires and heather... She loved living here, just outside Vence, half an hour's drive from Nice, but she couldn't help longing for a real Irish Christmas.

"Père Noël will still come at Christmas?" Kieran asked as if reading her thoughts.

"Of course. We must write him that letter and tell him what you want." She squeezed his hand. "Hey, come on. Let's do it now while Pierre's still asleep. Then Papa can post it on the way to the airport."

Kieran looked up at his mother. "Is he going away again?"

"Yes, but he'll be back at the weekend. He's going to do a photo shoot in Scotland."

"What's he going to shoot? Deer?"

Flora laughed. "No, it's not that kind of shooting. It's a photo shoot. Taking photographs for an advertisement. It's called a shoot. Don't know why, really. And we can't come because we'd be in the way, and he's only going for three days. But next time he's going to Ireland we can go with him and make it a holiday."

"Will he go there for Christmas?"

Flora sighed. "No. We'll have Christmas here. But that's okay, isn't it?" She looked up at the big, beautiful house looming above them. Surrounded by lawns and exotic trees and shrubs, with a large pool on the lower lawn and a terrace with views to die for, it was more than okay. It was the ideal home for any family. But she couldn't help missing her own family in Ireland and the little house where she had grown up. But maybe everyone felt like this at Christmas? A yearning for their childhood days when things had seemed so carefree and easy...

The phone rang inside the house. Flora picked Kieran up and ran with him to the living room. She picked up the phone before the voicemail kicked in.

"Hello?" she panted.

"Hi Flora," Daisy laughed. "You sound out of breath. Are those boys keeping you on your toes?"

"They sure are. You wouldn't know, being the mother of a dainty little girl."

"Not always so dainty. I have a feeling she'll be catching up with your little horrors soon."

"Looking forward to that. How are you?"

"I'm good. Trying to get back in shape, though. It's murder."

"Why bother? You're an old married woman now."

Daisy sighed. "Oh, shut up. So are you, but you manage to look great anyway. But there's an event coming up, so we have to look our very best."

Flora frowned. "We? I sense some kind of conspiracy."

"Not really. Just an evil plan. For Christmas. We're all feeling a little low just now, aren't we? Christmas is coming, the weather is too summery, and we're homesick for cold weather, blazing fires, and wearing that Santa sweater and so on, right?"

"True." Flora sank down in the sofa. "I'm glad I'm not alone. I'm always a little sad this time of year."

"We all are. And the saddest one of all this year is Marianne."

Flora felt a pang of guilt. "Of course. It must be very hard for her."

"Awful. But she's doing something about it. She's throwing the mother of all parties at Christmas. We're all invited, and I won't take no for an answer."

"But what about the kids? I mean, two wild little boys running around that perfect house with the white furniture and all those expensive ornaments ..." Flora shivered as she envisaged what the house would look like when her boys had raced through it.

"Marianne said she'll clear the decks and put covers on the sofas. And one of the maids has promised to do nanny duty."

"Sounds too good to be true. But I don't think I can

accept without asking Philippe first. He might want to stay at home. He loves a quiet Christmas and never wants to go out or anything. Not that it'll be that quiet with the boys, but—"

"Oh, come on, Flora, it'll be fun. You'll just have to convince Philippe. Marianne needs shaking up."

"I think we can deliver on that one," Flora said drily. She thought for a moment. It sounded nearly too good to be true: a big house with servants, some of whom would take the burden of chasing the boys around, good company, and excellent food cooked by someone else. Heaven. She cleared her throat. "You might be sorry I said it, but I accept the invitation. I'll just present Philippe with a *fait accompli*. It would be rude to cancel once we have accepted, wouldn't it?"

"Horribly rude," Daisy laughed. "I knew you wouldn't be able to say no."

"Are you kidding? How could I resist? I just hope Marianne will be able to stand the noise."

"I know. I'll be bringing two kids as well, remember? Tommy is quite grown up now, but he can act up if he gets excited. We'll have to bring his dog, too. And Clodagh is threatening to start walking any time soon. It'll be some circus with all that. But fun."

Flora jumped up as she heard screaming from upstairs. "Shit, Kieran wandered off while I was talking. He must have woken Pierre up. Must go before they kill each other. See you at Christmas, darlin'."

"I'll send you an invitation card," Daisy promised and hung up.

Flora ran up the stairs, singing "Jingle Bells," scooping both boys into her arms as they ran down to meet her. "We're going to a fun party for Christmas," she chanted, hugging them.

"Where?" Kieran asked. "Disneyland?"

Flora laughed and kissed him on the top of his head. "No, sweetheart, much better than that."

"Are we invited?"

"Of course! Everyone's invited. It's going to be the best Christmas ever."

"Christmas," Pierre said.

"What about Papa?" Kieran wriggled out of Flora's grip and landed on the bottom step. "Have you told him?"

Flora put Pierre on the floor and smoothed his hair. "No, I haven't told him yet."

"Have you told him about working?" Kieran asked.

Flora stared at him. "What are you talking about?"

"I heard you on the phone yesterday. You said you would love to get back to the office."

"Oh that," Flora laughed. "No, I haven't told him. It'll be a surprise."

3

Chantal hurried up the steps of the building with two big bags full of groceries. She was late again, but Gabriel was probably in his studio working on the final painting for the exhibition in Nice. She'd surprise him with a bouillabaisse made from scratch. He loved this fragrant fish soup so typical of Provence. Then cheese she got at the market, fresh bread still warm from the bakery, and, to finish, two small pots of chocolate mousse. She'd open that bottle of Rosé from St Croix, his favourite.

When she reached the landing, she put the bags on the floor and rummaged in her large handbag. Her phone rang as she extracted the keys, but she ignored it and let herself in, coming back for the groceries and carrying them into the small kitchen. She glanced at the caller ID. Daisy. Long time since she was in touch. Chantal poured herself a glass of wine, went out to the small terrace overlooking the harbour, and sat down in one of the wicker chairs. She needed to catch her breath before she called Daisy back.

The late-evening sun infused the harbour in a mellow light, the still water looking like melted gold and the boats moored at the marina like boats in a fairy-tale. *Gabriel should paint this*, Chantal thought as she sipped wine and enjoyed the soft breezes that brought the smell of seaweed and fish. She loved this part of Antibes. Her flat was perhaps too small for them, but she didn't want to move.

The best solution had been to hire a studio for Gabriel, high up in a building in the old town with large north-facing windows. Problem solved, except for Gabriel still complaining about the tiny bedroom and even tinier kitchen in their flat. Chantal stood her ground. This was her flat, her space, and if he didn't like it, he could move out. Harsh words, perhaps, but it all stemmed from a feeling of insecurity. If she gave up her independence, she'd have no security net should their relationship fail. She was terrified he'd take her at her words.

He was younger than her by ten years, and he could someday find a much younger and prettier woman—a woman who could give him children. She had never voiced her fears, knowing it would make him angry if she did. It would mean she didn't trust him, which was partly true. How could you trust a man with those looks and that talent? She often saw women come on to him, smile, flatter, and even touch him at public events. With his dark hair and eyes, engaging smile, and fit body, he was the kind of man women were drawn to. Added to his physical attributes were his deep voice and charming ways, especially with women. She trusted him, but sometimes that trust wore a little thin. Not his fault, of course. It was all in her head.

Chantal pushed the dark thoughts away and picked up her phone. She had to find out what Daisy wanted.

"Hi, Chantal!" Daisy chortled. "How are you? I haven't been in touch for a long time, but with the baby and everything..."

By "everything" Chantal knew Daisy meant a whole lot more than just her baby. How on earth did she manage to run the house, handle her business as website designer, and be a wife to Liam and a mother to Tommy and her new baby? Multitasking wasn't enough to cover all of that. "You're Superwoman," Chantal laughed. "I feel tired even thinking about all you have to do."

"Yeah, it gets a little overwhelming at times. I might have to hire a nanny now that Clodagh is crawling around."

"Sounds like a good idea."

"That's what Liam said. Anyway," Daisy breezed on, "what are you and that gorgeous man of yours doing for Christmas?"

Chantal took a sip of wine before she replied. "Christmas? I have no idea. We thought we might spend it with Gabriel's family, except I'm not that keen on it. They don't like me much. I suspect they were horrified he ended up with an older woman."

"Gee, you're not old," Daisy exclaimed. "You're so slim and gorgeous. I always feel dowdy in your company. But maybe that's what they don't like?"

"Thank you, *chérie*. That's very kind."

"I mean it. You're very intimidating. But I digress. Christmas. Have you definitely decided to go to Gabriel's family place in St Tropez?"

"Not really. We're trying to wriggle out of it."

"Then you can wriggle into a dress for Christmas at Marianne's. She's having a huge house party, and you and Gabriel are invited. Before you start backing out, I'll tell you that this is a way for her to cope with the loss of her husband. She found facing Christmas on her own too unbearable, so I suggested she invite a crowd just to take her mind off her sorrows." Daisy drew breath.

"Christmas at the house of Marianne Schlossenburgh? The one called Villa Farniente?"

"That's the one. Also known as the gem of the Riviera."

"It's fabulous. The interior was done by Giovanni Canova," Chantal said dreamily. "I saw a little bit of it when I came to the jewellery launch a year or two ago. I'd love to see the rest of it."

"Well, now's your chance. You'll be able to snoop around the whole house during the Christmas weekend."

"Well, I'd only snoop downstairs," Chantal laughed, her spirits lifting. Daisy was such a tonic. "But that sounds tempting. As it'll be in St Tropez, we can call in on the family while we're there. That way they can't say we ignored them. *D'accord, chérie*, we accept. I think Gabriel will like this idea."

"Fantastic!" Daisy exclaimed. "It'll be a full gala. Black tie and full-on glitz. I'll send you a fancy card to remind you."

Chantal smiled to herself when Daisy had hung up. This would be a good way to celebrate Christmas. Being with other people in that beautiful villa would be better than the strain of spending part of the holiday season with Gabriel's snooty family. They were St Tropez aristocracy, the family having lived in that old house for generations. Now she could give them the finger and have a good time instead. Her thought drifted to the house party. *Clothes*, she suddenly thought, *I have to look over my wardrobe... I've been compromising on style lately.*

A slow smile spread over her face as the delights of shopping for such a glitzy event went through her mind. Cocktails, followed by dinner, then Christmas Eve Mass. *Black tie, Daisy said, full gala. Hmm ... maybe that stylist in Nice is free? I'll show them true glamour! And Gabriel? He'll protest, say he's too busy, or that it isn't his style. Well he'll just have to put up with being arm candy.*

4

Marianne wandered through the empty reception rooms. Villa Farniente. From the Italian saying *dolce far niente*, the bliss of doing nothing. The name had been her idea when she and Klaus bought the house. It would be, like the name suggested, a place to relax, to have fun, and to welcome friends and family.

She remembered how she had spent months discussing the interiors with Giovanni Canova. Klaus had been mildly jealous, she remembered, which was understandable, considering Giovanni's good looks and flirtatious ways. But Marianne would only ever love Klaus, which she proved over and over again in their new bedroom on the top floor. A bedroom that now echoed with loneliness despite the beautiful décor and the private balcony overlooking the azure sea. A heavenly space were it not for the memories that lingered there.

Marianne ran her fingers over the smooth marble of the hall table and looked at her reflexion in the gold-framed mirror above it. Her blue eyes that used to sparkle with happiness were dull, her face pale, and her light-blonde hair limp. But who cared what she looked like? Her thoughts drifted to the Christmas party. Was it such a good idea? To fill the house with guests and pull out all the stops? It wouldn't bring Klaus back, nor would it fill the void he had left behind. But it would give her something to do, something to look forward to.

She nodded, a small spark igniting her fighting spirit. Yes, she'd do it. It would be good both for her and for her friends, many of whom were also sad at Christmastime. But there should be a theme or some kind of event to justify this big party. An idea popped into her mind, something she had briefly considered the other day. Christmas would be the perfect time... She walked into her study and picked up the phone.

"Daisy? Have you sent out the invitation cards yet?"

"I'm writing them out now," Daisy replied at the other end. "But I haven't sent any out yet."

"Brilliant," Marianne said, her voice bright. "I want you to add something to the cards."

* * *

"Fund raiser?" Molly asked, as Daisy called in to her workshop behind Liam's house.

"Yes," Daisy said, balancing Clodagh on her hip. "Brilliant idea, don't you think? Marianne wants to start a charity foundation in Klaus' name. Mainly to help refugees. So the Christmas party will kick start it big time. Apart from the house guests, she's going to invite a whole load of people from St Tropez and Nice. There's also going to be a raffle to raise money for the new fund she's setting up in Klaus' name. It's a charity for the refugee crisis."

"A raffle of what?"

"She's going to ask those of you who're artists to donate one of your pieces as a prize. So I was thinking..."

"I know. I'd donate one of my new pieces? Or a set of the silver-and-enamel design? Necklace and matching earrings? Of course I will." Molly held out her arms. "Give me that sweet baby."

Daisy plonked Clodagh on Molly's knees. "There you

go. I thought you might mind her for me while I go to the supermarket. She has started the bad habit of wriggling out of the trolley and pulling everything from the shelves."

Molly looked down at Clodagh's sweet face with the big brown eyes and dimples. "This cute angel? I can't believe that."

"Mo-mo," Clodagh said and pulled at Molly's red curls, so like her own.

Molly tickled Clodagh's bare feet, which made her laugh deliciously. "See? She says she didn't do it."

"You're worse than Liam. Spoils her rotten. Don't let her crawl around here and make a mess of all your pieces."

"I'll take her for a walk in her buggy while you're out."

Daisy leaned against the door frame and folded her arms. "Good idea. That should knock her out for a couple of hours." She yawned. "I wish someone would knock *me* out for a few hours. Little Miss Muffet here woke us up four thousand times last night. She's teething. Liam finally went into his study saying he was going to work on an idea before he forgot it. But I think he just went in there to catch some sleep."

"Sneaky bastard. Have you asked him if he'd donate a signed copy of his latest book?"

"I'll do better than that. I'll get him to sign the whole of the last series, all four books. Should be popular."

"Jay could offer to cook dinner one night in someone's house," Molly suggested. "His restaurant just got a great review by *Gault et Millau*, so he's raised his profile as a chef lately. Don't tell Marianne yet. I'll have to ask him first."

"Of course. Have you two moved in together yet?"

Molly laughed. "No. But now that we have the stairs between the apartments, it feels like the same place. I like it that way. It's like having your cake and eating it, too. Independence with a lover stashed away downstairs."

"The modern woman's dream existence," Daisy laughed.

"God, I sometimes wish I had my own place. To be able to put my feet up and watch romantic comedies on a loop. Bliss."

"Don't tell Liam. He'll have a blue fit."

Daisy sighed and detached herself from the door frame. "Hell, yeah, he would. Jesus, Irish men are so old fashioned!"

"I know," Molly laughed. "They still live in the nineteenth century when it comes to women. Nice when they're being polite and considerate, but perhaps a tad irritating if you're married to one."

Daisy rolled her eyes. "Tell me about it. But I'd better go if I'm to get some shopping done. I have to post the cards for the party, too. It's brilliant that everyone's able to donate something. They all said they would. Philippe is going to have one of his prize-winning photos framed. And Gabriel ..."

Molly's eyes widened. "He's agreed to donate a painting?"

"Uh, no, not yet. But Chantal said she'd persuade him."

"I wish her luck with that. I've heard he's become awfully precious since he was declared a genius. Not surprising. Those looks and that talent would easily make a man conceited if you let him."

"Maybe she hasn't let him?"

Molly kissed Clodagh on the top of her silky hair. "Who knows? But French men ..."

"Chantal can handle him." Daisy kissed her fingers. "Bye darlings, see you later," she chanted and skipped out the door and down the path to her car, mulling over the subject. Could Chantal handle Gabriel? He had seemed a little moody and almost snooty the last time they met. But that was just artistic temperament, wasn't it? Or...was there a real problem brewing?

5

Chantal frowned as she read the note that accompanied the invitation card. She looked across the breakfast table at Gabriel, who was arguing loudly with his agent on the phone, waving his hand.

"No, I will not have anything ready for that exhibition in London," he snapped. "You know I don't like to have my work exhibited with other artists. My style, my *art*, is too controversial, too avant-garde to be diluted by weaker and more populist stuff." He listened for a while, then rolled his eyes. "So what? I don't care what the hell the critics in London say. No, there's no use trying to persuade me. I want to work on my abstracts. I've moved on from landscapes and portraits. That's all I have to say." He hung up without saying goodbye, muttering to himself as he put away his phone and picked up his bowl of *café au lait*.

Chantal shook her head and picked up the card again. How rude and bad tempered he had sounded. How could she broach the subject of the Christmas party and the donation to him? He'd never agree to donate even a small painting, or a watercolour.

"What's up?" Gabriel asked. "You look worried. Bad news?"

She looked up. "No, just the confirmation card for Marianne's Christmas party. I already accepted for both of us."

He sighed. "*Oui, je sais*. Not that I'm over the moon about it, but okay. Better than a family Christmas with my lot, even if it is at the house of a *noveau riche*—"

Chantal shot him an angry look. "Don't be such a snob, *chéri*. Just because your family has lived in St Tropez since the crusades, there is no need to sneer. In any case, Marianne's not one of those billionaires who build huge ugly houses that they only use for two weeks of the year. Villa Farniente is her permanent home. And it's one of the most attractive new buildings in the town. You said so yourself."

He raised an eyebrow. "Did I? Must have forgotten."

"You forget a lot of things lately. You even forgot that we were supposed to have dinner at Le Perroquet last night. I sat there alone. You didn't answer your phone. I had to make up some story about you being ill. Then they served me their delicious seafood risotto on the house. I think they felt sorry for me. Lonely old woman stood up by her lover. How pathetic."

His expression softened. "I'm sorry about that, *mon chou*. I did forget. I was in the middle of a business meeting."

It was her turn to raise an eyebrow. "Business? Is that what they call it now?"

He looked suddenly angry. "Yes, business. I wasn't with another woman. I'm involved in something I can't reveal yet. But once it's all in place, I will. You'll be very happy about it, I swear." He reached across the table, took her hand, and kissed it. "I know I've been a bit distant lately. I'm sorry if it has upset you. Is there anything I can do to put that beautiful smile back on your face?"

Chantal didn't hesitate for a second. Here was her chance. She looked at his handsome face and smiled. "You can donate a small painting with your signature to Marianne's fund raiser. She's doing a raffle to raise money for Syrian refugees."

His eyes darkened. "Raffle? You want to see my work in a *raffle*?"

She swallowed, her courage waning. "Yes. What's so terrible about that? It's for the refugees." Chantal got up from the table and started pacing around the kitchen, waving her hands. "Think about it, Gabriel. Think about those poor people, those children fleeing from the hell that used to be their homes. They have nothing, absolutely nothing! If you want to see me smile, then donate a painting to Marianne's fund."

She walked out of the kitchen, through the living room and onto the balcony, staring blindly at the view of the marina and the blue sea stretching all the way to the horizon. *They're out there,* she thought, *out there in those boats. Those children, those mothers and fathers having to watch them starve and die.* It was unbearable to even think about it. *Why couldn't he—*

Gabriel caught her arm and pulled her close. "Of course I will donate a painting. I will even paint something especially for the raffle. Something a little more commercial than my abstracts."

She pressed her face against his chest. "Thank you," she whispered. She closed her eyes and thought about those days only two years earlier when they had been so in love they couldn't keep away from each other. Why was it so difficult now? Why did she have to manipulate him to get him to do the slightest thing? Were they slowly drifting apart? She breathed in the smell of soap and oil paints that always clung to his clothes. Maybe Marianne's Christmas would bring them together again...

* * *

She was always struck by how alike they were. Blond hair, bright-blue eyes, tall frame, even teeth, and a wide smile. At least Ross' smile was wide. Marianne rarely smiled these days, except for a polite grimace when she had to. But when Ross arrived and swept her into a bear hug, she laughed for the first time in over a year.

"Let go of me," she ordered and pulled out of his embrace. "I can't breathe." She stepped away from him in the hall where he had dumped his bag. "Let me look at you." She studied him for a moment. He looked good. Healthy, happy, a little older, and more polished than when she had seen him last. But still the same Ross who was like a younger brother to her, ever since those early days in the Bahamas when they'd spent a summer in the same villa.

Marianne's cousin had been married to Ross' billionaire father, and Marianne had come to spend her holidays there. Bored with the glitzy lifestyle, with nothing to do but drink champagne, lie in the sun, and gossip, Ross and Marianne had joined a Cuban dance school on the beach. Together, they learned the Salsa, Samba, and Lambada, swiftly becoming a celebrated double act at every party. *Those were the days*, Marianne thought. *Twenty years ago, and now we're all grown up and responsible.* "You look good," she finally said.

He grinned, his teeth gleaming against his tan. "Thank you. I feel good."

"And the shoulder? All better again?"

"Not quite. But getting there. Physiotherapy is hard work. But I'm doing everything I'm told."

"Good boy."

"Are you okay?" Ross asked. "You looked so sad there. I am so sorry about Klaus. And so upset I couldn't come to the funeral. But I was in Australia. Then I hurt my shoulder and had all that surgery and had to stay. That's why I decided to come a few days before your Christmas party, so we could talk."

Marianne put her hand on his chest. "It's okay. I know. Please don't feel bad about it. I loved the letter you sent. Such sweet things about Klaus. I know how fond of him you were."

"Yes, I was. I can't believe he's gone. I feel him still here, in this house."

"I know. He is. But I'm so glad you're here." She glanced at his bag. "Hey, why are we standing here in the hall? Come in, and we'll have a drink. Dinner in about half an hour. Maria will put your bag in your room. I put you in the one next to mine. That way you'll have the view of the sea. I know you love looking at the water."

"And I'll be close to you," Ross said, as he followed Marianne into the vast living room.

"Yes. That's true. I like the idea that you're close. You've been away far too long, cuz."

He laughed and took the ice-cold bottle of beer she handed him. "Cuz. Long time since you called me that."

She lifted her glass of Kir Royal. "About time I did, then. Here's to keeping in touch. And seeing each other more often."

He clinked his bottle against her glass. "Keeping in touch at least. Seeing each other perhaps not so often. I'll be off as soon as my shoulder has healed."

She stared at him, forgetting to drink. "What do you mean? 'Off'? You only live an hour away by car."

He took a swig of beer. "I've sold the house. I'm leaving on my boat as soon as I'm strong enough." He rolled his shoulder. "I'm nearly there."

Marianne's jaw dropped. "You sold the house? That gorgeous house you rebuilt nearly from scratch? I thought that would be your forever home. And that you'd fall in love with some lucky girl and live there with your family the rest of your life."

He shrugged and stared out the window. "I never found that lucky girl. Or, more realistically, the girl I fell for didn't feel so lucky. She's happy with someone else now."

Marianne sank down in the white sofa. "Daisy? I know she was very fond of you, though. Still is. You just weren't compatible." She stared at Ross. "Don't tell me you're still pining for her?"

He drained the bottle. "No, not really. There's just a sad little spot in my heart still." He smiled at her. "Don't worry about me, sweetheart. You have to look after yourself now. I'm here to make sure you do."

"For a moment before you take off again," she said, a bitter edge to her voice. "But that's life, I suppose. Everyone leaves sooner or later. You just have to learn to live alone. Is that what you're doing? Living alone so you can't be hurt?"

He joined her in the sofa. "I'm not sure. I don't have that clear, concise way of thinking like a Swede. I just feel what's right for me at the moment, and then I do it. The house is too big, and I never felt part of the community there. French people don't generally take foreigners to their bosoms. They're suspicious of us. We don't have the same points of reference or the same culture. So it got a little lonely up there on the hill. Lovely, yes, and stunningly beautiful. But not for me."

"Who bought it?"

"I don't know. Someone who wants to remain anonymous. But he paid top dollar, so I'm happy. I'm having a new boat built in Marseille. A catamaran. It will have all mod cons and room for guests. I'll be off to Africa after Christmas, then down the coast to Cape Town, and then either up the other side of Africa and the Indian Ocean or across the Atlantic to Brazil." His eyes sparkled.

"Sounds amazing."

His eyes were suddenly dreamy. "Oh, Marianne, you don't know the magic of sailing across the ocean. The skies, the sea, the marine life. And the nights. To look up at the vast canopy of stars in that dark-blue sky would blow your mind. You truly understand how vast the universe is. I'd love you to see it. Fancy joining me?"

Marianne sat up. "Me? Going around the world on a boat? Are you mad?"

"Why is that so mad? I know you're a great sailor. I remember you handling that little sailing boat in the Caribbean years ago. Maybe you could come for part of the trip? Or fly out to the Bahamas when I get there. I would love to do the Samba again with you on that beach."

Marianne didn't reply. His words had opened a door in her mind, and she saw, as if through a window, a glimpse, like a glittering sunlit sea, into a new life and all the things she could do if she wanted to. She hadn't realised before how free she really was. She could do anything now, go anywhere. But that would mean casting off from the house and the world she had lived in with Klaus. It would mean leaving him behind. She wasn't sure she was ready.

6

Marianne didn't have time to think much about what Ross had said as the preparations for the big Christmas fundraiser got under way. She did, however, get plenty of opportunity to see him. She hadn't realised that giving him the room next to hers would not only make her feel less lonely, but also give her a peek show to his fit (and scantily clad) body as he exercised in his briefs on his balcony every morning, followed by a swim in the pool. He didn't know she was watching him through her half-open shutters, and she would have been mortified if he had spotted her.

She knew she shouldn't behave like this, sneaking looks at him while he worked out, but she couldn't help herself. He was so beautiful standing there in the early-morning sunshine, the sweat glistening on his muscular torso and rippling thighs. He looked like one of those Greek statues, and she told herself it was the artist in her that made her wake up at seven every morning and tiptoe to the window. *What artist?* She asked herself. *You're nothing but a pervert, sneaking a peek at a gorgeous man's near-naked body.*

She giggled at the thought and felt no shame. Nor did she stop peeking. It made her mornings brighter and her days happier. There was a new energy in her body, and a feeling of life beginning again made her eyes come alive. She started to take better care of herself, getting a much needed haircut and facial at the beauty salon in St Tropez. The staff greeted her with great joy.

"We haven't seen Madame for over a year," the receptionist gushed. "We were so sad about your husband. A very nice man. So generous and kind."

Marianne sighed, thanked her, and let herself be looked after, the caring hands massaging and kneading, soothing, and re-energising. Then she had her hair cut into the pixie style Klaus had loved. She smiled as she remembered how she had suddenly changed her style from Barbie-doll to working-woman when she had taken on the job of running Mollie's budding jewellery-design business. It had been just for fun then, but now it was a thriving business with Daisy as web designer and Marianne as business and marketing manager. But during her self-imposed year of mourning, she had handed over her responsibilities to Molly, who had been forced to hire an accountant. That was not acceptable. It was time to get back to work.

Marianne sat up as the hairdresser whipped the cape from her shoulders and brushed stray hairs off her neck. She looked at her reflexion in the mirror. Her face was thin, and her eyes, although sad, had a new glimmer of determination and hope. Molly's business and the new charity would give her the incentive to get her life back on track. A life without Klaus, but, still, a life worth living.

She had friends who needed her and many years still to live. And Ross, what about him? A much younger man who still loved a girl he lost. *Not for me*, Marianne told herself as she drove home. *It'll only bring heartache and misery. Ross has always been like a younger brother, and that is the way it should always be. Okay, so he has this hot body, but it's up to you to stop looking...*

Marianne felt like physically slapping herself to get back to reality. Then she remembered that Daisy would be calling in later to go through the arrangements for the Christmas party. Ross would be at the house. How would he react to seeing Daisy again?

* * *

She was already there when Marianne arrived at the house. She could hear Daisy's trademark husky laugh in the living room and Ross saying something in a light, teasing voice.

Marianne walked softly toward the sound of voices. What were they talking about? Was the old chemistry still there? She stopped in the doorway and took in the scene: Ross on the sofa bouncing Clodagh on his knee and Daisy looking at them and laughing.

"I see you're a dab hand with babies," Daisy said.

Ross looked up. "Uh, no, not really. She seems to like me, though."

Clodagh reached up and grabbed a handful of Ross' hair, pulling hard.

"Ouch!" Ross struggled to untangle his hair from Clodagh's tight grip. "Stop pulling my hair."

Clodagh's face crumpled, and she started to cry. Ross looked at Daisy with panic in his eyes. "What do I do now? She's crying. How do I make it stop?" He held Clodagh as if she were a bomb that was about to explode. "Here. She wants her mom. She's wet too."

Laughing, Daisy relieved Ross of the crying baby. "You big chicken. How are you going to cope when you have your own kids?"

"I don't think that's going to happen," Ross muttered. "I'm not into fatherhood. Never have been."

Daisy stared at Ross over Clodagh's head. "I had no idea. Thank God we—us—never happened, then."

Ross shot her a glum look. "Yeah. I think that was probably a good thing."

"Yes, very good." Daisy busied herself with the baby, pushing a soother into her mouth when Marianne walked in.

"Oh, what a gorgeous little girl," Marianne exclaimed. She held out her arms. "May I hold her?"

"Not a very good idea at the moment," Daisy laughed. "She needs to be changed. I'll go and give her to Maria, so we can go through the party arrangements. Then, when she's all sweet and clean, you can cuddle her."

"Great." Marianne poured herself a glass of orange juice from the drinks trolley. "How about you, Ross? You want a beer?"

Ross got up. "No. I have to make a phone call and send a few e-mails. I'll see you at dinner, hon. Nice to see you again, Daisy. You're looking good."

"So are you, and that's an understatement," Daisy replied with a wink. "See you later, Ross. Won't be long, Marianne."

"So how did you feel when you saw Ross again?" Marianne asked later when they were sitting in the study looking at the plans for the party.

Daisy stared into the middle distance. "How did I feel? Weird. I saw him in a completely different light, especially when I noticed how uncomfortable he was around a baby." She laughed and shook her head. "He was scared to death when Clodagh started to yell. But, hey, apart from not being the ideal dad, he looks good enough to eat."

Marianne felt herself blush. "Yeah, I know. He's kind of hot, isn't he?"

Daisy's gaze homed in on Marianne. "Hot? Sizzling I'd say. He used to be quite nerdy, but here he is, giving Brad Pitt a run for his money. Don't tell me you haven't noticed."

"Uh, well... yeah, okay, I have." Marianne buried her face in her hands. "I can't take my eyes off him," she moaned. "Especially in the morning when he does his workout in these very tiny shorts. And... this morning he went down to the pool and swam naked." She lifted her face and stared at Daisy. "I'm a dirty old woman, aren't I? What am I going to do?"

"Do yourself a favour and sleep with him."

Marianne's jaw dropped. "What? How can you—"

"It would be good for you. I saw him looking at you when you came in. There was something in his eyes."

"You're making it up." Marianne pulled a piece of paper from the pile on the desk. "Stop this and concentrate. I have everything in place except the raffle tickets. And I have no idea how much to charge for them."

"With those prizes? I'd say fifty euros per ticket. At least."

"That's pretty steep," Marianne protested.

"Of course not. Imagine: the winner of any of those items will end up with something worth far more. Plus," Daisy added with an evil cackle, "those bitches will have to cough up some cash to look good."

Marianne smirked. Daisy's good mood was infectious. "That's mean, but I like it. Okay. We'll go for that. They can all afford it anyway. Can you have tickets made up that look fancy and expensive?"

"Sure. I'll go to the printers who made our wedding invitations. They do a lot of these things for top-notch fund raisers. So," Daisy continued, scanning the list. "Food, wine, table decorations... We have invited fifty people to the cocktail party, and that's when we'll do the raffle. Then we'll have the dinner for close friends afterwards, and we'll all go to midnight Mass together. Ten adults for the dinner, three little boys, and a baby. Is that right?"

"Yes." Marianne sighed. "This was all your idea. I don't know how on earth I'm going to make it all Christmassy." She gestured at the sunlit garden. "Look at the weather: still summery. If we were in the Alps, we'd have snow. But here? No chance. It hasn't snowed in St Tropez for over a hundred years. It never will again."

"Oh, we can make it Christmassy without snow. All it takes is a bit of imagination."

"What are you talking about?"

Daisy winked. "When there's a will, there's a way. Stop being so negative. Let's talk Christmas presents."

7

Daisy's words echoed in Marianne's mind during the next few days: *do yourself a favour and sleep with him.* She went to the window in the morning, as if pulled by invisible hands and peeped through the crack in the shutters. There he was, as beautiful as ever, working hard to heal his injured shoulder and to get fit for his trip around the world. It was something he had always dreamed of doing, and now he finally had the courage. She felt a dart of shame as she stood there, like some peeping Tom. But as soon as Christmas was over, he'd be gone, and they might never meet again. Why not enjoy the sight of his perfect, toned body while she still could?

But things swiftly changed as the weather turned colder. Arctic air suddenly descended over Europe, all the way to the Riviera. The garden was enveloped in a damp mist, and the sound of foghorns echoed across the water like ghosts calling ships to home. Ross changed his exercise routine, now doing his workout in the gym in the basement, wrapped up in sweatpants and a warm pullover. Marianne no longer had her early-morning peep show to look forward to—both a relief and a disappointment. She laughed at herself and turned her mind to the Christmas party, which demanded some last-minute preparations.

The night before Christmas Eve, everything was in place. The drawing room was ready, with socks hanging across the mantelpiece of the large fireplace and the Christmas tree beautifully decorated by Marianne and Ross, who showed surprising skills in that area. For all the children, there was a pile of presents wrapped in colourful paper under the tree.

Dressed in silk pyjamas, Marianne sat in one of the white sofas sipping mulled wine, admiring their handiwork, and enjoying the warmth of the fire, when Ross walked in dressed up in a Santa costume. She burst out laughing. "Where on earth did you get that?"

"Galeries Lafayette in Nice," Ross replied, his voice muffled by the white beard. "I thought the kids would enjoy meeting Santa." He stuck out his stomach. "But I'm lacking a bit of *embonpoint*, don'tcha think?"

"I'd say drink more beer and eat pizza for a month, but even that wouldn't work." She grabbed one of the silk cushions from the sofa and ran up to stuff it under the Santa jacket. Job done, she patted his now fuller stomach. "There. Better."

He grabbed her hand. "How about a kiss for Santa?" Before she knew what had happened, he dragged her to the sofa, sat down, and pulled her onto his lap. "Have you been a good girl?" he said in a low old-man voice

Marianne giggled. "No. I've been very, very bad." She planted a light kiss on his mouth. "There. That's for being Santa."

"You taste nice. What have you been drinking?"

"Mulled wine." She pulled off the beard. "This tickles."

Ross didn't reply. Their eyes met. Then Marianne took his face and kissed him hard on the mouth. Ross stiffened and tightened his arms around her and kissed her back. They collapsed among the silk cushions in a mess of Santa clothes, beard, and giggles, kissing and panting, legs entwined. The Santa costume came off, along with Marianne's silk pyjamas. She kicked off her slippers and slid her hands over his smooth torso. It was wrong and foolish, but it was too late. They had reached the road of no return.

Ross pulled them both onto the soft white carpet, and Marianne felt herself slide into a dreamlike state as she gave herself up to Ross' hands and loving kisses. It suddenly seemed as if this was meant to happen and that Ross had been waiting for her ever since they met on the beach all those years ago. They moved slowly at first until they were both carried away by a wave of lust and passion, Marianne on top, Ross holding her, making her meet him and moving with him in a rhythm more prefect than any of the Latin dance moves they had been so good at years before.

When they finally slowed to a stop, they looked at each other in mutual wonderment. Ross' expression made Marianne's eyes well up. She touched his face. "Oh, Ross. I ... It was..."

He caught her hand. "Marianne. I never thought... I didn't plan this. But I want to tell you that I have always had you in my heart. Like a loving sister, friend, whatever. You've always been *there*, like a solid wall of support, no matter where I was in the world. Do you know what I'm saying?"

Marianne grinned. "That you just made love to your mother?"

Her rolled her over and pinned her under him. "No. Just that... Oh, forget it. Let's not talk. Let's just have fun."

Marianne stretched and sighed. "Oh, yes. Let's not even think." She eased herself off him. "The pool is still heated. I forgot to turn it off. There's steam coming out of it. How about a little skinny dipping, Santa baby?"

He got up and started to gather his Santa costume and beard. "Sounds like a good idea."

She picked up her pyjamas. "I'd better go and get some towels. Thank goodness I gave the staff the day off today to do their Christmas shopping."

"What about the neighbours? Do they have the day off too?"

She shrugged. "Who cares? Why not make their Christmas extra special?" She stopped on her way to the door. "Just one thing."

He looked up. "Yes?"

"I love you, too. In the same way."

Ross nodded, but didn't reply. He didn't need to. The look in his eyes said it all.

* * *

Christmas Eve dawned with cold winds and a smattering of rain against the windows. Chantal looked out at the boats and the dark choppy sea, wondering what she should wear to the party. The off-the-shoulder silk dress she had laid out would now be too flimsy. She opened the door to the wardrobe and flicked through the clothes crammed into the small space. What a mess. Gabriel's clothes were pushed into a heap and his shoes piled on top of hers at the bottom of the tiny wardrobe.

She rummaged around and pulled out a pair of Yves St Laurent Palazzo pants. Years old, but still stylish. With that, she could wear the deep-blue cashmere top and Chanel sling backs, all classics and perfect for cooler days. She patted her hair, happy she had managed to get to the hairdresser to trim it before the Christmas rush. Pants, top, shoes, hair. All good. Then she'd have to pack an overnight bag for them both, get Gabriel to decide what to wear, and persuade him yet again that they had to go to both the cocktail party and the dinner afterwards. It would be rude not to. They could pop in and see his family the following day. It would all work out very neatly. If it wasn't for Gabriel's strange mood.

Chantal pulled out a pair of dark pants, a pale-pink Cardin shirt, and a navy blazer and laid them on Gabriel's side of the bed. Casual and trendy, perfect for the artistic look he liked. Good. Now they were both organised for the evening ahead. She pushed the rest of the clothes back into the wardrobe and wedged the door shut, banging her shin on the edge of the bed.

She sighed as she looked around the room. He was right. The apartment was too small for them both. This had begun to dawn on her as they spent more time indoors now that the weather had turned colder. They had to find another, bigger place, or Gabriel might get tired of living like this and leave. She was never sure of his moods or what they meant. It wasn't easy to live with a much younger man, especially one so famous and popular with women.

The front door banged. He was home.

Chantal rushed out to the tiny hall and found Gabriel leaning a small canvas against the wall. He looked up. "Oh, you're home. I just finished this, the thing for the charity."

She looked at the canvas. "Hold it up."

He turned the painting around and held it up for her to see. It was an oil painting of the harbour, with boats on the glittering azure sea. The sky was brilliantly blue with just a few clouds, and seagulls fluttering around the boats. The scene would have been a cliché, a picture-postcard pastiche like the usual tourist-Riviera daubs, if it were not for Gabriel's touch. There was something special about the light and the contours of people just visible on the quay that gave it an edge, a feel of the true spirit of Provence.

"It's wonderful," Chantal said. "Thank you for doing this. I know you're busy with the exhibition in Nice in the New Year, so I really appreciate it."

He glanced at her and pushed his floppy hair from his eyes. "I didn't do it for you. I did it for all those people. Especially the children."

"I know. I didn't mean—" She stopped. "Anyway, I put out your clothes and nearly finished packing the overnight bag, so we'll be ready to go soon."

He nodded, pushing past her into the living room.

"Good. Thanks. I just have to send a couple of e-mails and make a phone call, and then we can go."

"Okay. I'll just check that we have everything, and then you can add your personal stuff."

He didn't reply. She could hear him typing on his laptop at the little desk in the corner. She looked at his broad back as he wrote. What was biting him? He was so distant and cool these days. A cold hand of fear squeezed her heart. Was he growing tired of her? Had he met someone else? Someone younger, sexier, more exciting? Chantal sighed and went back into the bedroom. Life in a cramped flat with an older woman was probably losing its charm. Would this be their last Christmas together?

8

The cocktail party was in full swing when Daisy and Liam arrived with the children and their dog. Daisy looked around the crowded living room and laughed. "It's just like the old days when we met right here in this house. Remember, honey?"

Liam hoisted Clodagh higher in his arms. "Not quite. We didn't have this little bundle then."

Daisy laughed. "No, but it gives me a kind of *déjà vu* feeling all the same. Except I was thinner and wore designer clothes and that amazing jewellery."

"Borrowed feathers," Liam remarked. "I thought you were a rich heiress."

"Did you feel really stupid after the wedding, when you found out she was poor?" Tommy asked.

Liam ruffled his hair. "I found out long before that."

"Did you get a bad surprise when you found out Dad wasn't a billionaire?" Tommy asked Daisy. "I mean, if you thought he was rich, and he thought you were—" He stopped. "I mean if—"

"No, that's not quite how it was, Tommy," Daisy said. "But never mind. Here's Flora and the boys. Do you think they'd like to say hello to Asta?"

Liam bounced Clodagh. "I'd like to say hello to the nanny, so I can get myself a drink."

Marianne, looking amazing in a tight red dress, appeared

by their side with a smiling young woman. "Hi folks. This is Jeanne, the nanny for the night. She's Maria's daughter, and she loves kids. Tommy, say hi to Jeanne."

"Hi," Tommy said. "But I'm too big for nannies. You can have Clodagh. She's very noisy."

"Hello, Tommy." Jeanne laughed and reached out to take the baby. "And hello, Clodagh. What a beautiful baby."

"She'll cry," Tommy warned. "She doesn't like strangers."

But Clodagh didn't seem to mind. She stuck her thumb in her mouth and grabbed a strand of Jeanne's dark curly hair with her other hand.

"Sorry, she has this thing about pulling hair," Daisy said, untangling Jeanne's hair from Clodagh's eager fist.

"I know," Jeanne said. "They all do at this age." She pulled a colourful rattle from the pocket of her pink housecoat and handed it to Clodagh. "Here, *mon chou*, this is more fun than hair."

The sound of the rattle made Clodagh laugh, and she grabbed it with both hands. Jeanne turned to Tommy. "That's a very nice dog you have there. Do you think she'd like a bone? Come to the kitchen with me, and I'll see if we can find something nice for her. There's sausages and *frites*, too, if you feel hungry, Tommy."

"Yes, please," Tommy said. "I know where the kitchen is. Let's go!"

Liam smiled at Marianne. "You clever woman. Not only a nanny, but Mary Poppins, no less."

Marianne nodded. "Yes, she's amazing. I had no idea how good she was until she took care of Flora's boys. They're already in their pyjamas watching a Disney DVD in the little staff room beside the kitchen. Brilliant girl."

Liam let out a long sigh and put his arm around Daisy. "That's terrific. Now we can pretend we just met and get drunk and disorderly. I haven't had a moment alone with this babe for six months."

Marianne giggled. "Just try to behave, will you? My posh neighbours frown on public snogging."

"Is that Ross handing out drinks?" Liam asked.

Marianne glanced at Daisy. "Yes. He offered to help, so I accepted. He's been very... sweet."

"I'm going to get a beer," Liam announced. "What do you want, sweetie?"

"Champagne," Daisy replied.

"Of course, my princess," Liam said. "What else?"

"So what's going on with you?" Daisy asked, looking at Marianne's sparkling eyes and happy smile. "You're a different woman."

"I kissed Santa Claus," Marianne said cryptically. "Tell you later. More people coming up the steps."

Daisy looked at Marianne's slim form skipping down the steps, watching her greet new guests with a cheery "Hello." Something had happened since they had that talk. Marianne was a different woman. In that red dress and the new short hairdo, she looked years younger. But not only that, there was a happy look in her eyes and a lightness in her voice that spoke of something new and wonderful in her life. "I bet she had great sex," Daisy muttered to herself, taking the champagne flute Liam handed her. "And I bet it's someone we know very well."

"What are you muttering about?" Liam asked.

Daisy gestured at Marianne's distant figure. "Her. Marianne. She looks like she's won the lottery. Or that proverbial cat with the canary. She's transformed. Must be sex. Nothing else gives you that glow."

Liam drank from his bottle. "She looks incredible. Maybe she just had a makeover or some kind of yoga thing?"

Daisy drained her flute. "Whatever it is, I'm having some of that."

Liam pulled her close. "I'm sure that can be arranged," he muttered in her ear.

* * *

The sale of the lottery tickets got under way as soon as the guests had been served champagne, caviar, shrimp parcels with chili dipping sauce, foie gras, and other delicacies and the hum of polite conversation had turned to louder laughs and risqué jokes. Everyone was having a good time, and the festive mood was due more to the pleasure of seeing Marianne back to her old self than because of Christmas. Although there was a hint of sadness in her eyes and voice when she thanked her guests for their kindness during her hard time of mourning, she managed to make everyone feel welcome, even the "evil bitches," as Daisy called them.

Half an hour into the party, Marianne tapped her glass with a spoon. There was a hush in the room as she started to speak.

"Dear friends and neighbours. Thank you for coming to my little Christmas gathering, which, as you know, I organised for a reason. I know you are all very generous and often give money to charity. But I felt that we should gather force and give a big sum in one go to all those refugees landing on our shores, having left their homes and families, fleeing the hell of war and destruction. My heart goes out particularly to the children, and I often wonder what will happen to them. What future do they have? How will they cope with living in camps under horrible conditions? No child should have to go through that, yet they do in their thousands." She paused and made a sweeping gesture. "And here we are in the lap of luxury, enjoying the best food and wine, wearing designer clothes and feeling well and happy. Does this seem fair to you?"

There was a communal murmur of "No."

Marianne nodded. "Exactly. For that reason, I have decided to start a foundation in the name of my late husband,

Klaus, who you know was so generous and caring. This way, I feel his name will not die." Marianne stopped. Her mouth wobbled for a moment. She suddenly found it hard to speak.

Daisy ran to her side and put her arm around her waist. "Just to finish: to kick off the foundation," she shouted, "we're selling lottery tickets in a raffle with amazing prizes donated by local artists. Not your usual locals, but international names. There's a painting by Gabriel Sardou, signed copies of Liam Creedon's latest series, a set of exquisite enamel jewellery by Molly from her winter collection, a signed framed photograph by internationally acclaimed photographer Philippe Belcourt. Last but not least, Michelin star chef Jay will cook one of you a dinner in your own home. Howzat for great prizes, eh?"

The crowd broke into loud applause and shouts of "Bravo!"

Daisy waved a packet of lottery tickets in the air. "You can buy the tickets from me or Ross, that tall hunk over there who looks like Brad Pitt. The tickets are fifty euros each. Expensive, yes, but you can frigging afford it! In fact," she added, feeling inspired, "you can afford to buy several tickets each. The more you buy, the bigger the chance of winning. If you don't, you'll look like miserable stingy bastards. The draw will take place in exactly one hour, and after that you can go home because we have other things to do." She drew breath and beamed at Marianne. "There. How was my speech?"

Marianne wiped her eyes and laughed. "The best speech ever. Nobody can refuse a ticket now. Nor will anyone speak to me ever again."

Daisy looked at the elegant women, now all practically mobbing Ross for lottery tickets, some even throwing fifty-euro bills at him. "I wouldn't be too sure. Especially if you keep Ross around. He'll be the pet of St Tropez before long."

"He'd hate that. In any case, he's leaving after the holidays. His boat is ready and his injury practically healed."

"He's leaving?"

"Yes. Tomorrow. His boat is ready."

Daisy looked at Marianne's suddenly pale face. "You're doing it, aren't you?"

Marianne grinned. "Yes," she whispered. "And it's amazing."

"Good for you."

"But then what?" Marianne asked, a note of desperation in her voice. "I'll be all alone again."

"Go with him?"

"What? Leave everything and go around the world in a sailing boat?"

Daisy shrugged. "Sure. Why not? You're free to do what you want."

"But what about the foundation and the house, where Klaus and I were so happy?"

"All that can be solved. You just have to sort out your priorities." Daisy kissed Marianne's cheek. "I have to go sell tickets. I bet I can sell more than Ross."

"Thank you for all you've done."

"You're welcome. Think about what I said," Daisy said over her shoulder. "Life's so short."

"I know," Marianne whispered to herself. "So short and heart breaking." She pulled herself together, pasted on her hostess smile, and went back to the party.

9

Chantal looked around the table in the large, bright kitchen, while everyone was finding their seats. Marianne had given the staff the rest of the holidays off, so they could celebrate Christmas with their families. Before they left, they had laid the table and set up the buffet on the long counter beside the twin gas cookers.

"Beautiful kitchen," Chantal said to Gabriel.

"I think we could fit our entire apartment into it," he replied.

Chantal laughed, even though she didn't find it funny. There he went again, complaining about their flat. "I like the Provençal feel of it all," she continued, looking approvingly at the solid oak cupboards, terracotta floor tiles, and pine worktops.

"It's a very attractive room," Gabriel agreed and pulled out her chair.

Chantal sank down on the chair, grateful to rest after several hours of standing at the drinks party. Having the dinner in the kitchen was a good idea, making the gathering feel intimate and cosy. She glanced out the windows that overlooked the herb garden. She could still see the shapes of umbrella pines in the gathering dusk. She knew they shaded the plants from the worst heat of the sun. Today there had been no sun, however, and the dark clouds rolling in from the north spoke of bad weather to come. But in this bright, warm room, there was only a feeling of cheer and welcome, with everyone chatting and laughing and helping themselves from the platters giving off mouth-watering smells.

She looked around the table at the other couples: Molly and Jay, Flora and Philippe, Daisy and Liam, all looking happy and in tune with each other. Marianne, who had so recently lost her husband, was slowly coming back to life, even if she was still obviously grieving. Ross, that handsome American, seemed very close to her. Chantal had heard they had known each other a long time. She envied them all, even Marianne. None of them had to worry. They were loved and cherished. And not alone. Chantal shivered and tried to smile and chat as if she didn't have a care in the world. And she didn't, except for that niggling fear that she would soon be all alone.

"Help yourselves," Marianne shouted, taking a large ham out of the oven. I've cooked some Swedish specialities, but nobody's forced to eat it. There's plenty of other safer stuff if you don't feel brave enough."

But they all wanted to at least taste the Swedish Christmas food, digging in to pickled herring, cured salmon with mustard sauce, and that big glazed ham studded with cloves. But they stepped away from the rice pudding, preferring the more luscious French chocolate log.

"Sorry," Daisy said as she dug in to a huge slice. "But ya' know, chocolate wins over rice pudding any day, even more so at Christmas."

The door suddenly flew open with a bang, and everyone stopped talking, looking at a small pyjama-clad figure. "I can't sleep," Kieran sobbed. "I've been sitting in front of the fire waiting for Santa, but he won't come."

Flora rushed to his side and picked him up. "Sweetheart, he won't come if you sit there. You have to be asleep."

"But I can't," Kieran wailed and buried his face in Flora's bosom. "Maybe he won't come at all. Maybe he knows I was bad and broke your vase. Maybe—"

Ross got up and pulled out his phone. "I think we can check his progress on the Santa tracker here on my phone. Do you want to know where he is right now?"

Kieran glanced at Ross and nodded. "Yes, please," he whispered.

Ross switched on his phone and scrolled for a while. "Here he is," he said and showed the screen to Kieran. "See? He's in Russia. It'll take him a while to get down here. I mean think of all the children on the way—in Sweden and Denmark and Germany. So if you go back to bed, close your eyes, and make a wish, I bet you'll go to sleep and then, tomorrow morning—"

Kieran's eyes sparkled with new hope. "He'll have left me presents?"

"Not only that, but I have heard that Marianne is a very special friend of Santa because she is from Sweden, so..."

"What?" Kieran asked, his eyes on stalks.

"So he might even give you and the other children their presents himself."

Kieran shook his head. "Nah, he won't. That's a fib."

"It's not, I swear," Ross insisted.

Kieran looked doubtful. He leaned his head on Flora's shoulder looking suddenly sleepy.

"Let's get you to bed," Flora said. "Is Pierre asleep?"

Kieran nodded. "Yes." He yawned. "That girl sang him a song. The baby is asleep too, and the other boy and his dog. All asleep." He yawned again and rubbed his eyes.

"Come on," Flora said. "We'll go to bed together. You can sleep with us tonight." She glanced at Philippe at the other side of the table. "I'm taking him upstairs. That bed is so huge we'll all fit."

Philippe rolled his eyes, sighed, and laughed. "Of course. It's okay." He joined Flora at the door and took the sleepy little boy from her. "I'll take him up."

"Before you go," Daisy cut in, "I have to tell you all how much the lottery made for Klaus' foundation."

Philippe stopped. "Of course. How much did it bring in?"

"Amazingly, five thousand euros. Couldn't believe all the tickets people bought. Plus, one of the neighbours offered to help run it, and he'll even set up a Facebook page and do all the accounts. He owns a bank, so it should be right up his alley. It's François whatshisname, Marianne. His wife is that large woman who wore the dining room curtains. She is going to do a fundraiser for you when they come back from their cruise in the spring. Howzat, eh?"

"*Magnifique*," Philippe said before he left to put his son to bed.

"Brilliant," Marianne laughed. "Thank you for running this, Daisy. Nobody else could have blackmailed so many people into parting with their money."

Daisy shrugged. "It wasn't me—it was Ross. He just looked into their eyes, and they didn't even notice they were doing it. You'd go far as a con man, Ross."

Ross waggled his eyebrows. "Could be fun."

"But some of the women were disappointed you weren't one of the prizes," Molly laughed.

Ross coloured slightly. "Gee, no. I mean..."

"Can we leave now?" Gabriel whispered in Chantal's ear.

She looked at him and realised he was bored. "But everyone's going to Christmas Mass," she whispered back. "Then we're staying the night here. I *told* you that was the deal. Please, Gabriel, don't be rude."

"Very well." His eyes darkened, and she could feel his body stiffen beside her. "I'll stay."

"Good." With a heavy heart, she got up to help Daisy clear the plates and tidy up. It was no use. He was ready to leave her. How foolish it had been to think she could hold on to a younger man for any length of time. She had to face the truth and realise it was over. She couldn't go on like this any longer. They'd have to talk when they got back home the next day. Better to cut it off in one go than have it linger and fester.

"How are things at the agency?" Flora's voice cut into Chantal's thoughts.

"Hectic," Chantal replied and sat down beside Flora. "I only have one other person working with me at the moment. I need to hire someone else." She glanced at Flora. "You said you'd be interested?"

Flora's forkful of chocolate cake stopped in mid-air as she looked at Chantal thoughtfully. "I wasn't sure before, but now I think I'm ready."

Chantal stared at her. "Really? *Mon dieu*, I would love that! To run it with you again would be wonderful. You wouldn't have to work every day. How about three days a week?"

"Perfect." Flora beamed. "I'd just have to organise a minder for the kids, or Philippe could—"

"Philippe could what?" he cut in, as he came back into the kitchen.

Chantal turned to him. "Flora has just agreed to come back to the agency for three days a week. So we were discussing how she'd organise childcare."

"I see," Philippe drawled. He looked coldly at Flora. "And all this without asking your husband? I had no idea you were planning this."

"I wasn't planning anything," Flora shot back. "Chantal just mentioned it, and then I thought—I mean, I was going to tell you, but not until we got back home."

"You can stop thinking," he snapped, his French accent more pronounced than before. "There is no way you're going back to work when you have two small children and a husband to look after."

"A husband to look after," Daisy mimicked. "How about joining the twenty-first century?"

Philippe glowered at her. "Is this any of your business?"

"It is if you're being a sexist pig," Daisy retorted. "That attitude is so bourgeois."

Flora jumped up and pointed her spoon at Daisy. "Are you insulting my husband?"

"If the shoe fits," Daisy replied.

Chantal, horrified by the growing hostility, tried to soothe the ruffled feathers. "I'm sorry. I didn't realise this would cause you a problem, Flora. I didn't mean to start an argument here. It's just that you're the best assistant I ever had. Having you back, even on a part-time basis, would be a huge help."

"In your dreams," Philippe muttered, regaining his seat. "Flora, sit down. We'll have some more wine and talk about something else. The subject is closed." He raised his glass. "How about a toast to the lovely hostess?"

Nobody replied. Daisy muttered something and turned back to loading the dishwasher.

Liam drained his wine glass. "Listen, Philippe, my wife works and does a great job looking after the kids. But we share a lot of the chores. With a little organisation, I'm sure you could—"

"I don't think you heard what I said," Philippe replied, his voice smooth. "The discussion is closed. Isn't that right, Flora?"

Flora glared at him. "No, it's not, and you know it. But we'll get back to it in private."

"Philippe," Chantal started, "please reconsider. I'm not asking Flora to work full time after all, just three days a week. I'm sure you can find a good childminder if you put an ad in *Nice Matin*. Going back to work will be good for both Flora and the children."

Philippe stiffened. "You don't seem to have heard what I said, Chantal. I'm not going to talk about it anymore. Except perhaps to inquire what you know about having children."

Gabriel, who had been quiet all through the arguments, suddenly raised his voice. "That's an insensitive comment, I have to say."

Daisy slammed the door of the dishwasher. "Yeah, that's pretty mean, Philippe."

Flora started to say something, but Molly interrupted her. Then Daisy cut in on what Molly had said, Jay shouted back at her, and, suddenly, everyone in the room was yelling. Everyone except Ross and Marianne. Ross rolled his eyes and jerked his head toward the door. Marianne nodded.

Nobody noticed when they crept through the door and closed it softly behind them.

* * *

They stopped when they got to the hall.

"What's the matter with everyone?" Ross asked.

Marianne shrugged. "Don't know. Fatigue. Too much booze. Christmas nerves or something. But they'll calm down. Even Philippe. I've never known him to be so stupid. I bet he doesn't mean half the things he said."

"Maybe he just doesn't want to be contradicted?"

"Could be. Never knew he was so old fashioned. Or maybe he's jealous of Flora wanting to do something for herself?"

He put his hands on her arms. "Who cares? Leave them alone to sort it out. How about taking a little siesta?"

She leaned her cheek against his chest. "Sounds perfect. Except if you want to go to Christmas Mass?"

"Nah. I'm not Catholic. How about you?"

"Neither am I." She lifted her head and laughed. "But they all are. So they'll have to stop fighting and get themselves to church in about half an hour."

"I'm more of a Buddhist really."

"Me too. I believe in God, but not religion." Marianne hugged him close. "And I believe in Santa Claus."

He laughed and started to pull her to the stairs. "Then we'll have to see what Santa can do for you."

"I can't wait."

They walked up the stairs and into Ross' bedroom that they had made theirs and sank down on the bed, their arms around each other. Marianne touched his face. He'd be gone soon. All she'd have were the memories of this special Christmas. She closed her eyes and breathed in the smell of him, felt his breath in her hair and his gentle hands on her body. She turned her head to hide the tears that suddenly welled up. He didn't see them, but knew she was crying and hugged her hard, so hard she felt all her broken pieces fit back together again.

Ross, her new love and forever friend, would help her heal, even if they were apart for a while. She sighed and hugged him back. Then they made love like teenagers in the faint light of the moon.

10

Later that night, when they had come back after Mass, Philippe apologised. “I’m sorry,” he said and walked around the bed to put his arms around Flora. “I don’t know what came over me. Of course you should go back to work if you want. I’m sure we can find a minder for the three days a week. I mean that.”

Flora kissed him. “I know. Where’s Kieran? I thought he was sleeping with us tonight?”

“He fell asleep in my arms, so I carried him to his own bed and tucked him in.”

“Oh. Good. Thank you. I don’t know why I got so hot and bothered earlier,” she continued. “I don’t even care if I can work or not. It’ll mean a lot of organisation.”

“But in the end, you’ll be happy. And it’ll provide an income for you.”

She sat down on the bed, unbuttoning her silk shirt. “I’m too tired to think about that now. Let’s just go to sleep. I love you, Philippe.”

“Me too. You, I mean, *mon amour*.” he toppled her over onto the bed and smiled into her eyes. “I don’t know what was in that wine, but I feel suddenly very attracted to you, Madame Belcourt.”

“It was the champagne. You always get amorous when you drink champagne.”

“And argumentative when I drink too much red wine.

But the Mass and all that beautiful Christmas music made me feel guilty. I said some things I didn't mean. I hope you can forgive me."

"Of course, darlin'." Flora smiled. "We must go to Mass more often."

"It was a beautiful service." He smiled and winked. "But let's enjoy this wonderful bedroom and the enormous bed. Seems a shame not to use it to its full advantage, don't you think?"

"Oh yes," Flora sighed and threw her arms around him. "Let's see what we can get up to."

Philippe put his head on her chest. "You smell nice," he mumbled. "So very, very nice..." He closed his eyes and yawned.

Flora giggled as he began to snore and pulled the covers over them both. She closed her eyes and drifted off, first saying a prayer to the saint of working mothers. *Please send me a nice nanny so I can go back to work.*

* * *

Gabriel moved in the bed and put his hand on Chantal's shoulder. "Asleep, *mon amour*?" he whispered.

Chantal stirred. "No, not yet."

He moved closer and slid his arms around her from behind. "There's a beautiful moon."

"I know. Do you want me to close the shutters?"

"No. Let's lie here and look at it. Or let it look at us."

She looked up at the silver disc of the moon that seemed to hover over the dark, silent garden. "It really looks as if there's a man in the moon tonight. So magical. Such a still night, after the rain and clouds moved away. Tomorrow will be a nice day."

"I hope so. I have something to tell you. Something

important. But I'll wait until tomorrow when we're on our own."

"We're on our own now."

He kissed her neck. "Yes, but it's not the right time."

She twisted her head and tried to see his face, but it was too dark. "What is it about? What are you planning?"

He hugged her tight. "Shh. Not now. Go to sleep, *chérie*. I'll tell you all about it tomorrow."

She sighed, knowing it was no use. He wouldn't tell her until he was ready. But there was a tenderness in his voice that reassured her. Maybe he wasn't planning to leave her after all. Maybe...

"You will be happy, my darling," he said so softly the words sounded like part of his breath. "Tomorrow will bring good things for us both."

Her eyes closed and she drifted off, wondering if what he had just said was real or part of a dream.

* * *

"Seven o'clock," Ross moaned. "I'm barely awake."

Marianne stood by the bed holding the Santa costume. "I know, but those kids are waiting for Santa. This was all your idea, remember?"

He sat up and rubbed his head. "Yeah, I know. One of those things that seemed like a good idea at the time. Jesus, my head." He flopped back on the pillow. "Can I call in sick?"

"No, you can't. Come on, don't be such a wimp. I've been up since six thirty with Jeanne making breakfast. Get into that costume and do your stuff," Marianne ordered.

"Slave driver. But okay, if you say so." He got out of bed, stripped off his pyjamas and quickly donned the costume, not forgetting to stuff a pillow inside the pants. "How's this?" Ross held out his arms.

"Perfect." Marianne pulled down his beard and planted a kiss on his mouth. "The only problem is that I'll never be able to look at a Santa Claus without having dirty thoughts."

Ross laughed. "I know. Me neither." He looked around. "Where's the sack with the presents?"

"Here." Marianne pulled a hessian sack out of the wardrobe. "I hid it so they wouldn't find it."

Ross took the sack. "It's heavy."

"The parents gave me all the gifts from them and their aunts and uncles, too, so, yes, it would be a lot. Should keep them quiet for a while so we can have breakfast in peace."

Ross swung the sack over his shoulder. "What about the adults?"

"They all said they'd pass on the presents and give to Klaus' charity instead. Except for things they might want to give each other in private."

"Great idea. Okay, let's go. Where are the kids?"

Marianne picked Ross' pyjamas off the floor. "In the living room going crazy. I've just been down there to tell them Santa went down the wrong chimney and that I'd go and get him." She shooed Ross out the door. "Go on—it's your show."

He threw her a last look before he left. "I just want to say..."

She smiled. "I know. But we can talk when they're gone."

He held up his thumb. "It's a date."

In the living room, the children greeted Santa with shouts and laughter and were soon tearing the paper off the presents, discovering toys, books, and DVDs. Clodagh hugged her very first doll and proceeded to rip all the clothes off.

"Brilliant," Daisy laughed. "After all the trouble I had to find one with the cutest dress. But if she's happy, so am I."

When Ross had distributed the presents, he took the empty sack and headed for the door. "Bye now, children. See you next year."

Kieran looked up from his new Lego set. "What about the grownups? Don't they get anything?"

"No," Marianne said. "They've been bad, so they get nothing."

"What did they do?" Tommy asked.

"They were rude and nasty to each other," Liam said.

"Did they say sorry?" Kieran wanted to know.

"Not yet, but they will, or they'll get no breakfast," Marianne said. "How about it, gang? Say sorry to each other, and I'll give you fresh croissants."

"Sorry," everyone mumbled.

Flora giggled. "I bet everyone feels really stupid now."

Chantal couldn't help laughing. "I can't even remember what I said. Did I say something mean and nasty?"

"No," Philippe replied. "I was the nasty one." He took Flora's hand. "But I said sorry, and I told Flora I had no objections if she wants to go back to work with Chantal. How's that for an apology?"

Chantal beamed. "Excellent!"

"Provided we find a good childminder," Philippe added. "Not until then."

"Of course," Chantal said.

"Breakfast!" Marianne chanted. "Baguette, croissants, apricot jam, sausages, bacon, coffee, tea, waffles, hot chocolate, orange juice, and whatever else you'd like, all served in the kitchen. The fabulous Jeanne got up early and helped me. Anyone hungry?"

"I wasn't until I heard all of that." Liam got up from the sofa, pulling Daisy with him. "Come on, before it's all gone."

"Waffles!" Tommy shouted and raced to the kitchen, followed by Kieran and little Pierre shouting, "Waffeee!"

When everyone had left, Marianne tidied away the piles of torn gift paper from the floor, straightened the sofa cushions, and picked up a Christmas card that had fallen from the display on the mantelpiece. Her heart flipped as she caught sight of a photo taken two years earlier.

Klaus, wearing a ski jacket and hat, smiled at her against a background of snow-covered Alps and blue skies. It had been taken outside their chalet in St Moritz. Two years had passed since that photo was taken, but it felt like an eternity. Marianne twisted her rings around her finger—the wedding ring and the five-carat heart-shaped diamond that Klaus had pushed onto her finger only weeks after they met saying he knew she was the love of his life. And he had been hers. Always would be, whoever else she met and fell in love with.

Marianne nodded at Klaus. "Thank you," she whispered, looking at his brown eyes and warm smile. The sun glinted on the glass of the frame for an instant, making it look as if Klaus winked at her. She blinked and shook her head. No. Not possible. She took off her wedding ring and put it in the little china bowl beside the photo. She didn't feel married anymore. Klaus had set her free.

The diamond heart would stay on her finger for the rest of her life.

11

Later that day, when everyone had left, Marianne wandered around the house picking up bits of gift wrapping, ribbons, and forgotten items of clothing. She found a pink sock under the Christmas tree and a small Winnie the Pooh sweatshirt with chocolate stains down the front behind the sofa. She stepped on something sharp and yelped. What was it? Glass? She lifted her foot and saw that it was a piece of Lego and laughed. She put it with the other items for collection later. She straightened chairs, plumped up sofa cushions, and soon the room was back to its original pristine state, except for the echo of children's voices and the lingering memory of laughter among friends.

Ross met her in the hall. "Hi. Peace at last, eh?"

Marianne sighed. "Yes. But kind of dull and quiet, don't you think?"

He put his arms around her. "Feeling blue?"

She nodded, afraid to speak. He would be leaving soon, too. She swallowed and cleared her throat. "I'll be okay. Lots to do. Daisy drew up some plans for other fundraisers. She wants to get the mayor on board so we can do a charity walk. Then we'll have a stall at the market selling artisan craft. I'll be doing the accounts for the whole thing. And I'm taking charge of Molly's business again. So I'll be busy."

"I bet. Good for you." He put his hand under her chin and tilted her face up. "Are you sure you're going to be okay? I can stay a bit longer if—"

She backed away, blinking to stop the tears. "No. You should go. The boat is ready, and you need to start the first leg of your journey to get to Cape Town before the winter storms start here."

"Are you sure you'll be okay?"

She looked up at him and gave him a shaky smile. "I'll be fine. I feel this has been the start of the rest of my life, the rest of the journey. I have friends here, dear friends who are like family." She made a gesture to encompass the hall, the living room, and the rest of the house. "This is too big, though. I might move to something smaller and more manageable. It'll be hard to leave all the memories, but also a good thing. Healing, cleansing, if you know what I mean."

He nodded. "Yes, I do. I felt the same when I sold the house. I had put so much of myself into it. But in the end, it's just a house. My boat is my new home."

"But don't you have a base somewhere? On land, I mean."

"Sure. Forgot to tell you. I bought a flat in Nice. Great place with lovely views. That'll be where I'll go when I come back. Or so I thought," he added, looking unsure.

"How do you mean?"

"Well, you and me—us. It happened so fast I didn't have time to think. I have always been a lone wolf, never trusted anyone. But, now, I find myself pulled to you by invisible strings. You've always been there, in my thoughts, as someone I could turn to in a storm, if you know what I mean. Now you're much more than that." He caught her hand and looked at her with his honest blue eyes. "So here is what I think we should do. I'll go and get started on my trip. I need to be on my own for a bit, to think about what happened here. Is that okay?"

"Of course. I think I need to do that, too. And then?"

"Then maybe you'd like to join me in Cape Town? We could sail across the Atlantic together to Brazil." He squeezed her hand, his eyes bright. "Marianne, you have no idea what it's like to be in the middle of the ocean, all alone under the stars. The silence, the vast sky, the sheer enormity of the ocean. It's like sailing to heaven. I want to do that with you."

Marianne stared at him, taken aback by the passion in his voice and the fire in his eyes. "That sounds incredible. And I *will* come with you. One day. I'm not ready to cast off just yet. I might fly over to the Bahamas when you get there and spend a week or so on the boat. How's that?"

The light in his eyes died. "That would be great, too, of course, but not quite the same."

"I know. But—" She shivered. "I'm scared. As you said, it all happened so fast. I need to think, too."

He let go of her hand and started up the stairs. "I'll go pack. Nearly ready to go. I have to go to Nice first and collect the keys to my new flat. And then, tomorrow, I take delivery of some of the stuff from the house. And then—"

"Then you're off," Marianne said in a flat voice.

"Yes."

"I'll be in the garden, down by the beach. Come and say goodbye when you're ready to go."

He nodded. "Not goodbye. Just *au revoir*. Until we meet again in the Bahamas."

She smiled through her tears. "Yes. That's what I meant. Until we meet again."

* * *

"What are we doing here?" Chantal asked as Gabriel pulled up in front of the beach on Cap d'Antibes. "I need to get back home. I have things to do before we open again tomorrow."

He switched off the engine and rummaged in his pocket. "I have something for you. Your Christmas present." He handed her a small gift-wrapped parcel.

"What?" Chantal looked from his mischievous eyes to

the parcel. "A gift? But I thought we said—"

He laughed. "Yes, I know. We said no presents, blah, blah. But this is different. This is more than just a gift."

She tore the paper off and looked at the small box. "You bought me jewellery?" Her heart leapt. A ring, he had bought her a ring. But inside the box was a key. She stared at it. "What is this? A key to what?"

He took her hand. "It's the key to the rest of our lives, *mon coeur*." He started the car. "Close your eyes."

"Why? What?"

"Just do it."

"All right." She squeezed her eyes shut, feeling dizzy as the car moved around sharp bends, then up a steep hill, until it came to an abrupt stop.

"You can look now," he said, his voice full of laughter.

She opened her eyes and looked. They were in a leafy street shaded by umbrella pines and palms. This was very familiar. She stared at the big green gates of the house in front of them and read the name: *Les Temps Heureux*, The Happy Times. "It's... my house. I mean Ross' house. What are we doing here?" She looked at the key and finally understood. Tears stung her eyes as she looked at Gabriel. "You—you bought my house back?"

He took her hand and looked at her, his brown eyes full of emotion. "Yes, Chantal. I bought your house. But not only that, I bought it in both our names. It's *our* house. This is where we'll spend the rest of our lives."

"But I never saw it for sale."

"It was a private deal. It was never on the market."

Chantal didn't know what to say. This house must have cost several million euros. Ross had restored the house and spent a lot of money landscaping the grounds. As the house was in a prime location with stunning views, it would have fetched a huge sum on the open market. "Why didn't he get an agency to sell it for him? Not my agency, of course, but one of the bigger ones in Nice would have—" She was babbling, unable to take in the one big thing: Gabriel wanted to stay with her for good. He had spent millions to prove it to her.

She looked up at the house, the white façade of which had been newly painted. Her house, where she had grown up, where she and Jean had lived as newlyweds, and much later, where she had brought her young lover, Gabriel, for their secret trysts. Selling the house had been a painful wrench during that time when Jean had been so ill. She had needed the money for his medical bills, and selling the house was the only way she could meet the astronomical costs. Then Jean had chosen the spiritual path, entering an enclosed order of monks and in that way setting her free.

She sighed and closed her eyes. The journey had come full circle, and here she was again, moving into the house she had thought was lost. The enormity of Gabriel's gesture suddenly hit her like a sledgehammer. Chantal bent over and started to cry.

Gabriel took her hand. "What's the matter? Are you ill?"

She couldn't reply for a long while, giving herself up to the pent-up tension of so many weeks of worry and insecurity. Finally, the storm abated. She drew in a ragged breath and turned her tear-stained face to Gabriel. "I'm all right now. I just needed to let it all out." She smiled and handed him the key. "Let's go and inspect our home."

12

Marianne sat in the deck chair on the beach waiting for Ross. The sun was sinking into the sea, bathing the beach in a buttery light. The silence was broken only by the lapping of the waves and the plaintive cry of a seagull gliding over the calm waters of the bay. It would be dark soon. Where was Ross? Marianne shivered, despite the layers of cashmere. This was the moment she had dreaded—saying goodbye.

The French saying *partir, c'est un peu mourir*—to leave is to die a little—rang so true. That moment when you part from someone you love is indeed like a little death. But they'd meet again and pick up where they left off, she told herself. In the Bahamas, where they had first met and become such close friends. She'd go there when he sent a message that he had arrived. Could be months away, but by then she would have come a long way toward running the charity and got back to work as Molly's business manager. Things would have settled down, and she'd be able to take a long break. All of that would help her cope with missing Ross.

She knew he couldn't stay. It was impossible. He had to go on this round-the-world journey. It was his dream that he had worked so hard to realise. They couldn't live together in Klaus' house, where all the memories threatened to engulf her. She didn't even know if she could continue to live there herself. It was time to sell the house and move on. Not leave St Tropez, but buy a smaller house, easier to run, with no memories.

"Madame?"

Marianne looked up. "Maria? What are you doing here? I thought you weren't coming back until tomorrow."

"I came back today because I thought you might need help tidying up."

"That's very kind of you. But there was no rush. I cleaned up a bit, and then I thought the rest could wait until tomorrow."

Maria nodded. "I saw that." She held out a small bundle. "This is for you."

Marianne held out her hand. "I thought I said not to give me a present."

"It's not from me. It's from the young man, who just left. He said to give this to you."

Marianne jumped up. "He left? When? How?"

"In his car—a Jeep, no?"

"Yes, yes!" Marianne exclaimed. "Whatever. He's gone, you said? When?"

"About ten minutes ago. He drove away very fast. But he asked me to give you this and said he'd wait for you in—" Maria stopped. "I think he said 'under the stars.'"

Marianne took the bundle from Maria's hand. She looked at it more closely and discovered a Santa hat and an envelope. Ross. Leaving without saying goodbye. What did it mean? She sank down in the deck chair. "Thank you, Maria," she mumbled, holding the hat and letter to her heart.

"Are you all right?" Maria asked looking concerned.

"Yes. I'm fine. But I need a little space."

Maria backed away. "Of course, Madame. I'll be in the kitchen if you need anything."

Marianne didn't answer. While Maria walked away, she started to read the letter.

My darling cuz Marianne,

I know you will think me a coward for not staying for the tearful farewell. But I just couldn't face kissing you and then walking away. I couldn't bear the thought of looking into those beautiful dark-blue eyes that would be full of tears, hold you in my arms and know it was the last time. I know it's not forever, but that's the way it feels right now. Every hour, every day I'm away from you will feel like an eternity. When I set sail from Cape Town to go across the Atlantic in three weeks' time, I will look at the stars at night and think of you. I will feel the sun on my skin and think of you. I will look at the dolphins following my boat and think of you. All the beautiful sights will be a little less beautiful because you will not be with me to share them. You will be in my heart and mind every moment of every day until we meet again.

Lots more to say, but I'll save it for the Bahamas. I had hoped you could join me in Cape Town and then sail with me across the Atlantic, but you didn't feel ready to take that leap into the unknown. The week we spent together at your house, and the Christmas party were probably the happiest times in my life. The love and laughter lifted my spirits, and I could see you come out of the darkness and smile again. I know you will always carry Klaus in your heart, but I feel we can build something together and that he would smile if he knew about us.

That's all I can think of right now. Please forgive me for not saying goodbye, but I wanted to remember you the way you looked in the hall earlier, your eyes sparkling with new hope and happiness.

I will let you know when I arrive in the Bahamas. Could take a few months. Sailing is unpredictable, and you're never sure of weather and winds.

Take care. Be happy. Until we meet again,

Ross

Marianne blinked away the tears and folded the letter in her lap. She hung the Santa hat on the back of the deck chair and stared out to sea, watching the orange disc of the sun sink behind the horizon. She sat there for a while, her mind blank.

In the gathering dusk, she looked up Air France on her phone and booked a flight to Cape Town two weeks later. She'd be in the harbour when his boat docked.

THE END

About the author

Susanne O'Leary is the bestselling author of more than twenty novels, mainly in the romantic fiction genre. She has also written four crime novels and two in the historical fiction genre. She has been the wife of a diplomat (still is), a fitness teacher and a translator. She now writes full-time from either of two locations; a rambling house in County Tipperary, Ireland or a little cottage overlooking the Atlantic in Dingle, County Kerry. When she is not scaling the mountains of said counties, keeping fit in the local gym, or doing yoga, she keeps writing, producing a book every six months.

Find out more about Susanne and her books on her website: http://www.susannne-oleary.co.uk

Printed in Great Britain
by Amazon

42019496R10180